THE
STONE LIONS

The
Stone Lions

JULIA IATRIDIS

CONTENTS

CHAPTER 1

My Plot of Land

It's been quite a while since I decided on this lot, which is within the city limits. Today, I went to get my planning permission to build. I signed the documents clearly with my name, Panoria Fokianou, with well-rounded and beautiful letters, which took me a while. The clerk pulled the piece of paper towards him, looked at the signature and raised his eyes — like a bird's eyes — then turned them sharply on me.

"Alright", he said. He put the stamp and said something but I didn't understand, even though I was wearing my hearing aid. The battery must have run out. So, just in case, I replied: "Indeed."

My hearing was not very good. Throughout the years I was serving people — well, I had been in service — whenever I did not clearly hear, something that often occurred, I used to answer "Indeed." That word solves all problems. People like hearing it and you always benefit from giving people what they want, that's one thing I've learned. I took great care to do just that during the 32 years and seven months that I struggled to survive. If I hadn't been respectful and used that 'magic' word, I wouldn't have managed to save 930 gold pounds. Then, I wouldn't have been able to buy myself neither a lot nor a house.

Anyway, today I got my planning permission but, while I had less than 797 sovereigns and that cost me forty-three drachmas[1], the permit and the necessary papers for the lot were far more expensive.

---

[1] Greece's currency was replaced by the Euro in 2002.

With the permit in my hand, I went on the bus to Haravgi[2]. At the final stop, the builder was waiting for me in a *kafenion*[3] close by, as we had agreed. We talked with the planning permission laid out on the table. My master had given me his opinion on the plans for the house.

My master, I must say, is a real gentleman, remote and respectable. I've been with him since the German Occupation of Greece. He has helped me a lot. When he introduced me to the builder, he said: "He is a good man, he will take less from you than others."

"Are all builders on the take?"

"All. What do you think?" He asked.

"Are you afraid of the builders?"

"No, I'm not afraid of them, why should I be? Just because they are on the take. Isn't that what we all do in this world, to eat?"

The master looked at me the way he usually does when I tell him what I'm thinking. He didn't say anything else. I knew he wanted to get back to his papers rather than talk to me...

It was a sunny day. People were out in the streets, people in a hurry who seemed to be walking to the rhythm of the shaky song my heart suddenly started to sing: "Panoria, you have your land; Panoria you have your land. It's all yours. The lot today, the house tomorrow..."

Streets, shops, state buildings, people, cars were going fast, all for that same reason...I felt an urge to return to Haravgi, there where the grass was growing, to take in that spectacular view that would soothe my soul to the point that I would want to rise up and say "Glory to God!"

"Good luck!", the builder said as he left. He said something else

---

[2] A suburb of Athens in Greece where I bought a plot of land to build my house.
[3] Cafe or café.

too...something which sounded like "with your husband..." He looked rather shifty.

My happiness was ruined. I said to myself that my master was just making fun of me. I'm forty years old now, perhaps more. I am not really sure when I was born, nobody has ever told me. My day was spoiled. But, in time, I thought that with the few golden sovereigns I had left I might go to the dentist's to get the denture I needed to replace the four teeth he'd taken out. I'd kept postponing this job because I didn't want to spend any of the money I was saving for the house. Time, however, had also done its job on my teeth and a couple of them were ready to fall out.

I got scared and that helped me to think practically, as my master would have, "If they fall out and if I can't eat, I will lose weight and be in pain. I could even get ill, then what use would the house be to me? Why even build it?" So, I fixed them, but the dentures hurt and I couldn't eat. My gums had hurt me before because they were worn out. Then, though, they were hurting because the dentures were new. It seems like you always hurt, no matter what you do. I will get used to them, they say, I will chew well and even crack walnuts with my teeth...Amen to that!"

From up high on Haravgi, I forgot to say, you can see the sea. From there, where my house will be, you can see further away to the horizon. The world will be mine. All the shining world the midday blinding light falls on.

I am not happy though. Not for this world of mine, not for the unending sea which cools the spirit. No, not even for those things. Not for anything else. I must find a way to be happy.

If I can just sort out all the things that happened today. I got the planning permission, I came to Haravgi and spoke with the builder. On Monday he will lay the foundations. Monday! The foundations...! The foundations of my house...

I'm waiting.

Nothing, still.

My mood does not change.

I'm standing exactly where my house will be. A large stone in the middle of the lot is the marker. I look at the rock for some time.

My home, I say.

Nothing yet.

Time passes. It's nearly midday. Far away, the sea shimmers. It's as if it is showering light and its sparks are spreading all around.

Something flashes in my mind.

The Flight to Greece

From the depths of time, a thick smoke rises. Flames go up high, spread out, devouring and swallowing the whole world, our house and our balcony, which was supported by two stone lions.

We ran, and so did many others with us. The fire, with its heat, was following us and the thick smoke was choking us.

We ran and ran. My father, my mother, my sister and I, hands held tight.

We could see the boats. They got clearer through the smoke when bad things happened. The Earth tore up, the skies were pulled apart. All around us, debris made of burning wood, stones and clay was falling. The crashes thundered in my head. Then, I rolled down a dark cliff. I rolled for a long time down a cliff full of earth and mud until I could get up and run again. I kept on clutching my mother's hand and my mother held onto my sister's hand, while my father followed up at the back. We were all in a chain, holding on firmly, with all the strength we had so that we wouldn't lose each other.

After the warehouse exploded — it was a long time before I found out what it was — the world became silent. All the mists caused by the catastrophe reached me from afar. Just as if nothing had happened. My eyes could still see, and that's why I kept them wide open, as wide as I could to take in as much as possible about what was happening, to remember those bewildered faces, covered in sweat and smut, the people running.

They kept running - sometimes they would get scared and blackened, lost in the smoke, sometimes the light from the flames vanquished the smoke and came close, very close, magnified and increasing, shining a bright, fiery red.

Then, I found myself sitting on a boat. There, I realised that my hand was empty. I reached out to touch my mother but my search was in vain. I turned and saw a strange woman sitting on the seat above me. Next to her was another stranger, next to that one was another...all of them were strangers. No mother and no baby. None of those people was my mother. No father. None of them was my father. My sister wasn't there either.

The boat was leaving. Unending black clouds behind us struggled to swallow the sky, while the fire tore the sky with knives made of flames. I opened my mouth to scream but nothing came out, not one sound. Nothing.

On this overladen boat, I was sailing towards the world.

I could not speak. I could not hear. But, I could see. I kept looking, looking to find one of my own people among all those faces...searching...

Then I saw a woman, she beckoned to me. I went towards her. I noticed her lips moved, maybe she knew something.

"Come here", her hand was already holding me.

"My mother...?", is all I could say.

"There's no mother, you'll come with me. You are an orphan now and I..."

I didn't know what else she said, I was scared and ran away from her.

Among the legs, arms, bodies of people who were standing, sitting, half lying, however they could go in the boat, I kept searching.

A nurse with a blue scarf, with a red cross on it, came up to me, took a piece of bread out of a bag and gave it to me. I ate it and felt better, my whole body filled with warmth and I found my courage again. I took the nurse's hand and followed her like a little dog. Like that, between the arms, legs and bodies which filled the boat. I followed her.

Later on, the nurse pushed me gently into a corner and made me sit down. She told me I must rest. I didn't want to sleep, but I complied - I sat down. At least until she left, then I got up again. I continued my search, stumbling among all the people lying around, looking to see if I knew their faces. I had to find what I was looking for. I must find them. Find them...

I searched for two whole days and nights. Until all those people, the boat, the sea, the sun, the sky, the stars, a half-moon...until some long threads, active wires let's say, spread all over and bundled me up in a thick net that wouldn't let me walk or see. They closed my eyes, they imprisoned me. They weighed me down as if they wanted to throw me deep down, as deep as they could, into the dark depths of the world.

But I woke up, I got up and spoke. I began to ask. Not even the nurse who gave me the bread knew what to say to me, other than there were other children like me on the boat and all would get sorted out when we arrived to Piraeus[4].

I searched. Parents must be here, I said to myself, the ones I am looking for. I got my hopes up and found the strength to keep looking.

On the third day, I found an old neighbour of ours. I fell into her arms and cried with all my heart and soul. She battled to get me off of her, to untangle me from her, to push me gently away, but I insisted. Her lips were moving, but it took me a while to under-

---

[4] Port of Athens, the major port of Greece.

stand what she was saying:

"Off you go, you poor little thing, to find that woman whom you said spoke to you."

"The one who called me an orphan?"

"Yes, her! Off you go. If she's well, she'll take you with her. You may be lucky!"

"She'll take me with her?"

"Yes, silly. Off you go! You will eat well with her."

"I'll eat? Who says I want to eat?"

I moved away from the neighbour, but then I regretted it and was just going to go back to where I saw her. She put her hand into her bag and took something out. She hid it in her palm and started to eat. Every few minutes, she would steal a glance at me where I was sitting and pretending she couldn't see me, carried on eating. I was watching her for ages. All the time, she was chewing.

The night has fallen. By the little light of a lamp, I saw the nurses' dark scarf again. She came and gave me some bread. I found somewhere to sit next to an old man, and the nurse gave some food to him; also, the bread fell out of his hands. She picked it up and gave it to him again. He didn't want it. She let go, and it fell back. He was tired, although his eyes were open and they were looking at me.

"Your bread, grandpa..."

But although his lips wanted to break into a smile, they couldn't. I showed him the piece of bread and pretended that I was going to eat it, he signalled to me slowly, but I understood and I ate it. I enjoyed it.

Nighttime. Just a little light leaks out from the boat's lamp. We are travelling. The old man touches my hand. He is cold, frozen. It was the first night on the ship that I had slept with company, and I leant against the old man and held onto his hand until it started to warm up. I don't remember anything else.

The sun, which was coming up over the opposite shore, burned my eyes; a huge sun. At first, I was afraid that the fire was still following us and had reached our boat. I woke up, bodies all around me. The sea in front of us, red like blood. My companion, the old man, slept with his mouth open and his eyes open. I stood up, my legs touched his cold forehead. The cold I felt spread through my body and filled me with fear.

I got as far away as I could from there, as far as possible. I felt saliva rush into my mouth, hot saliva, I spat. It was blood. Something was moving in my gum, on the right at the top. I got a hold of it and pulled out a tooth.

I spat blood again. If I could just get up onto the gunwale of the boat...I struggled and prodded and pushed, and finally, I managed it. I could see the sea below, all foam, and that's where I threw my tooth. When we were at home, we would throw our teeth onto the roof tiles. Our mother told us that each tooth which came out would bring us more luck.

I don't know.

I don't remember how we arrived in Piraeus. I just saw something like a warehouse in my memory. There we all slept together. Everyone lies down on the slabs of the waterfront. We didn't all fit inside. I managed to fit in though, as I didn't take up much room and people felt sorry for me. I managed, alright. So, then, some well-dressed ladies came and gave out clothes.

They gave me an old jacket which reached below the knees. It was red. I liked it. Those ladies talked and laughed with the guards who had come with us. Holding a paper in their hands, they were writing too. I couldn't hear much, and I understood even less, but at least, I told myself: now we are lost, but we will surely be found. Didn't the nurse on the boat say that it would all be sorted out in Piraeus?

The woman who was lying next to me tore up the blanket to give me a piece so that I wouldn't get cold lying on the stones, she told me that boats were arriving all the time. Surely my family would come? She was also waiting for someone.

Some boats came, our people weren't on them. I stood there when they disembarked with the woman and others from the warehouse, we had climbed onto some crates to see better.

But one of those who were with us found his family, you should have seen the tears, hugs and kisses! All of us who had climbed up onto the crates were crying too.

Other boats arrive, but nothing.

Then, the other ladies came. They were to take people to their homes to work for them, they would feed them, they would dress them. Many said they wanted to go. One of the guards weighed me up and looked at me pityingly. He shook his head. Then, as if he'd just made a decision:

"I will write you down, as well. You'll do."

"What will I do?"

"You'll do to go to be in service."

He said it loudly and clearly, so I heard it. He wrote me down on a large piece of paper he was holding. He went a bit further on. Stood in front of a pretty girl. He looked at her and greeted her with a smile, showing all of his teeth in a white line. He writes her down too. We have to all go and sit outside the warehouse and not move from there.

They will come along and choose from us, a woman said.

The ladies who came had some sort of glasses on a handle. They screwed up their faces and walked away from a little, and screwed up their faces over there too. All the waterfront, as far as the eye could see, was full of people. Men and women, mostly children, who were waiting to be taken into service.

I was there for days waiting. They chose many and took them

away. They took the woman who had kept me company, and she left me the rest of her blanket. Before she went, I asked her what would happen to me if nobody chose me. She didn't know. However, she gave me some advice:

"Say you are ten or eleven years old because they see you so young and are afraid you wouldn't be able to stand the work."

But none of the ladies ever asked me my age so that I could say I was eleven years old. I didn't know exactly how old I was anyway. So, I remain among the last.

Other boats came. Other new people. Lots of them. I could see, from up on the crates. Nobody I knew. Nothing. Every day more and more I begged to be lucky and for some lady to choose me. When they looked through their lorgnettes — that's what I later learned the glasses with the handles were called — I even managed to smile as if to say pleadingly, "Take me too, also I am so young!" that it seemed that they started to like me more because they decided to pick me.

She stands in front of me. She is saying something. She looks at me hard. I said:

"I am a little hard of hearing."

Why did I have to tell her? That sent her away.

Some time passed, and I smiled again and waited. Then I saw her leave with a girl as small as me. She held her by the hand. That girl was doubtless not hard of hearing.

My First "Home"

Finally, there was a lady for me too.

We go into a train with brown wooden wagons. The lady sat next to the window, and I remained standing by her. While I saw so many people who had pushed us when we got on, I noticed a woman with a child, a boy. I thought: that could be his mother, why not? I turned around and looked at the window: houses, gardens, streets, trees rushed past, all gone, blurred and disappeared into the dust which whirled in the wind making large wheels which swirled, scattered, and became millions of small circles which only swirled and multiplied.

From the moment I arrived in the country, wheels had appeared before me.

It was noon. Everything blurred and became distant in the bright sunlight. From the sun, the light seemed to shoot out a flaming hand to my heart, and squeeze it strangely, sweet and yet painful. Then, suddenly, "Whoosh!" a robust and white wind, a person on a bicycle passed beneath our door where the mother stood grinding coffee.

Mother: "The barber."

"Who did you say?"

"Just now, didn't you see who went past?"

"Who went past?"

"The barber, on his bike, in his white uniform...yes, look there on the road, the cloud, it's from the dust kicked up by the wheels."

I see the cloud far off, on the edge of the sky. If the wind blows in this direction, it will bring the rain.

"Mother, didn't you see the barber? He has just passed by?"

"No, my daughter. I didn't see him, and he didn't pass by. You just saw his ghost. Different elves and spirits appear in the summer midday heat, but these noonday ghosts don't hurt you."

The person on the bicycle, whether it was a noontime ghost or not, spins me along with his wheels of time. Years. So, like the first time, when I continued my journey on the train, the wheels acquired pure white riders, and more and more bikes and riders filled the roads and fields that we passed; they overflowed. Some took the long way to the sky, others ran alongside the train. Now there are crowds of cycles. Millions of barbers making strange jeering grimaces, while their wheels are already beginning to grind into my body.

I don't remember how that train journey with its wheels ended. I just remember the lady's words when we finally arrived at the house near a cemetery on the street of Eternal Rest. There where the stonemasons made crosses and the florists sold flowers for the dead.

"You will help me with the housework. If you are a bright girl, you will become a proper person. You will enjoy your life." As she said this, she was half-laughing in a way that didn't fit her words. I would say, from then on, I began to realise that only if I was brilliant, would I be likely to enjoy my life.

What should I say about the housework, everyone more or less knows what it is. But this incident had burned into my memory: my lady had a weakness for the corners. When I was brushing and mopping, I had to reach into the last corner under the ward-robes, tables, whatever. And, well, I was bored. I decided not to enter the very last turn. She — the lady I mean — at the crack of dawn, who acted as the alarm by ringing a loud bell to wake me in the morning, was sleeping and didn't see me. But when she got up and suddenly appeared in front of me with her bright red dressing gown which opened in front higher than it should to where you could see everything, and at first, I flushed and didn't know where to look, but later on, I got used to it...What was I saying? Ah, yes about the day she appeared in front of me. She bent down and reached her hand to the corner and then held it up in front of me to show me the dust stuck on her fingers, and with these dirty hands, she gave me two good slaps.

My head was buzzing, just as it did with the explosion, and I felt my nose bleeding. For days, my ears would sound as if I had been pushed into a beehive. After that, I never left any dust in the corners nor in the dustbin, which I had to empty out and wash thoroughly. If I'd had a cent for all those cigarette stubs which I threw away from that house, I would be a really wealthy woman. Just as if they had nothing else to do all night but smoke...You ask me who? The lady and her friends. She lived alone, but accepted visitors. Men, of course, like that.

She gave me some of her old things, which suited me. She gave me a bed to sleep in. I had food to eat. Thank God, I had food. I was alright. She put money in the bank for me each month, she said. What more could I ask for? If I were smart, I would know how to enjoy my life, that's what she said.

I didn't even know if I was gifted. Finding that out about yourself can be problematic. It's just that there was something which I didn't like. I was not happy, although I should have been. I had everything. I was clothed, fed and paid - what else was there? I told myself I was ungrateful. Sometimes, a great sadness took hold of me and I just wanted to cry.

One day, I was in that kind of state when I took the first path I found and arrived at the gates of the cemetery. I saw the trees. The marble, when shining in the sun, weakened my senses. Visiting the cemetery became a habit of mine. I often went there and wandered among the trees and the headstones of the graves. If I happened to be there while a service or memorial was being performed, the ladies who attended would give me some *koliva*[5]. If it was a proper funeral, I would sit at a distance and watch in amazement as they brought large, broad wreaths tied with mauve ribbons with gold writing on them. It was wonderful.

Again, as I wandered through the small paths, I was attracted by the statues of men, women and even children, and I would always end up in front of a reclining, sleeping little girl made of marble. I would speak to her the same way I would talk to my mother. I told her my troubles and looked at her smiling face asking for advice, then I would cry. I felt better afterwards, lighter.

One dark and cloudy day, I left the house and ran to see "my mar-

---

[5] Or *kollyva* and *kollyba*. An ancient Greek sweet based on boiled wheat. Later, used in the Orthodox Church for funerals and memorials.

ble lady". When I got there, I knelt in front of her and left a bottle of perfume at her feet. I'd thought about it for a long time. Since I pondered on it so much, it had become evident for me that I needed to do something for my sleeping one, I owed her because she had supported me a lot. I wondered what I should do, how I should do it. Every night, my mind spinning around as I tried to come up with the perfect idea, until, finally, one morning, she — my mistress, I mean — had gone out and, as I cleaned up the mess she had left on her dressing table, I noticed that she had four small bottles of perfume. Did she need so many? It seemed like she wanted to have it all. So, I took one of them for my only friend, the one who championed and sustained me. I hadn't made friends with the neighbours because of my deafness.

A little girl lived in the house next door. In the beginning, it seemed that she'd like to speak to me. But it was as if she realised she would have to pay attention to how she talked to me, and it would be difficult not to shout, due to my impaired hearing, but then all our mistresses would hear us. So, she quickly got bored apparently. I would call her from the kitchen, but she would close the window. So, I never called again.

Time passed, more than a year, before I spoke to the grocer's son, Mihalis. He would make the shape of a horn with his hands around his mouth, put them near my ear and make a sound like a trumpet. This made him laugh out loud! And it made me laugh too, because I liked to see Mihalis laughing. That's how our friendship began. Mihalis went to night school and learned to write. I thought about doing it too. I could manage to go to night school, I don't think "she" would refuse if I asked her.

But I didn't. I was afraid that I wouldn't be able to hear the teacher. Not all the kids who went to night school were like Mihalis, who cupped his hands and whistled in my ear. So what would I do if I really couldn't hear?

That, and other things, kept me away from other people. This was the reason why I looked for comfort in "my marble lady", and why I stole one of the little bottles of perfume from my lady, who had made it crystal clear that she wanted me out of the house in the afternoons. She found all kinds of things she wanted me to buy: reels of cotton, lemons, milk, cigarettes. "Why don't you just go for a walk and get a bit of fresh air?"she had told me. I understood.

She wanted me out of the way. But she always made sure I would be back in time to make her evening meal, or to help her get dressed and put on her revealing clothes. This time she stayed out for a long time.

So, the day I took the bottle of perfume to "my marble lady", I returned home as soon as it got dark. I rang the bell. Once, twice, three times. I left some time between each ring, because she used to growl at me in an angry voice that I should know she wasn't deaf like me and other similar 'nice' things.

I rang again. Once, twice, three, four times. Jesus Christ! Mother of God! Has she gone out? Where could she have gone? What will become of me? The night was falling — where should I go? Then it started raining. I sat on the doorstep. I rang the bell again. Just then, the light went on in her bedroom. It was as if the light spreading in the room also spread within me, filling me with joy, deep in my bones. She opened the door and there she stood in her red dressing gown. I went in, straight to the kitchen. Straight to my corner, to sit on my trunk — that was my seat. I didn't like her expression. Probably, her "visit" hadn't gone well. I was scared. Who else would she take it out on, except me of course?

I sat and waited. It was getting dark. The kitchen window was like a big white stain. I couldn't turn the light on because the kitchen didn't have electricity, that was just for the other rooms, and the lady would bring me matches to light the petrol lamp if she needed me to cook or anything else. Otherwise, there was no point in me using the oil. So, I waited in the company of the dull stain that was the kitchen window.

You see, unlike other people, I couldn't learn things by listening to someone else's conversations from the keyholes of their doors like Mihalis had told me (apparently that is the only way to learn the most important things). But I would still be able to tell what was going on, good or bad, by the way the wind vibrated around me. So, when the wind gently caressed me, I would suddenly feel happy. Then, I knew that something good would happen. Maybe I would eat a sweet, perhaps I would have more food, they lady would give me some clothes or I would meet Mihalis in the street. If, however, the wind held back and blew so strong it would feel like a pair of pincers were grabbing me, crushing me and making me dizzy, then I knew bad things would be coming, as if all the bad things in the world were rushing in.

The darkness was divided into two by the light coming from the hall. The wind became ice-cold, it felt like steel blades cutting me, it was frightening. I was scared. I made a loud noise, so loud even I heard it! Suddenly, she lunged into the kitchen like a ghoul and slapped me in the face countless times. I thought I could hear her say something about a "bottle" and a "perfume"...but the steely shards of light were hurting me. Blood ran down from my nose as I suddenly disappeared, falling into a red darkness.

When I opened my eyes, little by little, I realised I was on her bed. I could make out her face and I saw a man next to her. My dress had been taken off, my underwear pulled down and my bodice opened...I nearly fainted again, this time from shame. They noticed my embarrassment, so the man grabbed the coverlet and pulled it over me. Then, she threw my dress at me and the man turned around towards the window and lit himself a cigarette.

"Come on, get up," she said, "you scared me to death."

Next to the bed, on the cupboard was a bowl of vinegar and a cloth. I realised that my forehead and my hair were dump. At the window, the man kept smoking. She said something while looking at him.

"I brought a doctor to look at you. There's nothing wrong. You just became a little dizzy..."

She said something else which I didn't hear, so I made for the kitchen but she ran behind me and stopped me: "Put some chips and eggs to fry. The doctor will eat with us. Here, take some matches for the lamp..."

The so-called doctor was watching her now. She told me this with round eyes, wide open like those of a hungry cow. My lady smiled at him, pleased with the hunger which showed in his eyes and said: "Oh, go on then! You can have an egg this evening too. It will give you strength!"

I really don't understand why such cow-eyes could have that much of an effect on me. Even I was pleased, although it was only for an egg.

From that evening on, the lady was nicer. She never shouted at me again. Maybe the so-called doctor told her that she shouldn't. She even sent me to fetch the dressmaker, Anetta, because she had bought me a dress.

The day the dressmaker came it was a sunny one. Just seeing a clear sky warms you up inside and makes life seem easy. Anetta took my measurements as instructed. Later, she cut the material and said: "Here's to a bridal gown, one day!"

She said it loudly, even I heard it. That day was so lovely, my duties seemed light and I finished them quickly, so I sat on the steps in the kitchen, enjoying the sunshine and the warmth. I felt like singing. I opened my mouth to sing one of the songs our mother had taught us. I could tell by the fluttering of my larynx that I was singing, but I couldn't hear any sound coming out of my mouth. I tried again and again, but I really couldn't. Maybe if I sang a bit louder, I'd be able to hear it, but I was afraid that my lady would hear it too and come out to hit me again. After all, she had hired me to work, not to sing. Never mind, I won't sing then, it's all fine anyway, and in a little while I will be trying my new dress.

It was blue, light blue, with a darker pattern. I tried it on at lunchtime. My lady's eyes lit on me strangely, while I undressed and on my underwear which was an old one of hers. I had taken it in and shortened it. It was rose-coloured and pretty and I liked it a lot. But her eyes, which were like the wind again, pinched and weighed me down like pincers. The bad feeling was lifted when Anetta very carefully — not to undo the pins — tried the dress on me.

On the second fitting, she let me look at myself in her wardrobe mirror. Then, I saw Anetta behind me shaking her head and smiling oddly with her nasty mouth. I didn't like that. Then I noticed myself in the other half of the mirror. I looked like someone else! Completely different from how I looked when I saw myself in the mirror when she went out. She had told me not to look in the mirror when she first brought me home.

"The mirror is Satan for young girls. For women like me, it is a comfort, and for old women, it's a curse."

Obviously, I shouldn't leave my duties for Satan to mess with my mind, and lots of other things she said at the beginning. That was a time when she was beautiful because she had a cousin who would often come around and they would go out together in the evenings. But when he stopped coming was when she started slapping me. Later on, others came.

I don't like the dress. It made me very different, and that different me when I first came across it in the mirror, frightened me. For days I thought about it, and for days a dark misery would torment me, and finally, I made up my mind. One evening when she told me that I could go out, I went to Anetta's house.

"I don't want it!"

She looked hard at me. A teasing glint in her eye and she said something. But I couldn't hear it.

"Why don't you like it?" she said louder.

I struggled and tried to find all the things I had been thinking to say. Finally, I said: "I don't like it because, well, Anetta, you can see for yourself. It makes me into a different person. It doesn't suit me. I just don't know how to say it...it doesn't suit me."

She took me by the hand and sat me on her trunk, which was

covered with an embroidered towel, and she sat next to me. She looked at me:

"Now listen carefully to what I am going to say to you. Once I've said it I want you to think about it on your own and then decide. You are not stupid. The dress which I sewed for you is just what the other one needs. As you said, someone your lady wants to make you."

"To make me into what?"

"A tart," she said more loudly and carried on: "Because you have no choice. Poor thing, you have to eat, dress, have somewhere to sleep. That's what she's paying for."

"She is not paying me for my work?"

"No. The payment is more."

"More? More what? Tell me!"

She didn't speak straight away. Finally, as if she'd made a difficult decision:

"With the dress, she made you, tight and short, she wants to see if you will do..."

"If I'll do for what?"

"You are still young, but learn this from now: you will either live decently and exhaust yourself in work, and you will never eat what you want, and you will never wear what you want, and you will never sleep long enough, or you live naughtily. Oh dear! What am I saying?"

"I am listening."

"You can live dishonourably like your lady, and you will have everything, and then, later on, you will have your own orphan to beat up."

Anetta's eyes suddenly filled with tears and started rolling down her cheeks, sallow and wrinkled. I felt sorry for her and took her hand.

"Anetta…So why do you…"

"Me? Me? Eh? Look at me well. I am honest and decent! Tomorrow, Sunday, I won't have even a mouthful of meat to eat. Look at my fingers worn out by the needle, my shoes without soles — if it rains I have to stuff them with newspaper…"

My heart had become a hard lump and hurt like a wound.

Anetta was speaking again. I was careful to not miss one word. What she was saying was very important.

"I didn't manage it. It needs a special talent. It's also a craft, like needlework."

"So, hard?"

"Even more difficult. Maybe you have the talent." She looked at me inquiringly:

"Maybe you could do it."

She wanted to give me hope.

"You'll be fine. Listen to me. I saw in her eyes when the lady was watching you try on the new dress. You are pretty and light. They will like you."

She got up off the trunk and looked at me from a bit further away and repeated, this time with malice: "They will like you, you'll do for that work."

Then I saw Anetta as if I saw her for the first time. Her long top lip, her beady little eyes, sparse eyebrows, with her thinning fringe and a hooked nose.

"What are you looking at? I am ugly, aren't I? Now you realise that I am ugly?"

She was getting angry and came at me with her arm upraised as if to beat me, but I moved away. I let her shout, I didn't know what she was saying. Some sort of hysteria had come over her so I left as fast as I could. I felt like bells were ringing inside my head, bells from all the churches in the world and all of them were thundering and saying: "You are pretty, you'll do for that kind of work." What work? Was it what I had seen a man doing to my lady when I watched through the keyhole? That was when I felt mud in the wind — hot mud. Had I run to the cemetery to cool off and stay there next to my marble lady? Then I had decided never to return to the lady's house? But the day was ending, the night was falling, and the guard came to get me out. I had to leave. I was hungry, and it was cold. I returned to the house, and my lady beat me because I got in late. I wanted to ask Anetta all those questions. Even about children. Was that the way children were got? What did I see through the keyhole? If so, why was it that all those who did that didn't have children? All the years with my lady and I never saw her have a child-nor had she had one before. I wanted to ask Anetta so many things but I couldn't. I had nobody else to ask.

I walked the streets aimlessly. The bells stopped thundering in my head because I thought of a reason which stopped them. The word which went with my new dress: "Shameless."

When the street lights came on, I found myself in front of the grocer's where Mihalis worked.

I remember that we needed tea. I found him, and he gave me some, and he slipped me two dried figs. Mihalis often gave me things. Sometimes a few almonds, a handful of raisins. But that evening, when he gave me the figs I felt a horrid tightening of the throat, and I started to cry, right here in the grocer's shop.

Mihalis pulled me into the back room and made me sit down on a small barrel and stood in front of me looking confused and watched me cry. After a while, he put his hand on my shoulder, his fingers gently squeezed me, and that's when my teeth started chattering. I was terrified and got up to leave. He wouldn't let me go. He was holding me tightly by the hand, and I could see his lips glistening.

"What's happening, Panoria. Did someone hurt you?"

"No! No! Nothing, nobody hurt me. Let me go!"

I battled with both my hands to push him to make him go. Then I realised that I still held the figs in one of my hands, something inside melted. I sat back down on the barrel and started to eat them. The more I ate, the better I felt. I calmed down so much that he came and sat down next to me. The backroom was rather dark as it was only lit by the light coming from the shop. Mihalis moved closer to me, he smelled of cheese and oil. I liked his smell and watched him. He was trying to say something:

"Panoria, you know, Panoria..."

He stopped. I bit into another fig.

Someone came into the shop, and Mihalis got up and went out. I stayed. I wasn't afraid anymore. He returned and brought me some almonds and raisins, tipping them into my apron, and sat next to me again on the barrel. We didn't speak again.

We never said anything else that evening. But as I ran home because I was late, splashing through the mud in the street, I wanted to both laugh and cry.

There was a light on in the house. It took a while before the door was opened, and instead of her, the doctor opened it. He was at the house day and night. He half-smiled when he saw me and pinched my cheek. I went into the kitchen and lit the lamp because I was going to fry some chips. I washed up, got the brush, and scrubbed the sink, making it shine. Then she appeared in the kitchen, told me to put on my white apron and go to open the door. It was someone new. The three of them were closeted in the dining room. I stayed outside for a bit in the dark corridor and tried to calm myself down, to understand, to guess a world of secrets only from the strip of light appearing from underneath the closed door where three people were inside and talking about things.

I don't know how long I sat there. I ate a few of the little raisins and cracked two of the last almonds which Mihalis had given me, with my teeth. After a bit, the strip of light from the door began to tease me. Sometimes it would blur, then it would flow, and it seemed to jump around in front of my eyes and makes me dizzy. It wanted me to sleep. That shouldn't be allowed. What if they suddenly came out? So, stumbling as if I was drunk, I went and shut myself up in my little room. Thus, I escaped from the strip of light, from my fear.

From the next day, everything changed in our house: We rented out my lady's room. I didn't say we rented, I said we rented it out. Because these tenants would just come for an hour or so and then would leave. There were proper gentlemen, and ladies with veils who would get out of carriages or cars, like those new ones with the little flag and a chauffeur. The doctor would turn up late in the evening, and my lady never hit me after that. On the contrary, she would explain some things to me in a lovely way. Her words were significant, and I wasn't to forget even one of them. She had called me to her bedroom.

"Sit down," she said.

I hesitated, maybe I hadn't heard right, she'd never asked me to sit down before.

"Sit down," she said again.

I sat down on the little low stool which she used to rest her feet on when she was sewing.

"You are a big girl now, almost a woman. You have already become one, haven't you? She smiled knowingly. I was embarrassed, I was very embarrassed, but I knew I must listen to what she was saying, and that it would be necessary for me.

"I want to speak to you as a person who needs to know the good and the bad sides of the world."

I couldn't ask anything more, and my eyes were fastened to her lips. The thin rose-red lips near which her skin had small wrinkles in, this was the first time I'd noticed that.

"Times are hard. The campaign in Asia Minor killed many people. That was where I lost my *fiancé*[6]."

She stopped and sighed. Then continued:

"I was left alone in the world. I was lucky I left before the catastrophe. I brought some money with me..."

So, she was also from that part of the world? All on her own as well, like me? She continued, and I listened:

"Money runs out. Do you know how fast it runs out?"

How would I know? I'd never had any.

"Something had to be done. Do you understand?" The rooms we let out will benefit you as well."

"How? Benefit you said?"

"But, of course. The visitors will give where..."

"What will they give?"

"Tips"

Money, in other words, for me. I was pleased. I grabbed a hold of her hand and kissed it. She pulled it away and carried on:

"I shall put double the amount in the bank for you, and it will start building up. Later on, after a few years, you could even buy a plot of land..."

"Me? A plot of land?"

"Yes, you, why not? Later on, if you've got any brains, you'll start building"

"I will build?"

---

6 A man to whom a woman is engaged to be married *(The Oxford Dictionary of English)*.

"Yes, silly, you'll make just one room, and then afterwards…"

I was stunned! What she'd said was far more critical than I'd imagined. I would have, in other words, a house of my own…

I couldn't sleep from the excitement that night. I would build a house. With a balcony. I would put two stone lions to support it. I would buy a coffee grinder, and I would go out onto the stoop and grind the coffee. The sun would glint with golden sparks on the copper, and my daughter would ask me if I had seen the barber go by on his bicycle. I'll just go on grinding the coffee…and the barber would pass by.

My head filled with wheels. The wheels would slowly grind my mind slowly, and beautifully until I finally fell asleep.

I got up at dawn at that time. In the winter, I would go down to the laundry, put in the kindling and light the fire, and while I waited for the water to heat up, I took the sheets and threw them in the trough to soak in cold water first. You see, with the new situation we required a lot of linen, we changed them every day even though sometimes the sheets were almost clean and only smelled from the lady's perfume — in that case, I just soaked them in hot water and didn't scrub them. That's what she had told me. Sometimes though they had large yellow stains and then I soaped them well and felt something akin to nausea. My tummy was to blame, of course. It must have been some sort of weakness because whenever I washed the toilet, I would feel the same kind of thing. Some kind of all mixed up. You can say that every job has its difficulties and mine weren't other than to clean up other people's dirt. The more I cleaned, the more they dirtied them. Eventually, I learned something from the unwashed linen. You could call them secrets. A mark, a strange crease, a stain would excite my mind which would present different ugly and unspeakable things.

So, one morning I noticed how the last sheet which I put to soak had blood on it. I know that it was from the two I'd seen where the lady had a thick mauve veil and the man with gold-rimmed glasses who held her by the hand when they left the room and wanted to go with her. She pushed him away and left on her own.

He stood for a while outside the closed door, he waited for a little, then looking at his watch, made to go. Then my lady came out of the salon. He said something to her, and she shook her head.. No! I suppose he must have said something awful because he looked at me at once. The tenant opened his wallet, he gave her some money and then he left.

After counting the money again, my lady put a drachma in my hands without saying anything. It was the first time I'd ever held cash of my own. That would be what she meant by "tips" I felt a strange and different joy.

Later, she came into the room which I had swept out and was making the bed with fresh sheets, she said clearly, looking me in the eye: "Hurry up, some more are coming."

An officer with gold buttons arrived, which shone beautifully. With him was a tall and slim brunette with devilish eyes and a hat pulled well down over her forehead. They shut the door and turned the light on. The only thing left to see was the strip of light under the door.

The doctor came that night, entered the dining room, and they closed the door. I had yet another strip of light to look at. I looked from one to the other, in my pocket I felt the drachma, I stroked it, it was warm, and I was happy that its warmth was mine, all mine, because I had it with me, the drachma. I went to bed, I was tired.

Next morning, I found the sheets used by the officer with the "devil eyes" in the kitchen thrown into a basket. I took them and immediately put them in the water to soak, later I soaped them well because they needed it.

When I'd finished with them and hung them out completely clean in the sun, I peeled her apple. She always ate a piece of fruit in the morning as soon as she opened her eyes. I made coffee for the doctor as we called him and took them upstairs. He had already got up, got dressed and was getting ready to leave. As soon as he saw me with the coffee, he motioned to me to leave his coffee outside on the little table. He came closer to me as I was doing this and just stood there. I suddenly felt the beating of his heart, a thousand sirens going off in my body and a hot awful feeling like warm mud surrounded me when his two fat lips, cold and wet landed on my mouth...His tongue battled to get between my teeth, his hand was trying to get inside me, and his weight paralysed me. Then, courage gave me the strength to push with all my might against his hard body to free myself. I went to scream, but he closed my mouth with his dirty hand while frightening me with his eyes which were lit up. I gave him a hard bite on his side, and he laughed. He liked it, he said. But he didn't do anything else apart from looking at me with his fiery eyes. Then he put his hand in his pocket and gave me some money. He told me that if I were okay, he would give me more," You hear? Think about it" he said.

What could I think, when with his money in my hand I felt that I was sinking further into real flames. In all of the fiery depths, I could see a small white spot which grew until it looked like a house. It had a balcony. Two stone lions to support it. I smiled at that. He, the idiot was pleased and said clearly close to my ear so that I would be sure to hear: "You are a bright girl. You know what is in your interests. You will be nice to me. I'm going now, be quiet and let her sleep, we were late last night."

He left half-smiling, and I could still see his yellow teeth even when he'd closed the door.

Five whole drachmas he gave me. I tied them up along with the other one in a knot in my scarf and stuffed it into my pocket. When the lady got up, she hardly looked to see if I'd cleaned up or even asked about the doctor, nor spoke about food, and I didn't hear her dressing. Without even telling me if any strangers might turn up so that I could get things ready, she left as if she was being hunted.

So, anyway, I made the beds up with clean sheets, and by the time I'd done it, I had made the decision: I would give the money to Mihalis. He'd look after it for me. Because if she found my five drachmas and she was in a bad mood, she could easily say that I'd stolen them. But by the time I'd gone into the kitchen, something hurt inside me: "No, not Mihalis. It's not right. He would ask me how..."

I put the fava on to cook. That's all we had in the house, and we would have to eat at lunchtime. Again, I thought about Mihalis, and I wanted to cry when I heard the bell. She had made it louder, and it was like a church bell. It will be strangers, I said to myself. Just as well I'd got the bedroom ready. I ran and opened it.' Jesus Christ'! How didn't faint from the shock I'll never know. A policeman stood in front of me. He was saying something. I couldn't hear him. I told him, "I don't hear well." Then he came inside and shut the door. He observed me from top to toe and again from toe to the top, gathered his heavy eyebrows and stroked his moustache and said: "Who lives here?"

I answer "Mrs..."

"Where is she?"

"She went out."

"Will she be late?"

"I don't know."

"Are you her servant?"

"Yes."

"What do you see in here?"

He pursed his lips strangely and knowingly, he looked just like a scorpion.

"What do you mean, what do I see? You mean people?

"They pay you a lot, do they? Eh?" and stroked his moustache again.

"Who?"

"The people. Don't pretend to be stupid."

He smiled craftily and nudged me with his elbow.

"Why should they pay me?"

"Why? Because you serve them. Go on admit it. Admit it, and you'll see how good it is to make a clean breast of it."

Everything around me went dark, and I thought I wanted to die. I couldn't hear what he was saying. Amid the darkness, I'd fallen into, I only knew that he took me by the hand and made me sit on a chair.

I breathed deeply. I could tell him. At that moment, the door opened, and it was her. She looked at me, then she saw the policeman. He spoke to her from under his lowering eyebrows. But she said something to him, with the same sharp tone she uses to me sometimes, and then he raised his hand to his cap, while she, laughing the while, opened the door for him. Thus, the policeman left.

I took a breath again.

"Next time, if someone like that comes, you won't speak to them at all!"

"But he frightened me!"

"I said, you won't speak at all. Not at all. Nothing. You must make signs to them that you are dumb."

"Dumb?"

"Exactly. It's not so hard. Your deafness will help. Do you understand?" She put her finger in her mouth. "No sound!"

Then she continued more gently:

"So you can see how I will look after you, from tomorrow. I will take you with me to the bank so that you can get your hands on your own bank book. Who knows how much money you have. You'll be able to take it on your own."

"What will I have to do for the bank book, to get the money?"

"You have to sign for it. You write your name on a piece of paper."

"My name? I don't…"

She seemed pleased:

"Of course, I forgot, you don't know how to write."

I was shaken. It was as if my mind had been pierced by a hot needle. Because I can't write, I won't be able to take my money out. I won't be able to build a house. It was as though from far away, I could see her licking her lips, which were saying something I didn't understand.

In the afternoon, I went to the grocers. She sent me to get some biscuits and butter. I found Mihalis. I sign to him that I wanted him to come out so that I could tell him something and I left because his boss was there too. In a bit, he caught me up the street. Again, he put some raisins in my apron pocket. I felt my heart inside me was torn like a little fluttering bird as I settled into his hand the money I'd been given. Mihalis was confused:

"She paid your wages? So why me?"

"Keep them safe."

Mihalis put them inside a wallet he carried, and we separated. But somehow it looked to me that Mihalis had grown taller and more good looking and, in spite of that, I was sad. An uncontrollable desire made me want to run to the cemetery to tell everything to my marble lady. But I didn't go. She was waiting for me at home because we'd be having people for tea. We would get the silver tray out, the good napkins, and the porcelain cups.

When the doorbell rang, and I opened the door, I saw another policeman.

One of those grand ones with lots of gold braids. He asked me something. I couldn't hear him, my head was buzzing, and I thought, whatever happens, I'm not speaking. I pretended to be dumb. My lady came and welcomed him in. Nothing happened, they just went to drink tea with the excellent tea service in the bedroom.

I sat in my corner in the kitchen, without the lamp on. Through the window, I could see the full moon. I was frightened. As if that cold fear wasn't enough, I could hear the bell tolling. Something kept me sitting there on my stool. I didn't budge. Maybe it was the moon with its white threads of light. A few minutes passed. I knew that it would be that devil, the doctor. He would find her. No, the world could come to an end, I wasn't going to open the door. A little time passed, and the bell rang again. I did nothing. The bell rang again. I didn't move. More time passed. The moon had tied me up well, there in my corner where I could hear my heart beating in my ears. In my tongue.

Eventually, she turned up in the kitchen. Her hair was rumpled, her gown half undone, stark naked underneath as I could see in the light of the moon which fell on her and lit her up.

"What are you doing here? Why are you like this? Are you ill?"

I got up. No, I wasn't ill.

"The bell rang."

"Right, it did."

"You didn't open the door?"

"No!"

She didn't say anything more. She went out. She left the kitchen door open, and I saw that all the rest of the house was in darkness. Just me and the moon. I took a couple of steps into the corridor. There wasn't even any light in the bedroom. The strip of view couldn't be seen underneath. The grand policeman had left? He hadn't moved.

And how long would this darkness last? I wish I could have gone out, could have run to the grocer. It was just around the block, only a little way. I could have seen Mihalis. When I got back home again, they would turn the lights on. Everything would have been calmer.

But no. There was more to happen that evening: The bell rang again. The grand policeman, with his shiny buttons, came into the kitchen and gave me some matches. I lit the lamp. He was still buttoning up his jacket. He smiled and said:

"Go on now, open the door." And he put some money in my hand and went towards the kitchen door. I stayed stock still when I saw him unlocking it.

"Go on, I said, open up! And smiling horribly and oddly, to frighten me.

I pushed the money into my bodice, lit the light in the corridor and opened the door. The doctor said:

"Where were you?" His eyes were shining.

"I was here."

Didn't you hear the bell?"

"No."

"And you heard it?"

"I heard it."

"Where were you earlier?"

The stress was driving me mad. What could I say? Suddenly it came to me: "I was sleeping."

His eyes fastened on my chest where I had stuffed the other one's money, I felt something tearing inside me he went straight into the bedroom which had lights on, and the door was wide open. I stayed in the corridor to see what would happen. She went inside but didn't close the door. She was sitting at her dressing table, calmly powdering her face. He stood behind her and said something.

She smiled at him through the mirror, like the devil. Then she got up, went close to him, very close and rubbed herself against him like a cat, coaxingly she opened her white arms to embrace him. Then he smacked her across her face and again and again. She tried to get away from him, stumbling. He hit her harder, which knocked her down. Her gown became undone, the red one, and she lay on the floor stark naked. The man was so angry, he looked like a real monster as he grabbed her hair and pulled her upright. She looked so different with her naked breasts shaking, unable to lift her head as if she'd been strangled, and he had no pity but hit her with his fist in the eye. She tried to kick him, and they both fell on the floor, rolling like animals.

What should I do?

He jumped on her again and started hitting her. He was surely going to kill her. I rushed in and grabbed a dense metal top brush which I found in front of me and with all my strength, I hit him across the head. He let her go. He stepped back, stumbling like a drunk, his eyes turned up, and he lost consciousness. They were both on the ground. Him motionless, while she was scrambling about trying to get her dressing gown on and cover herself up, one of her eyes was closed entirely, and blood was oozing from her nose.

Something flashed through my mind. It was as though I saw in front of me the grand policeman, accusing me of killing them both. He would send me to prison! Even though this was going through my mind, I ran into the kitchen and got the vinegar, the water jug and towels, and ran back to the bedroom.

They were still on the ground, She was in the same place, crying, and had spotted the little rug in front of the bed with blood on it. He was still cold and I was more afraid of him. I threw a wet towel and went to him. I wet a cloth with vinegar and water and put it on his face. Then he moved and sighed. Thank god! He was alive. I put the towel with vinegar and water on his head. He opened his eyes and saw me, with his eyes still on me he got up:

"Did you hit me?"

I hung my head and waited. My last hour had come. He put his hand on his shoulder- I watched him, I thought I would beg him to have mercy on me.

"You are a good girl," he said, "we'll see each other soon."

Without a glance at her, he picked up his hat from the chair and left like a thief.

"Shall I make you a hot drink?"

Nothing. Silence. I thought that a hot drink couldn't hurt. When I went back into the room to give it to her, she was still sitting there, on the floor. As she lifted her head, the bloody towel she'd held to her face fell down, and I beheld...I will never forget as long as I live what her lovely face had become. I burst into tears. She watched me out of her one right eye. The other one had swollen up. I left the hot chamomile to one side and took her hand and cried. She wanted to kiss me. I put my cheek on her swollen trembling lips. Apart from my mother, so many years ago, nobody had kissed me like that. Something inside me twisted, and I cried even more from happiness. I stayed with her all night. I fed her the chamomile tea at first with a spoon as her mouth was too swollen to open wide enough to drink it. I helped her to put on her nightdress, and I continuously bathed her face with a damp cloth, until dawn came and I fell asleep. I was lying on the rug by the feet of her bed. After I had soaped it and cleaned the blood off, I fell asleep on the dusty corner of the carpet. I slept profoundly and sweetly without dreaming. She didn't go out for four days. We carried on with cold compresses on the eye. She wouldn't let me open the shutters, not the door, no matter how long and hard they rang the bell. For all our needs I used the kitchen door, the key was still in from when the grand policeman had used it.

I met Mihalis.

"I want to talk to you: You should take back the money you gave me."

"Why should I take it?"

"You should put it in the bank. Didn't your lady say she'd give you a bank book?"

He said: "Put that money with the rest."

"But she has the bank book."

"Well, you should ask her for it, and take it. You should have it. Don't leave it. Don't leave it with her. Are you listening?"

"Okay, I won't leave it with her. But please keep the money until she gives it to me."

He made me leave and then I said:

"Mihalis, you know I'd like to learn to write my name. How can I do it? I want to be able to..."

"Sign?"

"Is it tough?"

He looked at me. He became amazing, taller and older. He took up more room on the pavement on which we were standing.

"I will teach you," he said and left.

The day became lovely. Only then did I see that the sun was out. I wanted to run and jump and shout so that all the passers-by, and all those in their cars, carriages and houses would hear; "Mihalis is going to teach me to write!"

I turned the corner on my way home and stopped abruptly. There was a carriage in front of our house. Worst of all: the grand policeman, he who we'd given tea to on the excellent service was ringing the bell. I hid. It was better if he didn't see me. I gratefully thought that I had locked the kitchen door because he knew where it was and he could get into the house through there.

Yes, he was ringing the bell again! Of course, nobody was going to open it. I was terrorized even more. I squeezed myself into the corner and waited for quite a while. I looked out carefully so that he wouldn't see me. He was knocking with his fist on the door. I went back into the corner. I waited. I don't know how long I waited there. I only know that a tradesman came and left his cart, full of vegetables, on the pavement. He looked at me strangely, said something and smiled, just like a fox. I moved away.

He pulled his cart along and said something else. What was I to do? I couldn't leave, I had to stay there and watch what would happen. I had a bad feeling. The wind had become pincer-like, which upset me. The fox with his cart was just there. He took an apple from the cart and showed it to me.

Oh god! What do I need with you and your apple? So, I gave him the finger, and he spat at me but moved his cart away.

That was something anyway, and I calmed down a bit. I moved forward to see the street. The policeman was still there, but he wasn't knocking any more. He was walking up and down the road. She was too afraid to open the door. From that awful day she hadn't spoken, hadn't eaten anything, and didn't open the door to anyone, she just cried all the time. I made her something to eat from what we had; rice, pulses, something for me to eat too. So, what was going to happen? Did she want me to starve to death? We didn't have any tenants anymore, so we didn't get any money. Yesterday I couldn't pay the grocer for the soap, Mihalis' boss speaks and I am listening as best I can;

"You should leave there if you don't want to end up like her. Do you hear me?"

I was watching his lips. He was the right person, and I respected him. I noticed the little bit of foam that gathered on his mouth at the right, where he was missing a tooth.

"I know a noble house. They will pay you well, and you won't have these complications. Are you listening?"

I was.

"One day, you poor thing, you'll end up in a situation which you won't be able to get out of, ever. And that would be a shame.

"In prison?" I asked

"If it was the only prison...there are prisons for girls, other types of prisons which are much worse."

So, one way and another, he leaned closer to me, and I learned awful things. They will close her down, he said, she'll go to prison. One of the worst types of prison — in a house. That's what is waiting for her in the carriage. The grand policeman came for tea at that time, to be sure of what was going on.

"To be sure?"

"Yes," said Mr Vassilis, "only for that."

"But he went into the bedroom?"

"That's how they make sure of such things. Now, he is betraying her. Stay here. God lit your way here. It's better if none of them see you."

"The other one, the doctor, is a pimp. Someone told Mr Vassilis at the *kafenion*. Sure thing. He sells young girls to rich old men."

My head was spinning, I couldn't take all this in. My stomach started to heave, and I felt dizzy. I stayed where I was in the back-room. Mr Vassilis is speaking;

"You were lucky to get away. Don't you budge from here. In the evening, I will take you to a new house. They are decent people, Christians, with their children, with everything. They will look after you. If you are good, they will find you a husband as well."

"But what about my things?" Mr Vassilis responded angrily: "Do you hear me?!"

I heard him. But something else was worrying me. Crying, I begged:

"Oh, Mr Vassilis, my bank book. All those years of work for

nothing. She has it. My money...the house I want to build..."

"Your bank book, she ever shows it to you?"

"No, but she told me about it all the time."

"Oh, you poor thing. I too, with just words alone, can build palaces..." He laughed. Then added:

"You had no bank book and no money. She told you to make your work better and not complain."

I was silent. But my mind was working overtime until I realized this; if I hadn't given Mihalis those 21 drachmas, I wouldn't have earned a farthing all those years. Seven years for 21 drachmas.

When he shut the shop up at lunchtime, we sat down to eat. Sardines, olives, and cheese, which I love. I had a little wine, it tasted like poison to me. But I couldn't eat all that lovely food. It was impossible. My stomach, you see, was upset again.

Later we went with Mihalis to the house to see what had happened. As we came out of the corner, we saw two policemen standing in front of the house. We stopped at the edge, and Mihalis took my hand. The carriage was still there. Our door was open, my lady came out. She had a yellow scarf around her face so she wouldn't be seen. She walked like a drunk. One of the policemen pushed her into the carriage from which a hand emerged to pull her quickly inside. The policeman turned and closed the door of the house. He stuck a piece of paper on it and got into the carriage.

They set off.

The piece of paper shone white on the front door.

From the back window of the carriage, which was negotiating the potholes of the street, I could see part of my lady's yellow scarf.

CHAPTER 2

The Foundation Stone

We will start with the house on Monday, we said. I got up at dawn on Monday and took the bus to Haravgi, the sun wasn't out yet, and it was all dark. The streets were shiny with dew as if they'd just been scrubbed. There were only two men on the bus with me. Of course, I'd started early! But how could I have stayed at home? How could I have slept? Happiness brings worry and sleeplessness. I learned that recently and wondered why they always say that happiness relaxes one. It really doesn't look as if there is only one rest. We all know what that is.

On arriving in Haravgi, I went straight to my plot. "My plot of land" Mine. Mine! How could I possibly sleep? Mine is not a little word!

The coincidence was that as soon as I arrived at the top, the sun suddenly shot out a beam of light and started to rise correctly, admittedly. It's a beautiful thing to stand on the massive mountain with the sun aflame to light up my plot of land, even better! A cold wind blew and reached into the depths of my lungs, cooling my heart and giving me strength. That flame had reached quite high in the sky by the time the builder, Mr Manthos, arrived with two workers.

"Welcome!" they said, with their eyes on my handbag.

I understood what that was about and said: "Ok, don't rush, I'll give it to you in due course!"

Mr Manthos looked at me curiously.

"Where is the priest?"

The priest? In my excitement, I'd forgotten.

He continued:

"And the cockerel?"

I'll go, I'll run and find a priest and a cockerel! We went down the hill, the three men and myself, to the *kafenion*. We sat down.

The owner brought us a cockerel, his own one actually, and he sent the boy to fetch the priest. I paid. I held the bird while the men finished their coffees. I drank lemonade because my throat felt dry. The priest appeared.

So now here we all are, going up the hill again, me holding the cockerel which was trying to escape — flapping helplessly, angrily, even though he didn't know that he was going to be sacrificed for my house. On my left, the priest puffed on the climb and kept singing. On my right, the builder holding the knife the owner of the *kafenion* had given him. I wished one of those photographers would appear to take a photograph, and I could write underneath: "Panoria lays the foundation stone of her house..."

Everything went smoothly. The priest intoned his blessing, the cockerel was sacrificed. The stone was laid, and they all said "Welcome and Happy Landings" again. I gave the priest 50 and 20 to both workmen. These ceremonies certainly cost money.

The sun rose higher, and the world got hotter. We parted. I left on the bus, which also stopped at the Athens cemetery. I felt as if I'd suddenly become small. As if I was the other Panoria. I got off. I wanted to go and see the marble lady, my protector, to tell her about my house. It would be good just to see her again, without speaking to her. With her marble smile, she would have understood. Then I was ashamed. No, I am no longer that Panoria! An adult woman like me can't go visiting without good reason. I repeat "without good reason." The statues in the cemetery, and moreover I certainly can't speak to them.

Was I crazy? I turned back even though I had already reached the big gate at the end of the Eternal Rest Street. I took the other bus and arrived home.

My master was sitting in his office, as always. He lifted his head and struggled to smile:

"Happy landings," he said.

At least this time I don't have to pay anyone! I thought.

"Thank you."

"You don't look very pleased."

"No. Of course I am! Why wouldn't I be?"

True. What would happen if I wasn't pleased? You have to be pleased. You must. Do you hear it?

New Job

The world opened up another door to me and I went to a decent family this time. I learned how to stand nicely in front of my superiors, I learned to smile at those who paid me. They dressed me in a dark dress, with a white apron and cap for the visitors, and I was to laugh at them too. I learned to iron well. I struggled so hard with the shirts. In the "proper" houses, they roll differently, make the beds conversely and cook separately.

They taught me economics. "Economy", a word I never expected was my destiny to hear so many times from the old lady in the long dark dress, as if she herself was Fate. She often hit me. To "teach me."

It's difficult to learn things well, I realised that and I made my mind up. I got used to it. Sometimes my head would buzz when she slapped me, my left ear more, it was the most damaged. They used red thorny wheels to grind me, my whole body hurt. But, as I said, I got used to that. After those valuable lessons, God's doctrine always followed: You must learn. You need to know these things. When in the future you have your own house and become a housewife, that's the only way you'll manage: by being thrifty. That "when you have your own house" went through my damaged hearing and spread through me like a balsam. So I learned to respect those who knew how to be stronger.

At night I was in my little room, in the attic, and I didn't care if my legs and feet hurt from standing, from all the work. I focused on the pain that wracked my needy bones from my waist down. Never mind. I ran up the metal stairs and into my small room, my own little world.

There, "proper" people couldn't see me. Their eyes were not judging me to see if I was worthy, and how much I was worth. I felt free. It will sound silly, but that was my playground.

I was the lady of the house there. I ordered my servant around, the one in my mind, whom I saw in the broken glass of the mirror which I had found in the rubbish bin on the first day I arrived at the house.

I had put it on the plank which hung from the wall near my bed, with its clean straw mattress, with the striped sheets and its warm blanket. Beside the mirror, there was a clock. It had yellow hours, and a bell on top. The watch accelerated time during the night.

Every evening I gave it to the "grand lady" so she could wind it up, she set it at five in the summer, six in the winter, seven on Sundays and days off. I stood in front of the mirror and undid my hair and, as I brushed it, I spoke (always loudly, which I liked best) to my reflection. I mean, to my servant. I told her about Mihalis. I explained that Mihalis was my husband and her master. "Master…" It sounded strange to me when I first said it. I continued: it was the iron master's shirt.

"Don't be lazy, be economical!" Order and economy. She should get it clear that her master doesn't like mistakes. She must be careful when cooking the meat the master brings home. "Don't use too much butter…make soup for the children…" I said to myself, I was the only one who heard it and I alone argued with my servant because she was cheeky. She made fun of my economy and even dared say I was miserly...do you hear that? Miserly! I should hit her so she would learn. But no. I didn't want to catch those who needed me. Those were some of the things I said and did until I could no longer keep my eyes open from how tired I was and went to sleep.

There were two children in the house. The evening that Mr Vassilis first took me to the new lady I stood in front of her, afraid that I might not hear everything she would say to me, so I told her about my disability, to which she replied:

"It doesn't matter. It's better this way, you won't be able to hear things you shouldn't. They won't fill your mind with...foolishness."

She asked if I had any other relatives apart from Mr Vassilis. He, out of kindness, said that I was a distant relative of his. No. I had nobody else in the world.

She was pleased.

"Good", she said, without any joy. While she said that, she was studying me and weighing me up, and I felt as if she was sprinkling finely-sifted sand onto me...this sand had started to bury me, when one of the children's head popped up from the door - it was Nikaki. His eyes fixed on me, he began to dig me out of the sand. Later on, Stratis, the eldest, appeared as well. I smiled at them both with all my heart, thinking about the good they had done to me.

But I must listen, the lady was speaking: "You like children. That's good. Take care, though."

She was getting angry and the sand was rising up again. She wanted to finish her job and bury me underneath it.

"Be careful, I don't want you to caress them or speak to them. Don't even think of kissing the children, or I will throw you out. Not even parents should do that, because it spoils them. So, certainly strangers cannot."

Whether or not I was a stranger, however, the children wanted me. I did my best to make sure they needed me, because I surely needed them. I pretended they were my lost siblings. I told them stories so they would eat their food. Stratis and Nikakis rode horses, a white and a black one, through the Earth's most dangerous places. Oh, how they loved hearing their names! They slayed the seven-headed monster, speared and killed infidels and dervishes who tortured Christian slaves, and kept on riding in search of new adventures. The Earth was not large enough for them to dominate, their strength was such that they took to the skies, their horses grew massive wings and searched for places to right the wrongs, even in the countries and the flaming worlds of the West.

The words came quick to my lips, coming as they did from the depths of time, from a voice which sounded like my mother's.

Once they had been fed, the children would be taken to their beds by the old lady. After they'd made the sign of the cross and the old lady had turned the light out, I hung around — when I could manage to do so. I pretended I had something to tidy up, until the old lady eventually left. I would stay in the room for a while until my eyes got used to the dark and I could see the children's heads on their pillows and my mind would pause for a moment so I could enjoy this new strange warmth.

My body would tingle and I would miss Mihalis. It was strange and I found it very upsetting. The strangeness continued even when I'd left the room. Then, I would rush to the kitchen, finish my jobs and climb the metal staircase to the roof. Sitting on the ledge, I would look at the stars for ages. There, somewhere hidden inside my furthermost corners, a sob would rise. Huddled-up, I cried and felt better.

The house wasn't much further from the grocer's than the other one was, just in the opposite direction, below the Acropolis in a small street. To get to Mihalis, I had to go out onto the avenue, turn right at Hadrian's Arch, and go back onto the short road to find the yard where Mr Vassilis and Mihalis lived. Mrs Foto let out other rooms too. Mr Vassilis would smoke his *narghilé*[7] in the yard. Mihalis whistled while he washed clothes. He was also working to pay off all he owed to Mr Vassilis, who had adopted him. Whenever I saw him doing this, I would grab the clothes from him and wash them myself. I liked doing it because then my mind was busy working. I imagined our house, with the balcony and the two lions. They were my husband's shirts, I held on to them tight. I felt as if by holding the shirts I was holding his hand, I tried with all my heart and soul not to let go so as to never lose him. My chest hurt from the grave and painful joy I felt all the time, as long as I was there, as long as I cleaned and washed, and scrubbed, and even more when I was in Mihalis's room and he made me read my new lessons from the book. I wrote my name clearly on the paper: Panoria Fokianou.

I could get my money out of the bank whenever I want. My bank book, the real one this time, was kept by the lady. She put fifty drachmas a month in my account and brought it to show me.

On a Palm Sunday after I had finished work, I polished the copper saucepan and the taps in the kitchen and Mr Vassilis gave Mihalis some money so we could go to church and light a couple of candles, one for him. He stayed in the yard with his *narghile*. He looked at us quietly and tenderly from under his half-closed eyes as we left.

I set off for the graveyard. Mihalis stopped.

"Why this way?"

"The church is this way, and it's closer."

"It may be closer, but I'm afraid of ghosts. I will see dead people in my dreams at night. I'm not going."

"Oh, come on!" I pulled him. The dead can't hurt the living. Come on, I want to show you something, I want to show you a statue. Don't be scared."

---

[7] An oriental tobacco pipe with a long tube that draws the smoke through water; a hookah *(The Oxford Dictionary for English).*

"I'm not scared!" Mihalis was angry.

We went into the church and a priest was intoning on his own. Candlelights shone in the semi-darkness. As they melted, the flames shook the body of the candles. We put the money for our three candles in the box. Later, we went to see my marble lady. I could tell that Mihalis was afraid, but I couldn't help it. We had to go. The time had come when I had to introduce my marble lady to Mihalis. I, in my head, of course, would say to her "We came marble lady, we came...Please give us your blessing, Mihalis and I..."

Mihalis pulled me by the hand. He couldn't understand the beauty of the moment. In fact, he was cross. He left my grip. He wanted to go. I was stunned. I couldn't stand that he would spoil the moment. He mustn't, it was such a shame...but Mihalis lost his temper. He shouted: "What are you looking at? Do you see now who is afraid of the statues and cries? Now, who's scared?"

The cypress trees got taller, the night was on its way, and I, the ungrateful one, made a decision. Following that living person, with his hot, sweaty hand pulling me, I could see the marble lady all alone drown in the dark without me having said anything to her of all that I had been thinking of telling her for so many days and nights.

"What, are you dumb?"

Mihalis stood in the middle of the road, in front of the marble sellers with crosses all in line.

"After all, you wanted to go to the grave, so what's stopping you?"

"What's stopping me, what do you mean?"

"Fear, deaf donkey. What else? Fear..."

I managed to pull out a smile, because I liked it when he called me a deaf donkey, it felt like a caress. We found ourselves at a crossroads, all gravel and rocks, which led uphill to isolated places. We sat on a rock and in front of us the lights were coming on in Athens.

More and more lights were coming on and a tingle spread through me as Mihalis embraced me, this sensation tortured my body more and more - I knew Mihalis was becoming a man.

The same man as the one called "doctor" — a friend of the woman who was taken away in the police carriage, the same it seems with the one, who, when he kissed me in that horrible way, had given me money.

Mihalis's eyes had begun to redden, he was so close to me. I couldn't swallow. Thousands of hot threads came from the lights of Athens, from Mihalis's fingers, and they pressed me firmly to his lips to make me melt, to make me lose myself. But no! I won't get lost! I pushed him away with all my strength. I took a deep breath and went running along the path like a goat, scrambling downwards, stumbling. Mihalis was coming along behind me, saying something, but I couldn't understand. He laughed.

Then something broke inside me, spread through my throat trying to strangle me. I would have died if I hadn't laughed with all my heart. Mihalis took my hands and looked me in the eyes, then bent to kiss me on the cheek.

We got home late. It was the first time I was that late. Stratis opened the door for me and said something, but I couldn't hear it. See, the children were waiting for me. My siblings. It's adorable to have siblings. It makes the world a sweeter place and makes you happy to be alive.

It wasn't long before the lady appeared. With her long blue dressing gown with its gold buttons, she looked like a queen. I smiled happily at her and went off to get undressed, without looking at her. I could feel something like a cold snake running through me. I turned around. The lady was staring at me.

Christ, what on Earth didn't she like about me? My dress? My jacket? She didn't even give them to me, they are so lovely. She weighed me up. She lifted my chin with one finger, as though she found me repellent, and spoke clearly so that I could hear her, she seemed to spit out her words:

"Shame on you! Good girls don't do that!"

She gave me a hard slap and shouted:

"Go and get undressed. Go and brush your dress, you should be ashamed, where did you go and roll around?"

She hit me again on the other cheek so that it didn't feel left out. There was some soil on my dress and some dried grass.

She didn't say another word.

All that week I tried hard to please her. Just like a dog looks at its master, every time before she spoke, I decided to try and guess what she wanted and do it before she could order me. The fear that she might throw me out was driving me mad. What would become of me if I ended up with someone else, like the lady who was taken by that carriage, or some slave-trader? I had bad dreams. Monsters and lizards wanted to kill me. I didn't even want to go out on the second day of Easter, which was my day off, in case she told me to go back. I said to her: "If you need me, that's fine, I won't go out." She calmly and slowly replied: "Go out. Go with the old lady and the children to the Columns of Olympian Zeus, they will come and find me afterwards here. You can go and see your uncle. Be sure not to be late."

There were crowds at the columns. Men, women, children. Enough children to fill your spirit and most of them were flying kites which adorned the sky and filled it with hope. If I hadn't been unhappy, scared that they would throw me out, that would have been one of the most beautiful days of my life. I felt full of joy though! I had the company of the children. I helped them, first one then the other, to fly their two kites. Even so, I couldn't wholeheartedly enjoy it. When I forgot about it for a while, distracted by the colours of the kites which floated up there in the sky, or by the many people around me who were trying to make me feel good and glad that I wasn't on my own, suddenly a trem-

or gripped my heart as if suggesting I should take care because I could still easily find myself alone.

When the old lady said we should go, I went off to see Mr Vassilis. What did I see the moment I entered the yard? My lady! My head started to spin, everything went dark and I could hear a voice inside me saying she didn't want me in her house!

My lady was speaking with Mr Vassilis. They turned around and saw me, Mr Vassilis smiled, or maybe I imagined it, I was so dazed. Then, my lady started to walk away but stopped and said to me: "Be sure not to be late. You have the key."

"Come and sit down," Mr Vassilis told me once she'd gone. Mihalis wasn't there. I sat down, trembling and watching his mouth. There was a swollen bit on the left, a tooth was missing.

"She's a good lady. Very decent. You are lucky."

"Oh, come on Mr Vassilis, don't tease me anymore, say it. Say it and let's get it over with. She wants to throw me out."

"Oh, you silly, what on Earth are you saying? No, she doesn't want to throw you out!"

I wanted him to repeat it, maybe I hadn't heard him right.

"What? Tell me!"

"Silly thing, no, she doesn't want to throw you out, she's very pleased with your work. If you carry on like this, she will arrange for you to marry Mihalis. She was asking me about him. I told her that he is also an orphan. He has nobody but me. I have no children...If it wasn't for..."

He kept talking, but I couldn't hear him anymore, I could just see his eyes grow sad. My head was spinning. There was so much to take in. How could I possibly hold the weight of so much happiness?

Then, Mr Vassilis stopped talking, puffed on his *narghilé* and let his mind roam free. Later on, as if he suddenly realised I was still there, he spoke again:

"Call me uncle, that would be the best. Call me uncle." He repeated.

When Mihalis returned from his errands, we told him what had been decided and "uncle" left his *narghilé*, took us to a patisserie and treated us to a cake each, he ordered a cognac. He looked at us.

He didn't speak, he gulped down his drink. He became a bit different and after a while he stopped talking. Mihalis and I didn't say anything. It was as if we weren't ourselves either. We ate our cakes and looked at each other. Like that.

People were walking along the sidewalks. Maybe one of those passers-by who saw us thought: "There's a father who has taken his children out for a bit." I wanted to say something about this lovely situation but I was unable to. When we got back to the yard, I started soaping some of the clothes, I put them out to dry and left again. I wanted to get home early, as my lady had recommended I did.

It was 7pm when I arrived. I had the key so I opened up. The whole of the corridor smelled of cigarettes. The light in the dining room was on. There, through the blue smoke rings, I saw the tableau - it had been altered. It was like a fake from another world. There, my master and a stranger sat. They didn't see me. I stood in the darkness of the corridor. I could see a large leather bag open in the middle of the table. The stranger took a bundle of money from the opening, tore a paper, wetted the tips of his fingers in a glass of water and started to count. Those fingers drew me like a magnet. They were yellow, long, gnarled, ugly. Every two or three bundles, he would wet his fingers again and carry on counting. Eventually, the master put out his hand. He touched the money, looking at the stranger through his gold-rimmed glasses, then took it. He put it back in the bag and closed it. The other person got up, I saw how short he was, like half a person. I left tip-toeing, trying not to make any noise so they would not hear me. The master came into the kitchen, he was a middle-aged man and his eyes through the glasses looked larger and angrier, as if he was displeased that I was there. He said:

"You are back already? Prepare some cheese and bring us some glasses for *ouzo*[8]."

"The good ones?"

"Whatever they are. It's not..."

I couldn't hear what else he said, then he left. It must have meant something. I like finishing conversations that I don't understand, or I get upset.

The bag with the money stayed in the house. The master locked it in the cupboard in his office and nothing changed at first — after the suitcase incident I mean — other than the fact that the master went out more often in the evening. He was often late and I left his food in the kitchen, covered up. My lady would give it to him when he came in.

In my little room, I watched the yellow hours on my clock ticking the night away. I saw the lights of the sky spreading their rays to hold me there, on the ledge of the roof, and remembered my conversation with Mihalis about our bank accounts and how many years I would have to work to earn enough money to build a room and a kitchen and put a balcony supported by two lions. When I first told Mihalis about it he laughed, he thought it was amusing and teased me, saying I obviously had a lot of money to spare to spend it on such fantasies...but Mr Vassilis agreed with me. In fact, he said that he would chip some money in so that we could have a bigger house and he could come and stay with us. He would have company in his old age. I hoped for all these things while sitting on the roof during spring nights, when the wind blew warm with the smells of the flowers I couldn't see.

At the time of the bag incident, I changed the stories I told the children. The horses had become cars and each child had their own, their wheels rolled over the whole world to cities with names like Paris, Berlin, New York. I didn't even know what I was saying,

---

[8] A Greek aniseed-flavoured spirit *(The Oxford Dictionary of English)*.

but when the old lady heard me, we were just the two of us at that point with the children, because those days the lady often went out with the master in the evenings. They even had new clothes especially for them, the lady's dress was made of silk, it looked royal with its open back, while the master had a black suit with satin lapels and even got new gold frames for his glasses.

"How do you know about such places?", the old lady surprisingly asked me.

"From the newspaper," I explained. I had been reading newspapers for a while, and I liked the world that appeared on paper.

She didn't say a word, it was as though she'd been bitten by a snake and was disgusted when she heard about the newspaper. She raised her eyes from behind her glasses, which slid down her nose, and looked intensely at me: "Since when is it your business to read newspapers? Papers are for the gentry, not for the servants. What's next? You've really got to keep your station, I don't like you nosing around, do you hear me? In fact, I don't like you at all! You can stop all that rubbish...come on children, eat up", she then turned to the children, who were all but interested in eating.

My supporters sat as still as statues. The old lady became furious and aimed a slap at Stratis — that was it! They started crying and shouting and kicking...plates, forks and glasses got smashed, it was a mess.

The old lady tried to slap everyone, without managing to, so, as if she had become embarrassed for being so clumsy, she left and shut herself in her room. She had turned quite livid with fury and was holding her stomach.

As she left, she said that the three of us would be in trouble the next day.

From all this upsetting situation, however, I gained something precious. Before eventually falling asleep that night, I couldn't think of anything else. She said "the three of you", meaning that she was including me, as an equal with her grandchildren. That evening I actually loved the old lady.

The next day, something that looked a lot like a siren made its astounding appearance in the house. My lady showed up early in the kitchen in her new crimson-coloured dressing gown and tried to enchant me again with her gaze, the specks in her eyes reminded me of a finely-sifted sand sprinkled like a fairy dust used to cast spells. She said, loud and clear:

"Where did you learn to read?"

"I learned...by myself."

"Very good. If you want to read, you can take the children's old books - I never want to see you with a newspaper in your hands again, is that understood?"

"Yes."

"Just a 'yes' won't do. You won't reread the paper. Good girls don't read newspapers! For Heaven's sake, if you get into those kinds of habits, you won't be any good as a servant. Do you understand?"

I didn't, but I didn't say so. What could I say?

They hid the newspapers and didn't leave any lying about no more. If we needed wrapping paper, I had to ask the lady. Then, they started smacking and punishing the children because they didn't want to eat without listening to some stories. They were supposed to go to school to learn, to become proper people. Up until then, it seems, they weren't. Is that why they needed me? I felt a bitterness seeping through me, so profoundly that I couldn't sleep at night. Sometimes I managed to grab a small piece of an old newspaper from a package and to take it to my room to read and learn something about the world. But it didn't make me happy anymore.

That's how things were until the old lady became ill and they sent the children to school. Stratis went to second grade — he had already had a few lessons at home — and Nikakis was in first grade. Money began to make its miracles more visibly now. The children were given their parents' beds, and parents bought new ones for themselves. They were made of wood and they were so low they hurt my back whenever I had to make them. Blankets and new mattresses were purchased, too. All the furniture from the front room was replaced with new items. A junk dealer came by with his cart and took all the old stuff away. I was sad, upset. I wanted to say something, but I was afraid they would think that I was speaking above my station. I wanted to ask the lady for some of her old furniture for my own house. We could have put some things in Mr Vassilis's place for the time being, I could have even paid her as much as the junk dealer, I wouldn't have expected it for free. There was also a stove - in the winter we could have lit it and sat around it, we would have cooked our food on it and saved money. What a shame I couldn't get myself to speak. The door was open and I could see the junk dealer on his loaded cart, leaving with all the things he'd bought off us.

That day the lady went to the hairdresser's. I heard her say it quite distinctly and I couldn't believe it. What was she doing, going to the hairdresser's? It's not like she was a man. It was the first time such a thing happened in our house. On top of that, she came back late. I had to go to the old lady to give her the medicine.

She was bedridden for days. Even though I wasn't a doctor, I could see that her days were numbered...well, what do you expect when someone only drinks chamomile? I was sorry for the old lady. I was more sad than I expected to be for her. Then suddenly one night on the roof, I understood that I wasn't sad for the old lady - I was only sad because she made me realize that people can end up like that. This made me ponder about becoming old. Skin withers, eyes dim, your body shrivels up and becomes thin, noses stick out in an ugly way and mouths become empty holes. It will happen, I thought, to everyone...to you and me, too.

I took the spoon out of her mouth and was about to leave when she put her hand out as if she was trying to reach out to me. Her hand looked like a bone with some skin attached. Her lips were moving. I couldn't understand. She made signs to me to open the drawer, where I found some photographs tied in a bundle with a faded ribbon, it was probably rose-red once. I gave her the pictures and she took them, trying to find one in particular. Her fingers were trembling and the pictures fell to the floor. They were scattered everywhere, I picked them up, gave them back to the lady and, finally, she found the one she was looking for. It was a photo of her as a young woman, holding a baby. Behind her, a palm tree spread its spiked leaves in the sky. Next to her stood a man with a moustache with waxed ends, he looked like a crook. I wanted to see what she looked like in the photo. She made a gesture that said I should put the other pictures where I found them and leave that one there. I rearranged the bedside table so that it rested against the medicine bottle. She was happy, I could see in her eyes that she her mind had started drifting away, going back in time.

That night I was scared to see the yellow eyes on my clock. They really frightened me and I couldn't get away from them even if I turned out the light. Instead, they got brighter and brighter and spread their rays as far as my bed. The rays would eventually land on top of me, they whirled and became like hot metal wheels that ground me up.

For the first time in 17 years, I woke up in the morning with a bad headache. So I said, with some satisfaction: "Now, I have a headache, like ladies do."

The wind blowing outside was ice-cold, the skies were heavy and white, down by Zappeion Gardens[9] and the clouds above the columns were of unusual and strange shapes: carriages, boats, horses. I kept walking, going further away, my legs strutting. I looked at the clouds changing shapes as the wind kept blowing.

It was Nikaki's name day. I wanted to get him a present, but I didn't have any money. However, I thought of something and

---

[9] National gardens in Athens. Called Zappeion Gardens because of Zappeion Manson, a neoclassical building in the heart of the Gardens which is used by Greek premiers as their office, for official and private meetings and ceremonies.

told Mihalis — we would be able to arrange it. I was given all the ingredients that had been bought at the grocer's and I made almond cakes. I had just finished them, when the sun spread its beams across the house opposite ours. Its inhabitants were all still sleeping. The lady did not get up early again, so I gave the children their morning milk. That day was Saint Nicholas' Day and the master got up first. He was all ready to go out and held his glasses as he cleaned them with his handkerchief — he didn't use it to blow his nose any more. He saw me through his window and smiled. I didn't like it. He said:

"Good morning."

"Good morning, sir."

His eyes were upon me. Suddenly, he asked:

"Why are you looking at me like that?"

Was I looking at him or was he looking at me? For goodness' sake, first thing in the morning.

Then I remembered: "You must be proud of Nikaki, may he live for you."

He scrutinised me:

"Thank you. You should get married soon and have children."

I was embarrassed, but he continued and I listened carefully as he added:

 "It won't be long before..."

I couldn't hear what he said after that. He realised and repeated: "It won't be long before you marry. After all, you've already found him..."

I still couldn't hear the end of the sentence, but I could tell he was still looking at me up and down. Suddenly, though, he embraced me and pulled me onto him while watching me through his glasses:

"We will pay for the wedding if you are a good girl!"

Here we go again. The "good girl" bit. He wanted to kiss me. I pushed him hard. I don't know where I found the courage. I mean, the courage to do such a thing. It looks as though my mind wasn't working correctly at that time to not think that he had the power to sack me. I said trembling,

"If you do something like that again, I shall tell my lady."

He let me go and didn't say a word, not a sound. But his eyes flashed dangerously. He grabbed ahold of my hand as I was about to go and said: "Be careful you don't regret it."

He went out into the corridor, and I held his coat out to put it on as I did every day, just as if nothing had happened. He left.

I went into the old ladies' room to tidy up. I changed the sheets because she had dirtied them. I washed her down. I pulled her up as far as I could, although she didn't weigh more than a little child, and I put a clean sheet underneath her and brought her the chamomile tea. She only drank two sips. I cleaned up her room, and then she made some signs to me again to open the drawer. She wanted her money. I counted it in front of her. She wet her lips and counted with me as if she was praying. Seven hundred and eighty it was. I folded it away again as she told me, leaving out two eighty, which she gave me.

"Because you look after me," she said. She made me sit near her. I tried to understand what she wanted to tell me. She was speaking about the mistress. She looked angry.

"She lost her mind."

She gestured to her head, her white hair. As she spoke, she was dribbling from her empty mouth. I see, and I watch. I must understand what she is saying. She should be ashamed to cut it... You..."

Me what? I try to guess.

"You. Do you like it?"

Ah, I see. She's talking about the mistress. I forgot to say that the day she went to the hairdressers, she came back with shingled hair. How people can change! She lost all her charm. She was no longer like a queen. The long crimson robe hung on her like it didn't belong to her. It made her smaller. She just looked like a bad girl. I didn't like it. But how should I tell the old lady this?

"You, do you like it?" she asked again. She had dribbled a lot onto the sheet, and some droplets had fallen onto my hand, I wiped them off with my apron and I was surprised by this new thing. "Stop, now, as we count my opinion how can I not tell her the truth, which in all honesty doesn't flatter my mistress? How can I not reveal the truth to someone like the old lady who is already on her way to the grave?' So, I thought that it wasn't really my place to say "No, I don't like it," abruptly. I thought of a better and more polite way to say it: She was prettier before. The old lady was satisfied. I am watching, she is saying something else, and I am battling to understand:

"Money spoils..."

I added what I couldn't hear "...people" was what she would have said, that's what would fit, and the same thing went around my mind. I couldn't understand how money, which could bring so much happiness — a home I waited to build and all the joys that would follow — how it could spoil instead of a fix? I didn't understand. Of course, the mistress was ruined, proof that the old lady had said it. But still, I couldn't get it straight in my head as it thought the very opposite was true until one evening sometime later, there on my rooftop where I was again thinking of it. I suddenly said to myself: "Do you remember when I get what I want, and Mihalis makes money, and we also get rich — all the strangest things happen in the world and we watch them happen — do you want me to be spoilt?"

I remember what I said then. "Never mind just let me get rich, even if I do get spoilt in the meantime, just to see what it's like!"

That day, the celebration of Saint Nicholas, when I brought the almond cakes for Nikaki to the table at lunchtime, the lady smiled beautifully, the children clapped their hands, and the master looked at me and said: "Bravo! You're a good girl!"

The good girl spoilt the festivities for me, I wish he hadn't said it, at least then, with his ulterior motive. Happiness came again when the sun came later and spread over the marble of the sink and shone on the taps, lighting up the shelf with the copper kettles. I took the warmth of the light deep inside me, and it brought the image of Mihalis to mind and enthroned him in my heart, like a king on a velvet throne and...

I felt someone tapping me on the shoulder. The lady. I had lost myself in my thoughts and didn't notice the door. That should never happen. Because I've lost the sense of hearing, it's vital that I have my wits about me, and I hate being surprised. I'm concentrating on what the lady's saying:

"Leave everything and run to the doctor. Tell him he must come immediately. The old lady isn't well."

"Now she tells us! Has she only just realised that the old lady isn't well? And what did she want the doctor for? Just send me out onto the streets when the children will start arriving for Nikakis party, and I have to get the plates, spoons and cups ready because they'll be drinking tea. Now there's a new fashion. Tea! Did you hear that?! They will spill it all over the place and make a mess!" I was brave enough to say: "We didn't give them tea last year." She interrupted "Last year was different. This year, more children will be coming, and we will be giving them tea." And she said it in such a satisfactory way that she seemed to me to get taller, and as she got taller, I got smaller. I was thinking about all of this and found that I was already outside and on my way back from the doctor; he said he'd be about 15 minutes. If you'd asked me, I would have said they should have fetched the priest. But of course, nobody asked for my opinion.

The first children were already standing at the door, accompanied by a skinny teacher. Last year we didn't have either teachers or tea, and this year it looks, we have both! I rushed to put on my uniform, a blue dress with a white apron and a cap, and I can't stand the heat, and I would love to tear it to pieces and shove it in the rubbish bin. The bell is ringing again, and more children are arriving, most of whom I've never seen before. All with their teachers. They were all seated in armchairs. They didn't leave like the servant girls when they leave the children at the door, and I had to give cakes to *mademoiselle* and the *fräulein*. "That's what I think she said, and cognac, did you hear that?! Cognac!" They didn't even let their eyes light on me, they were more important you see. Only a step up actually, they were servants too, they were paid as well. It seems that the distance of one step is considerable when you see this from above; and small, non-existent, when viewed from below.

The doctor turned up just as I was serving tea to the children. I left the teapot in one of the teacher's hands; one who had come to drink the cognac, eat and sit, and went with the lady into the old lady's room. The doctor took her pulse while watching the seconds pass on a watch with a chain and yellow numbers. It was like mine. I helped the lady lift the old woman who was swaying like a heavy barrel, to settle her on the pillows better, and she opened her eyes. Large, dark eyes, full of fear for what they were already beginning to see. The doctor left, and the lady stayed with the frightened old girl, and I went back to the children.

We had opened up the dining room and the living room. The children sat around the table, eating and drinking, and behaving so well I could hardly believe my eyes. I felt like laughing out loud when I saw them all like little lambs. That was because across from them were the skinny ones, just like Cerberus! But Nikakis saw me and noticed my eyes and was tempted as if to say, "Just wait and see."

He gave the child next to him a push, that was the signal, the child pushed the one next to him, and the one further down the line fell off his chair, and someone else, by mistake, fell on top of him.

Another one pulled the tablecloth with all the plates, glasses and spoons on the Cerberus attached, one of them held onto the tablecloth. I caught the porcelain teapot. "We wouldn't want to lose that, would we?" The skinny ones started giving out slaps, and shouting, squeals, laughter and crying, which even deafened me, so you can imagine what it was like for everyone else! They started to run around the table, slipping and trampling, turning the chairs upside down. It was incredible how the lambs turned suddenly into wolves.

We had some breakages: four cups, three plates, the sugar bowl! That's not counting the cake trampled into the carpet, and some spots and marks that looked like blood.

Just then, the lady comes in. She said something to the teachers, and they collected the children and made them sit on the chairs and play some quiet games, and she took me back inside.

The old lady was slumped on the pillows with her mouth open, and her eyes turned back. Her forehead was shiny. The lady gave me a damp cloth to wipe her forehead with and left. I was alone with her.

The night has many shadows which swallow things up in the dark. After there was nothing left, I began to feel that the shadows were coming to swallow me up too, and fear gripped me, I got up, stumbling, with my hands outstretched to repel the shadows as much as I could. I got as far as the door frame, I found, feeling with my hands, the light switch and turned it on. The old lady's eyelids fluttered — I saw it, and my stomach churned, for goodness sake! It was hours since she did that. I took the damp cloth which had fallen on the floor and shook it out and cooled it and put it on her forehead. She didn't seem to notice. I left it there and stayed near her, rubbing my tummy to warm it up, which seemed to help. Eventually, my lady came to let me go.

I went inside and cleared the table, took all of the teacups into the kitchen and threw the broken pieces in the rubbish.

The children played peacefully with their teachers. They ran around the chairs which were all in a row, and one of the skinny teachers had a trumpet — it was Stratis' – and when she blew it, all the children had to find a seat. What a stupid kind of game that was!

But Stratis, who wasn't playing the silly game, appeared with two balls. He throws first one and then the other one straight at the children, ruining the stupid game. Each one tried to catch the balls wherever they landed, and they were thrown again, while the Cerberus was running to get ahold of them. They knocked a vase down and smashed the window in the balcony door through which the wild, cold wind blew and shocked us all. Even the children stopped suddenly in their tracks. Then one of the skinny ones began: she took the two children that she brought, home. I picked up one of the cushions from the sofa and stuffed it into the hole in the window to stop the horrid cold that was filling the room. The lady appeared to see what was going on; she was crying. The teachers took the children, and the girls came to pick up those who were left. But Stratis was cross. He went and beat the cushion I had put in the window with his fists — thank goodness, I'd rammed it firmly in and it didn't fall. I pulled him, I don't know what came over me, I gave him two good slaps. How could I have been so bold, and nobody said anything? But the whole day and night of this Saint Nicholas celebration were strange.

The light alone stood vigil in the old lady's room when my lady sent me back there. The sweat stood in droplets on her forehead. But she saw me and was struggling to tell me something. How could I understand? I sat next to her and held her cold hand. She squeezed it, I don't know where she found the strength. Her hand warmed up in mine. Her hand became one with mine, and from the depths of time, it brought the memory of flames leaping up and fire. A boat...and the sea spread through all my mind. From all that unending deep water, one by one, hands shot up; living hands with rings which hooked onto the wind, which fought to grab something, not to drown...the agony of the memory seemed to go on for a long time. The old lady's glassy eyes were fixed on mine, alive.

They wanted something. I made to pull my hand away from hers because mine was beginning to get cold, but she wouldn't let me. I was obliged to follow her gaze was fixed on the icons.

Next to them was a candle. I got up and lit a candle and put it in front of the icons. It looks as if that was what she wanted. I went back to her. No, she beckoned with her hand, as if she wanted me to stay there. She continued to watch the icons trembling by the light of the candle. I stood by the flame in front of the faces, which seemed to come alive again. I made one odd prayer of my own. I don't know where it suddenly came from: "Saints, please don't let her struggle any more; take her soul. Ease her way so that she won't suffer. Now that she is at death's door, please open it so that she can go into her kingdom and be at peace." I don't remember what else I said. When I turned to look at the old lady, she was still with her eyes open. I went and sat next to her without holding her hand. Again, the flames began to fill my mind. Back, the sea...the hands...

Until I felt someone tap me on the shoulder. I shot upright...The lady. She bent down to the old lady and closed her eyes.

I was still trembling when I went to the children. I picked up the balls, the trumpet, and some other toys they had got out. I put them away. They were cross and wanted to carry on playing. Then I told them that their grandma had died. So, they wouldn't be frightened, I said to them:

"She's gone on a journey."

"With what?" Nikakis asked me.

I was confused, but I didn't take long to find an answer:

"With her soul," I said, and was pleased with myself.

They looked at me in disbelief; I explained.

"Don't make a fuss because it will confuse her soul, and her soul will lose its way to heaven."

"Then where will it go?"

"It will come back," said Stratis, and looked at me as if he was making fun of me.

"No, it won't turn back. Come on now, time to eat supper."

When they were undressed and in their beds, the little one pulled on my apron.

"Sit here. Don't turn the light off."

He was afraid. I was scared too, and I would have liked to have stayed there all night. I would have told them a story of the soul and its journey, which would have gone until the sun came up again in the morning.

But I couldn't. There was a lot to do tonight for the dead woman. I washed her in water and vinegar, as my lady told me, and the pain in my stomach had become so bad it was making me dizzy. She helped a bit, just a few things; she couldn't do more. She slumped in a chair and looked yellow. I was scared. I left the old dead and rushed to the living. I gave her a whiff of vinegar, and she came around. Then I went back to the corpse.

What can I say? I had a hard time dressing her, to tie up her chin, closing up once and for all the dark hole of her mouth. Later, I took the comb from my lady's hand, which was shaking, and combed her thin hair, and tied a small plait on the top of her head. Some hairs remained in the comb, hairs that the dead leave for the world of the living. I pulled them out of the comb, tied them in a knot, and put them in the pocket of my apron, along with a button from Nikaki's trousers, found when I was picking up the toys. I would sow it on tomorrow. I left a candle burning in her room and my lady's, and I went. My sink was like a boat with all the plates I had to wash, and then I tidied up. The master came, and I served their food. Afterwards, he asked me to stay with the corpse so that his wife could relax, as she was exhausted. He went out to see if he was in time for the newspapers to print details about the funeral.

When I read the newspapers myself, I saw it: Funeral, Mourning.

Just as it should be. When you get married, or you die, and you have money to pay, they write your name in the newspaper.

My mind was full of these things while I was sitting next to the dead woman, when the master suddenly appeared. He came close to me and stroked my cheek. I got up; I wanted to get out.

"You are a good girl."

The candlelight was flickering in his eyes and filling them with little flames. They glowed and became fire. I wanted to scream. He shut my mouth. He's saying something, but I don't understand. But he won't let me go. He is holding me firmly by the shoulders like Satan himself.

"We will all end up like that." He is speaking clearly and is indicating the dead woman. "It's a shame not to…"

I pushed him. Tried to get away. He holds me again. He speaks more softly.

"Don't be afraid. I don't want to force you. When you want to…"

He leaves me. Goes to the door. Stands there. He looks at me. I'm afraid of him. "Come here; I want to tell you something," he beckons. I went as if I wasn't myself. As if it was someone else who was nearer to him, and I was her. So he speaks and is it I who understands him, or the other one?

"You have got prettier, did you know?"

He bends down and puts dry and hot lips on my cheek. His hand grips my waist. I feel a strange coldness, as if a window has suddenly opened and all the north wind has blown in. As if the corpse had got up and weighed us up…on my bones, another iciness comes…

"Don't! The dead woman!" I shouted.

He turned pale and left. He went out as if he was being chased.

So I kept the old lady company all through the night of Saint

Nicholas. It was a very long night, one of the longest of the year. So long that my body got a chance to rest and stop freezing and shaking. My mind cleared as the night progressed...and took her shadows far away.

The comfort of the dawning day seeped through the grilles and slats of the shutters when I managed, through the line of time, to see my white house with the balcony and the two stone lions holding it up.

I could see two children on the balcony, like Stratis and Nikakis, playing...Later, they would grow up and marry. I would become an old lady, like the dead one on the bed. I might even have been rich; they would write my name in the newspapers too.

Like a shiny black boat, the hearse came and stood in front of the house. Four columns on each corner held by a black kneeling angel. Four horses, anxious to take the old lady. The street was full of cars. The dining room and the front office, the corridors were full of people. Relatives, others I knew, some not; there were strangers. I thought I saw that short one who had counted my master's money that Sunday. My head was buzzing; I saw and didn't feel what I saw. I saw people come out of the living room where they had put the coffin, and when I saw the gravediggers go and get her, I ran into my room, dressed in my good frock, to follow behind the hearse.

I was already in a car with some unknown ladies when my master pulled me out. He was furious and about to say something when he suddenly softened and smiled sweetly, but not at me, at the ladies who were greeting him from inside the car. When the car started to move, he turned to me, angry again:

"Are you crazy? where do you think you are going?"

"To the cemetery. Isn't that where we were going?

"We are going there. But not you. I said not you. Did you hear?"

I heard. Not me. I was supposed to stay at home and get the coffee ready for everyone when they returned from the funeral.

I turned back to the empty house. I swept, tidied up, and opened the dresser to put out the cups. All the cups, the good ones and the common ones. I took them to the kitchen on a tray and counted them. Twenty-three, twenty-four, and six common ones that made thirty, and six others with golden handles — thirty-six... And as I was counting, I was crying, which was something that lightened my heart.

I hadn't thought that the house would seem so empty without the old lady. I would be working in the kitchen, and she used to come in with me and stand there. She wanted to complain because I had tied up her jaw. Why had I put her in her shroud? She did not want to leave the world and leave her photograph, which was on her dressing table. She didn't want that. I was trembling and too scared to turn my head towards the door in case I might see her. I was so sure she was standing there, ready to be angry with me. It's a dreadful thing to have a dead person mad at you.

One day, Stratis said to me:

"Come on, silly! What was that you were saying about grandma going on a journey? She died, did you hear? She died, and don't treat us like babies."

"They gave her a first-class funeral!" said the other one, "and wrote our names in the newspaper: The grandchildren Efstratios and Nikolaos."

Efstratios. Nikolaos. Those names sounded strange to me. I couldn't see that they suited the children...."my brothers" And I was "silly." They shouted it loud enough that I would hear it. Maybe I was silly. I said it before, I'm sure, that in this upside-down world, how do you know if you are stupid or smart?

At the new year they gave me a tablecloth and six towels for my household, the lady said. They also gave me a raise. They would put 100 drachmas a month into my bank account.

Overjoyed, I ran to tell Mr Vassilis and Mihalis on Sunday, and I took the package with the tablecloth and towels to show them.

That Sunday, they didn't allow me to tidy up. I found everything clean and tidy, and that made me sad; I didn't want Mihalis to have to do those kinds of jobs. It was my house as well. I was angry, and I told them so. Mr Vassilis wasn't smoking his *narghile*. He looked at me thoughtfully while counting his worry beads one by one:

"Don't get so worked up," he said, "when you come here, you should be able to rest. They work you hard enough at that house…"

Mihalis was looking into the distance, as if he didn't see me. There was something wrong. A horrid feeling of unhappiness filled me. I didn't know what to do, so I went into the kitchen to make some coffee. When I took it to Mr Vassilis, he forced a smile, while Mihalis seemed to have come to a decision, and said clearly enough for me to hear:

"Let's tell her, she won't be offended."

Mr Vassilis nodded his consent and carried on counting his beads, Mihalis was speaking, and I was concentrating as hard as I could: "Listen Panoria, something has happened to our uncle, he hasn't been paid some money that's owed to him. He has to pay an account by Saturday."

"What is that? What did you say?"

"An account, a debt. A piece of paper which, if he doesn't pay, will mean he will go to prison."

Mihalis didn't say anything more. I was waiting. My mind was dazed, dizzy with the word "prison" which I had heard, and it couldn't contain it. I notice Mihalis is speaking again:

"We thought perhaps you could give us the money…if you wanted to…"

My mind cleared suddenly. That was it; I could help them! Why didn't they say so all along? "Of course! Happily! How much is it?"

"Four hundred and eighty drachmas," Mihalis answered.

We made our plans immediately. I would ask my lady for my bank book to give to my uncle, who looks after it for me. That's what we said. That's what happened, my lady had no problems with that, and I felt proud, and foremost, when on Friday Mr Vassilis came to fetch me from the house, and we went to the bank together. I wore my best frock, and I signed. Indeed! I wrote my name with large letters on the paper just where the man pointed with his finger from the other side of the little barred window. Lots of people around and they all saw me sign my name and wondered how I knew how to write and how was it that I had money in the bank?

And they were serious people with big bags and briefcases, with papers in their hands which they were taking around hurriedly, while a massive silver shiny clock watched all that rushing about hither and yon.

When we came out of the bank, my uncle thanked me and said: "You are a good girl." He didn't say it like the other one did, the master of the house I mean. It was a beautiful day with a few clouds so that the sun didn't blind you, and the roads were full of people and trams and cars. I marched along with the crowds. A person like me could help a friend at a difficult time. All-day my heart sang!

At noon, my lady returned from the hairdressers. She was so different, I didn't recognise her, and slapped my hand across my mouth so that I wouldn't scream. She realised and said: "I dyed it. I think blonde hair goes well with my black clothes. It's in fashion."

She'd changed a lot recently. When she asked what I had done with my uncle, she didn't even ask for the bank book back. Her head inside and out was filled with the fact that blonde hair went well with mourning. That it was fashionable. The children liked the change in their mother, they told me that she had become more beautiful, like a painting. The master watched her all the time they were eating, and looked again and said something whilst smiling, and she was so proud. My lady's hair that day filled the house with happiness. If you asked me, I wouldn't know if it was better or worse, but it was certainly different. A third woman. One, a proper lady — the one I met first. The second lady was the one with her hair cut who looked younger, and looked cheaper with more money, now the third...I don't know what to say any more...Only that I can't use it - when she first appeared I was afraid, it was as though there'd been a mistake and I was in a different house. Well, be that as it may, it's her hair, and she has the right to dye it green if it's fashionable and goes with the mourning.

The next Sunday it was raining, and I found Mihalis alone at the house. He was cleaning the sink. "Move over," I said and gave him a push. He hugged me, and his lips hurt me. His body had become a flame of steel as he dragged me to Mr Vassili's bed. He was struggling to push me deeper into the hot mud.

From far off, foreign, I heard my voice saying: "Don't...don't. Don't." Something inside me didn't want this, something which shouted without being heard, that this was not right, while the hot steel flame waved above me and the hot mud increased...until...I don't know how...some unknown strength maybe that which suddenly appeared from that "it's not right" cry, separated us. I found myself, I don't know how, perhaps I'd run there, in the kitchen, I locked the door and turned on the tap, pouring cold water on me and ended up stark naked and wet. The kitchen was soaking. Later I dressed, cleaned up and mopped, I was in a hurry, I wanted to leave before Mr Vassilis came back. He mustn't see me and confront me.

Mihalis was huddled in the corner. He watched me with fear, his eyes cast down. I went to the door. He didn't speak. I opened it, and I left.

I hadn't walked far along the street, and my legs felt heavy, my body felt strange, and then I felt that I should go back, go back and hug him, fall and burn his fire, because my body had flared up with the cold water I had poured on it. It tortured me mercilessly.

That torture didn't leave me. The days passed well enough with more work...But the nights, and the more I was tortured, the more afraid I was of Mihalis. I upset him too, whenever we saw each other. I didn't let him touch me. Because if he felt me, I would have died. I would have been lost in lust and shame. Sometimes I thought I would go mad. I nearly did.

One night, I was on the roof in my shirt standing half-naked under the stars. They, in turn with their light, poured thousands of needles through me. They brought me a strange feeling. Their light came together and poured onto me, became steel flames. My lips whispered: Mihalis, Mihalis and I trembled all over, while my hands pulled the shirt off and I ended up naked under the stars, until I became aware of my body and unstoppable sobbing...Afterwards, dreadfully ashamed, I ran and jumped into bed, shaking with cold as if I was in a snowy tomb. Things like that happened often, and I suffered during the nights and I got thinner as the spring warmed up as it became summer.

I cried a lot at that time, while my clock showed me with its yellow eyes the passing of time. The Sunday after that one with Mihalis, I went to see my marble lady. There were two red roses on her crossed hands. Who on earth could have put them there? I sat down near her, I didn't speak to her, I couldn't say anything. I just looked at those red roses. For a long time. Eventually, a little drop, a glimpse, showed behind the cypresses the full moon. Then I wanted to ask something. I said: I would like to be stone as well if only I could become stone. I would stay in the world forever and I wouldn't suffer.

Night had fallen by the time I left for Mr Vassilis' house, Mihalis wouldn't be on his own at this time. The yard was in darkness, and there was nobody inside. The house was closed up. I stood and looked at the sealed door. They weren't waiting for me, not even Mihalis was waiting for me. There was only light in Mrs Foto's window, but I didn't knock. I left. On the road, I was thinking: How big the world is. So many people. I thought about all those many, foreign and unknown.

It was Sunday. This, I knew. I had no other relatives. The girl they had taken recently on the other floor of our house who smiles whenever she says anything to me as if she is making fun, or because she feels sorry for me, and passes by. People get bored with me because they have to take care of how they speak to me if I am to understand them. So, with a nice bit of food which I save for her sometimes, so that she will like me and not find me annoying when they give me cakes and sweets, I keep them for her to please her, and that way, gradually, I got her to talk to me a little. I learned that she has a brother who is a soldier. That she comes from an island. She told me the name of the island twice, but I couldn't make it out. Now I pretend I know it because I'm too embarrassed to ask her again. I wanted her to be my friend. I would like to have invited her to my room so that I could have a visitor. But she was either afraid of her mistress, or as I said before, she found me annoying and showed no inclination to come. Every Sunday, her older sisters came to fetch her, and the three of them go out.

I am alone. I'm alone in the house as well. The lady has left everything up to me and goes out more often, we have more work, never mind the clothes she has made for her. They have put the children in the most expensive school, and even they don't come back at lunchtime to eat.

That was how I went along the road that Sunday, with everything going around in my mind when I felt someone grab my arm. The lights had already come on. My heart fluttered, Mihalis said. It was Anetta, the dressmaker. I hadn't seen her since my previous house, the one where they took my lady away. Anetta smiled with her crooked lips. "Well, Panoria, how are you?"

She kissed me on both cheeks, and I kissed her as well. Oh, how good it was, my eyes filled with tears from happiness. Anetta took me by the hand, we went after the corner, to her house she opened her door and turned on the light. She made me sit on the same sofa as I'd sat in the past, all those years ago.

Seven, eight years? Only the covering was different, it was embroidered. She had a new bed, and she didn't seem to be so ugly.

She was wearing a lovely dress. She opened the dresser and gave me a mandarin sweetmeat. I told her what had happened. I told her about Mr Vassilis and Mihalis.

"So are you going to marry Mihalis? I hope it works out."

She said something else that I didn't hear. Later on, after she told me all about her news and wondered and was shocked at what can happen in this world. She had, she said, an elderly gentleman who she kept company with. They go to the cinema, even the theatre and he has taken her to a restaurant. He gives her presents. She's thrilled.

"Don't you sew anymore?"

"Of course, I do not hear myself, though, just what I can manage. I go out! I want to taste life, Panoria, to live!

"And...is he too old?"

She laughed and pouted, which showed her dull teeth.

"Not that old...just..."

"How old? What did you say?"

"Around sixty-five..." She shouted it, so that I would hear it.

"And did you know...?" She went on coming closer to me, and I can feel her hot breath. She smells of onions. "Old men look after you. They take care. You don't have problems."

"What sort of problems?"

"Oh, don't tell me you don't understand, silly."

I didn't know whether I understood and what I understood and what I didn't, but what I could see was that Anetta looked very happy and that all this happiness was due to an old man. She'd become more beautiful, and she went on.

"Bravo to you. You are a clever girl. You are bound to have lots of savings after they put it in the bank for you. But be careful.

Keep your wits about you. Don't ever give any of your money to anyone. Do you hear it? Not to anyone."

"Not even to Mihalis?"

"No, not even to Mihalis. Listen to me, and you will remember what I said to you."

I left Anetta's house quite late, and when I got home, there was nobody there. I started getting the food ready in the kitchen when Stratis and Nikakis rushed in. They'd been to play with a friend of theirs from school, and their eyes were shining.

"Well, it looks as if you had a good time. Did you play well?"

"We played," said Stratis. He said "we played!" in a strange way.

"So, what did you play?"

They looked at one another, half-smiling, but they didn't answer.

"Why don't you say anything? Are you going to tell me what you played?"

Stratis changed his expression and said quickly, "Many different games."

The younger boy seconded that and said like his older brother. He's ten this year, and the other is twelve.

"Lots of different ones."

"I can ask what are those "lots of different games?"

Suddenly I notice that Stratis's eyes have a strange glint of cunning, like an adult, while asking the most unanswerable question I have ever heard

, "Why don't you tell us what you do every Sunday with your Mihalis."

The younger one added, "With your grocer's boy."

If a thunderbolt hit me on the head, I don't think it would have shaken me as much. I couldn't think of anything to say. I just went to the sink and grabbed a clean plate, and pretended to be washing it, and without turning around, I said:

"Go and get undressed. I'll put your food on the table."

They left the kitchen without saying anything. I put their food out, and they ate it up without saying another word to me. I didn't open my mouth either.

Maybe from that day, or maybe a little earlier, began to be "bosses." Couldn't pretend any longer that they could have been mine, my brothers. Not any more.

It was during those days that they had bought Stratis his first pair of long trousers. When he put them on, he looked to me like a younger version of his father. Later on, one day, when Stratis had gone out, the younger one came into the kitchen.

"Panoria, remember last time when I called 'your Mihalis' the grocer's boy?"

"Well, he is."

He half turned and looked at me. He wanted something. In a little while:

"Panoria. Hey Panoria, are you listening?"

"I'm listening."

"Tell me...are you going to marry Mihalis?"

"Yes."

"Every Sunday you go out for a walk together?"

"Yes, we do."

"And...is it a nice walk?"

"It is."

"The other day when we didn't want to tell you, do you know what we were playing?"

"What were you playing?"

"Grown-ups."

"What do you mean?"

"We pretended to be you and Mihalis. Mothers and fathers."

"How do you play this?"

"Well, each of us has his wife or his *fiancé*. Some of the bigger ones said that they wouldn't marry their girlfriends. The girls laughed."

"You had girls with you? Did you have a girl?"

"I did, yes!"

"Who?"

"Aliki. Stratis had Lena. We asked them to come when we go to the new house as well."

"What? Where are we going?"

"To our new house. You, a silly deaf thing. Didn't you know?"

"No. What new house are you talking about?"

"Oh, poor wretch. Haven't you heard the talk about it? And we are always talking about it...and you don't know about it. I can't believe it! Papa wanted a villa in Kifissia. Mama[10] said though, that all the posh people go to Kolonaki."

"Well?"

"Well, we bought a house in Kolonaki. Seven rooms. Two drawing rooms, an office for papa..."

---

[10] Mother or mom in the Greek language.

That evening I was shocked at how much could be going on around me that I wasn't aware of. They only tell me what they want me to know, and I wait for them to want to tell me. Why would they want to? What have they got to gain from me? If they needed me, perhaps for my money, for example, then...maybe. I got confused and felt dizzy and didn't know how to make sense of it all.

A woman came to help with the move. Two men from the master's office, and a moving van. Really enormous. I went inside. It was the first time I'd been in a lorry. They made me sit up high with the things so that I could hold onto the large mirror from the dresser so that it wouldn't break. Stratis rode next to the driver to show him the way. The others all came by taxi. I was like a queen on her throne where I was sitting on an armchair up high. The lorry went so fast and shook all the things around, and I was concentrating on holding onto the massive mirror, and I could see from the inside that we were passing through Athens with its houses, with its columns with the stadium and Zappeion Gardens with its gardens and tall trees, and the palace, and Syntagma Square with its people darkening, dots on its squares, and the hotels, and we turned from Kifisias Avenue where it is called Vassilisis Sofias so that we could enter the realms of the posh people. The lorry strained on the hill. I held tight onto the mirror, so tight that my hands were hurting. Above us loured Likavitos Hill. The world was opening another, bigger door for me to see what was happening inside. To understand. I felt a pang in my heart as if I had been stung by a wasp. All that I was seeing receded and I could only see in my mind the little room I had left, the roof with its stars, the cemetery with the marble lady, Mr Vassilis' grocers, the yard. All gone. They'd left me...Of course, I would go on Sunday to find them, all those that I had loved for so many years. I went. But it wasn't the same. Everything had changed. Even people. Mr Vassilis. Mihalis. I said as much:

"They have a marble bath. A toilet just for the servants and one for the guests."

"A lot of work for you to have to clean all those places," smiled

Mr Vassilis.

"The work never ends. It's a real palace though. You should see the white doors. You should see the drawing rooms and the parquet floors."

Mihalis who until then hadn't said anything, he said in a complaining tone, "Ah, that's why your nose is in the air and you don't come early any more to help us wash and clear up."

They both seemed to be complaining. I went quickly into the kitchen and found lots of dirty clothes. I started to wash them. I always liked washing and cleaning. I imagine those people who I can see as clear as at the cinema at the moment. They make stains on their clothes. I always feel ashamed of thinking like this, so I rub the clothes extra hard to get them clean and get rid of both marks and images from my mind.

"They'll be paying you more that you have more work to do," Mr Vassilis said.

"Yes, they have given me a raise. So, the uncle could you give my bank book back so that I can put this month's money in the bank?"

Mr Vassilis went out, and in a little while, he put the bank book on the table. He didn't say anything to me about what he owed. I finished my jobs and got ready to leave.

"Stay a bit. Let's talk," said Mihalis.

I sat down. He was opposite me, with the table between us. At that moment, it seemed to me that our lives were all over. That we were an old couple sitting opposite each other, while something trembled inside me.

Mihalis spoke:

"You know, I am leaving."

"How? What did you say?"

"I am leaving."

"Where are you going?"

"To join the army. On Thursday, I have to be in Corinth. In the infantry. I have to stay there for forty days."

"And then?"

"Then, who knows where they will send me."

I couldn't see anything across from me. My eyes had darkened...

"You could do something for me if you want."

"Say it. Go on. What can I do?"

"Your master. From what you say, he has become a key person. He will know people. Here, take this. Here is written my name and whatever else is necessary for him to speak to the administration in Corinth. Or maybe they know some other crucial general who could arrange for me to be sent to Athens so that I don't get sent far away? What will happen to Uncle, to you, to me...if there is a war?

"A war? Why?"

"You never know what's going to happen. Hitler in Germany..."

I can't remember when I got up from opposite him where I was sitting, or how we found ourselves embracing. How I sank and burned and melted under the iron flame of his body. Then, heaven opened to me, and I drowned in unspeakable joy.

I left him all the money I had, and I had quite a lot with me. My lady had given it to me when I passed by to pay the dressmaker. I told her she wasn't at home and took my own money and went to the dressmaker again in the afternoon on Wednesday, and then left to see Mihalis. Mr Vassilis wasn't there, and we were a couple back.

I cried in my new bedroom, which once again was above the kitchen. Opposite me, I had Likavitos Hill, and the all-white church of Saint George, which I beseeched to look after my Mihalis. I had all my things to support me: the clock with its yellow hours, a lovely little table which they gave me because they didn't want it any more, a completely new armchair, just a little damaged, and I had even hung a picture on the wall, one which they didn't like. They said it didn't go with the new house. My bedroom had become a real sitting room. Even had curtains.

Never mind the mirror. They gave me that because it was broken on one edge as if I needed a new one without damage to see the woman I had become. The woman who cried and filled her face with wrinkles. I cried a lot in that room for my man.

I had become a different woman — a married woman — and I searched in vain for the girl who stayed in the piece of broken mirror which had been thrown in the rubbish. Then I threw it in there again when we left for the new house.

I gave the document to the master to look out for Mihalis. He said he didn't know anyone in the army, but he would ask at the stock market. That was the first time I heard the words, and he repeated it for me: "Stock Market."

On Sunday, Mr Vassilis struggled to explain to me that complicated thing that the stock market was. About the games which were played with money. There were people who bought and sold air. Where, if they were smart, they could win. It seems that the master was clever. Bravo to him!

Mr Vassilis looked at me through the shining slits of his half-closed eyes. He wants to speak, and I am listening:

"I had also been clever..."

He was silent. I wait.

"I was a sailor. Charcoal was our cargo. Some smart guys in there had a different cargo though."

"Like what?"

"Oh, never mind, you wouldn't know. Let's say it was, something to smoke."

"Smoke?"

"Something that you can make into cigarettes, and when you smoke it, you dream. Many people want to dream. They pay a lot for it. They wanted to bring me into the game, and in just three voyages I would have had enough money to buy a new house. But I was afraid."

He lit a cigarette — lately, he'd given up the *narghile*, he'd got bored of it — he carried on looking at me.

I am listening.

"So, I lost her."

"What? The ship?"

"No, the woman."

"I don't understand, uncle."

He got angry:

"Yes, stupid. It was smuggling. Understand? If you're found they throw you in jail to rot."

"So, it was good that you didn't get involved."

"No."

"Why, no?" "That wouldn't have been honest money, uncle.'

"There's no such thing as "honest money" There's just money."

"What of the woman?"

The mermaid...she has stayed here forever. Look at her!"

He unbuttoned his shirt, pulled his vest up, and over his heart on this chest was the tattoo of a mermaid, a woman's face, long black hair, beautiful, mythical and with the turned-up tail of a fish. It was the first time I'd seen such a thing. I was stunned!

"In Genoa, there was a Japanese man. I held her photograph in front of his eyes, and he made the tattoo."

"Did it hurt?"

"It hurt. That was why I did it. So that it would hurt."

He went silent again. I wanted to know the woman's story.

"Dear uncle, won't you..."

"No. Not today. Today my heart hurts inside here as if the Japanese were tattooing it. I'll tell you the story some other time. I'll let you know how a woman can be caught by money alone. But with a lot of money.

He buttoned up his shirt, and looked at me as though he'd noticed me for the first time, and smiled:

"You are the only one I've known to be different. Strange, of course..."

He lit another cigarette, which was weird. In a while, he got up and came up to me. So, close, that I could feel the heat of his body, which bothered me. I moved away from him a little, without meaning to. He carried on looking at me through his half-closed eyes with the shining slits. I felt my heart beating. I didn't budge. Suddenly he became angry as if something was making him very sad:

"Come on now, off you go. It's too late."

The tattooed mermaid on Mr Vassilis' chest kept me company all the way home. I tried to make something of that mixed up story, but I couldn't manage to. Maybe because a dreadful flame was bothering me. A yearning which made me long even more for Mihalis. At least perhaps the master can bring him back again. But he didn't say anything, as if he'd forgotten all about it.

One morning when I took him his coffee, I screwed up my courage and took a deep breath and asked him. He looked at me from top to toe and then from toe to top as though he was enjoying the study he was making of me. He took his glasses off and put them carefully next to the coffee. He took my hand and pulled me close to him. I felt like giving him a good slap, but I didn't because I was afraid to hit such an important man who knows how to play with money. But I managed to get away from him and ran and locked myself in the kitchen.

He didn't speak to me again. Nor did I talk to him again about Mihalis. When his wife wasn't there, he had started to look at me strangely, as if he was studying me. I got away from him at every opportunity and huddled in my kitchen — a white kitchen —, where I was the mistress and the boss. I grabbed the saucepans and I also had the habit of banging them on the marble sink. Bam! Boom! I enjoyed hearing the noise. I opened the drawers and shook them. I could listen to them, and I was happy. The same with the cupboards. Then I started to feel less angry.

One day when he had studied me again, and I had gone to the kitchen and started banging. The door of the cupboard annoyed me, and I gave it a strong kick and marked it and sat later to clean it. The lady appeared. She was wearing a pure silk dressing gown which had no buttons but closes with a sash, and it was open because I could see as far as I shouldn't have been able to see.

It seemed as though I was looking at the one who was taken by the carriage. Never mind, the blonde hair which spoiled her and made her look different, worse, of course. But then, hadn't we all become different? Even the master had white hairs over his ears which shone and made him look more cunning, like a fox. Anyway, I was talking about something else. About that time with the banging. She suddenly appeared in front of me. She was in a bad mood and shouting. "Are you mad? What is that noise? Why are you banging those things around? If you are in a bad mood, you should get over it somewhere else, and not with our things. Do you understand?"

I didn't say a word. She shouted louder: "I am talking to you. Do you understand?"

Not a word from me.

"Why don't you say anything?" She asked.

I don't know what came over me, but I said: "Because I don't want to."

She was furious and wild enough to eat me. She ranted and raved. I heard some things, but I didn't care a lot.

She was going on and on, and I was holding a knife as though I was cleaning it. Inside something was building up. Something terrible that had never affected me before. I wanted to be able to pass a knife right through her throat, to see if she would still shout then. I was afraid of the awful flash that blinded my mind and dropped the knife. In spite of myself, the badness was building up and taking me over. It brought the wheels to grind my head, to grind me up completely.

I found myself sitting on the kitchen chair. A strong smell of vinegar made me open my eyes. My lady, with the bottle still in her hand, was overseeing me. She was studying me in the same way as her husband did. I was embarrassed and made to get up, but she took me by the hand and made me sit down. She spoke clearly, loudly, and calmly.

"You became dizzy. Be careful. I hope you haven't done anything silly with your *fiancé*..."

I didn't speak. As if I was made of stone.

"I am talking to you. You have to tell me."

I didn't open my mouth.

"For your own shake, you must tell me. We can take some steps..."

"Take some steps? I felt as though my lips were whispering.

"Do not be silly. If you are pregnant, you will have to get rid of it. Otherwise, I will throw you out."

I sat and listened to her. She explained everything.

I stayed up all night. I was so sad. If I was? I didn't know for sure. If I was? Can you believe it? I spent some nights talking to it, petting it, singing lullabies as if I already had it with me. I even caressed the wind which blew over my pillow. I could see there Mihalis's eyes. They were the same. He was his real son. Its nose, and the mouth. Ah, the cheeky one, you're hungry again...you will suck everything out of me...you will...

It was something like madness. I tried everything I could to recover from it. I followed the lady's advice. I lifted heavy objects. The walnut table in the dining room. I raised on my own without the children's help, as usually happens. I pulled the carpet from under one side and then from the other. I brought the sheets down from the rooftop while they were wet during a rainstorm and took them back up again afterwards on the metal fire escape. I did lots of different things, but finally, everything was organised and I couldn't say any more if I was, because it was sure that I wasn't. Thus, I couldn't sing lullabies to him or anything. With all that my body hurt, I couldn't get comfortable on my mattress and slowly I got better. My lady gave me aspirin.

And so, I avoided the shame, because as she explained, it wouldn't have been shameful if we already had our own home. If...

Mihalis wrote often. One day he wrote: "worried about your health. I had a dream." I replied, "Don't worry, I'm fine."

I sat in my room to read an old book of Stratis in the evening. They had thrown it away during the move, and I had taken it.

I had also taken some half-filled exercise books, and there, I struggled to get used to writing nicely. I can't tell you how happy I was when I wrote my first letter to Mihalis. Nor will it ever be said.

And once again the newspapers kept me company. I get through. They opened my eyes and showed me the panorama of the world, and I even felt better about my ears. When you can learn, it's almost as though you can hear.

All that lightened the torment of longing which filled my body. The longing named "Mihalis" came and filled the room and held out its hands and pulled me into its embrace, and I melted.

It was summer and we went off to the country. When I first saw the magnitude of the sea, I was terrified. My mind filled with the smoke and fire and hands looking for help, hands grabbing at the wind and trying to hold the water. At nights, all the wet darkness spread out in front of me, filled with the heads of the drowned.

I ran and hid in the campaign bed — that's what they called the linen folding bed which they had given me — and tried to sleep to get away from all those ugly memories. I was afraid of the sea, but, in spite of the fear, I felt its pull.

Slowly, the images from my memory began to fade. When the sunset and the sky went red and painted the water, I couldn't help but watch. I let my eyes follow the red waves and I felt the sea breeze cool me off, when the blood-red sun below the hills of Piraeus and the first star appeared to hang over the water like a trembling light. Then I left at peace and all my bad memories were finally gone.

The house was right on the sea. It had a garden, a large pine tree, two eucalyptus trees and at the edge of the garden was a small room, mine. Whenever my master left, I went and sat on the patio steps and just gazed away. When the first star appeared, and before all the others came out in the heavens, the boats left the shore and went out to the sea, little fishing skiffs and big ships from Piraeus. I watched them as they got smaller and smaller until they became little dots far away in the sea, where the sea and the heavens became one. My mind took flight and I found myself on the balcony of my house, the one held up by the two stone lions.

I could see Mihalis coming back there. At first, he was a tiny dot in the distance then he gradually got bigger and bigger. My happiness increased because I was holding our child by the hand and we ran to meet him. We opened the door of our home...but, just as I was opening the door in my dreams one day, a car came and stopped outside my master's house. A real car. The master was at the wheel, the lady was next to him and the children sat behind. They made signs, laughing, that I should go to them. I ran. The master said: "Get in the back with the children, we are going for a ride."

My lady added: "Lock the front door first and bring the key."

I locked the house and got in the car, sitting behind with the children. We went to Varkiza. It was their own car. They had bought it that same day, and that day I ate with them all at the same table for the first time and I didn't take the plates away, I didn't wash them either. Unbelievable. But it really did happen.

We got back home early because some of their friends had arrived - there was a couple and the short guy with the briefcase who had counted out the money for my master. He was no longer carrying a briefcase, although occasionally he would take a piece of paper out of his pocket and give it to the master who, adjusting his golden framed spectacles, would read it, sign it and give it back to him. That's all. It seems that for some decent and smart people money just kept increasing, enough for them to buy cars and for me to eat at a restaurant and drink beer, and for a waiter to take my plate away. Bravo to my master! God, give him a long life.

That evening, when I brought them their coffees, I saw that they were having a lively discussion, surrounded by a few newspapers. They seemed pleased, their eyes were shining and they all spoke at once. I made out the word "war", which upset me, then I told myself I couldn't have heard right, so I managed to get some sleep.

In the morning, I gathered all the newspapers which were lying around the patio. I took them to my room, next to the pine tree, to read in the afternoon. I managed to see a large print which said: "The Danzig issue is at a critical phase. The Germans fear a coup.

A lot of young people are moving into Danzig from Poland." It had a map of Europe, with black lines drawn on it, which said 'Map of Europe' on top.

I told myself I would read those papers in the afternoon, even though I didn't understand what dangerous things were happening in Danzig. It was terribly hot and the pine tree smelled of resin, which made me dizzy, so I went to have a swim in the sea.

My lady had given me an old swimsuit of hers, it was red. At first, I was too scared to go into the water, but after seeing my master and other neighbours do it, I made my decision. Of course, I didn't know how to swim, which was why I just lolled about in the shallow during the siesta when everyone else was napping. I kicked around in the water and when I splashed it, it caught the sunrays — it looked like flying diamonds. I moved around, with one leg floating and kicking, splashing the water and making more diamonds, standing on the other and hopping around while my arms were making the proper movements that I had seen others do. It was amazing. I called Mihalis and he came to me, into the water, so he could see how well I performed the trick. I spoke to him aloud, and he said:

"Lift up the other leg if you can. Go on, silly. What are you afraid of? I am here, I'll catch you."

I replied: "No! I don't want you to catch me. I don't want you to!"

He added: "Since when? You are mine, aren't you? Isn't that why we married? Isn't that why our uncle blessed us?"

"Yes, of course. But not now. Not here in the sea. Don't! Stop... we'll drown...you shouldn't...Don't...", and I quickly swam back to the shore. I sat on a rock. The sun was burning me and I hurt as if I was ill.

The days passed. I really did get sunburned. I slept well though, I felt strong and crossed myself and gave my thanks to God.

Later on, England declared war against Germany. I read that in the newspapers, it was written everywhere, with big letters. Mihalis accompanied me more often now, on the land as well as in the sea.

He watched me from the photograph he had recently sent me from Serres. He was wearing a uniform.

"Don't be afraid, Panoria, let the important people in England and Germany quarrel between themselves. We smaller countries have no reason for going to war. Don't be afraid." That was what he said in his last letter.

I wasn't afraid, but I questioned my master and he answered:

"Maybe it's not out of the question that we could get involved in the war."

He said it as though it pleased him.

"Would the war be good or bad for us?"

"What do you mean?"

"Well, I mean...if we are the winners, will they give us back what we lost?"

"Who?"

Then he understood. He looked at me with pity and said:

"No. We won't get them back. They've gone forever, they gave them to Turkey."

"They gave them?"

"Now we must look after your *fiancé*. Where is he?"

It was as if he had given me a gift! I was dizzy with happiness and I ran to get the envelope with the address.

"Give me a pen to make a note of it."

"It doesn't matter. Keep it. I've got it written somewhere else too."

"You mean you can write? When did you learn to write, you sly little thing?"

"I learned on my own."

"Bravo. You are not one who will get lost in life."

Why I should get lost, I didn't know. Never mind. He looked at me. He didn't speak, just watched me. I began to feel bad, because I realised what was in his eyes and I wanted to go, to run into the kitchen and start banging the saucepans around to let off some steam. But I couldn't. I had to learn more, I had to take care of Mihalis.

"We won't get involved just yet," he said. Better never to get involved, then we all become wealthy. He bent over and kissed my hands — the first time he did such a thing. My hands...he seemed to get really angry, more than any other time he had approached me, and again he sent me away.

He will look for Mihalis. The thing I couldn't understand was why we were going to be rich. Why many, as he said, were going to be killed but we would survive.

On Sunday I got on the bus and I went to Athens. I found Mr Vassilis and he told me of totally different developments, of which he was most afraid:

"Panoria, we are going to get lost..."

"How? Why? Mihalis?"

"The poor one. Pity for our child."

"Speak, uncle, what happened? Did you learn anything?"

"What's more to learn, poor you. Don't you know that there is a war going on?"

"Of course, I know."

"What more do you want, then?"

"Did something wrong happen to Mihalis?"

"For the moment, nothing has happened to him. Something could, though. Pity for the poor orphan."

"But Greece is not at war..."

"How do you know? Did the prime minister, Metaxas[11], tell you?"

"No, my master told me."

"So, that's what he said himself?"

"So he told me."

"Then go and tell him he is wrong and he has not a lot of time left to celebrate."

"How? Who? What are we talking about?"

"Listen to what I say. Some people like him took their chances to win the war. How could I explain how businesses develop and money goes to the clever ones, like your master? Let it go."

I gave him some money because we had to buy some provisions for the shop as long as they were still available, in the future we would no longer be able to find them.

During the week, I went back. The masters had all gone on a day trip in their car. Mr Vassilis came with me to the bank and took out the money. In fact, he told me that it would be a good thing to take all the money out of the bank as banks were no longer safe. Then, as if he regretted what he'd said, he continued: "Ask your master, who is sharp and knows about these sorts of things, to tell you what you should do."

The following Sunday I said I wouldn't go out, I stayed in all afternoon then decided to go into Athens. I didn't go to see Mr Vassilis, it was too late, and I wouldn't have found him at home

---

[11] Ioannis Metaxas, Greek general, premier and dictator, was born in 1871 and died in 1941.

anyway. I decided to go and see the 'Marble Lady', even though I wouldn't speak to her. What could I say? There were so many thoughts whirling around my mind. But I still wanted to see her. I was turning around the Columns when I saw that it was getting late. In the autumn, the night was quick to arrive and it started to get dark very soon.

I couldn't go to the 'Marble Lady', one only visits graves and monuments in the bright light of day. I started going back down the street called Eternal Peace and suddenly stood still - wasn't this where Anneta's house was? Just around the corner.

I found her in a dreadful state. She had become ugly again, a monster! She hadn't combed her hair, her nose hung down and she'd gotten fatter. I was shocked to see her like this and wanted to leave, but she held me fast with her gnarled hands.

"Sit here and listen."

Her voice was something like a whistle, an extraordinary thing. Imagine how loud it must have been for me to have heard it.

Well, her old man was lost. He was not even in his house. She'd been and asked:

"Is he dead?"

I said,

"No!"

"So?"

"He left"

"Where did he go?"

She answered something, but I couldn't understand it. She repeated it, stressing the word "spy."

"How do you know this?"

"What do you care? I just know. This is war, and that's happening in wars. Everything changes from one minute to the next."

"But what spy? On whose side? I didn't really know what I wanted to say, but I had to say something to show I was interested.

"What does it matter on whose side? It could be one, or it could be another. The good spies are like that.

You see, with all the secrets that they learn, they can serve both sides. I've noticed that in the cinema. It was a great film. We'd been to see it together."

"Why didn't he tell you that he would leave?"

"Why? Why? Do you think that they talk? That spies give out such information? If they did that, they wouldn't be spies then. They'd be just agents."

"Agents? Why?

"Oh, you poor thing. Don't be silly."

She smiled, showing all her yellow teeth, just like the witches in the stories which I read with the children when they were little. With Stratis and Nikaki, I mean. I never had any other children.

"So, can you imagine how a spy talks, especially when they are playing a double game?"

She was like a madwoman. Her eyes were shining. She always talked about spies and wars. She told me the whole story from the film she'd seen and didn't even ask me how I was, and I didn't have the chance to say anything. She talked all the time. She also said she was going to get a new friend.

"Don't look at me in the state I'm now. I'll have a bath tomorrow and wash my hair. I'll get myself dressed up, and I'll go out..."

"Where will you go?"

"To the street. You should see how many will beg me to go with them. Do you know why?"

With a triumphant air, with bright red flames in her eyes, she shouted:

"Why? Because I have my own house, my lady. Indeed my own house! And because I'm on my own."

"How? Because you have a house? And..."

"It's not easy these days for a man to find somewhere where he can be with a woman for a short time, that is clean and tidy and quiet."

"Oh, I see. You will rent rooms out for this sort of thing. Don't do it. You really shouldn't. You saw what happened to my previous lady who did that..."

Oh, leave me alone. Always the same thing. Those were different times, and your other lady was stupid. Anyway, who said I would rent out rooms?"

"But you did, just now..."

"I'm not that stupid to rent out only rooms, and I would just watch them coming and going. No thanks! I'm going to rent out myself as well. Do you get it?

She waited to see what effect that shocking news would have on me. I spoke to her when she let me as logically as I was able. I said I would ask my mistress to take her on as a seamstress, to help her. She has a lot of friends. She was furious at that, went wild almost as if she would eat me! Me with the needle? Me with scissors, thread, a sewing machine going 'grouk, grouk, grouk?' No! No! I tell you I would rather die! No more sewing machines for me. I'm to rent myself out with the room and enjoy it at the same time. Or don't you think I'll be wanted? You see!"

At that moment, she started pulling at her dress and took all her clothes off, standing stark naked. I didn't know what to do! Some mania had seized her. There she stood in front of me, her white body stretched out in front of me, her breasts shaking...I didn't know what to do.

"Don't you think they'll want me? No, what were you thinking? Look at this flesh.

"Look…" And she slapped her thighs, laughing strangely.

I felt I was going mad and got up to leave. "It's late, I'll get told off."

"No. Look. You have to look and see how much my body is worth, do you understand? Oh, go on then…Off you go if you want to. But know that from now on, I will be for hire, ok? For hire!"

She slapped herself again, very pleased, and the truth was that the ugliest thing about her was her face.

I left then, and I never saw Anneta again. I passed by her house once, but it was locked and shuttered. I knocked, but she didn't open the door. Was she inside and renting herself out at that moment? Or had she left to try and find her old guy the spy? I never found out, and I'd lost yet another person who talked to me.

Autumn progressed, and it rained a couple of times. We left our summer house. My master took my money out of the bank and turned it into golden sovereigns. He brought them to me, nicely wrapped up in packets, and a piece of paper on each pack which wrote how much money was in each. He gave them to me, took his glasses off, wiped them, put them back on again and looked at me sternly.

"Have you heard from your *fiancé*?"

"I have."

"Is he well?"

"Yes, thank you."

"If you change your mind, we can bring him back."

I didn't speak. I moved away from him, holding onto the packages with my money. To cut it short, when we were still on holiday, he had told me clearly, if I want Mihalis to come back, I would have to let him one evening to my bedroom. I was to tell him myself when I wanted him to come, whenever the fancy took me. The way he said "fancy"; he said it strangely and laughed so shamelessly that I realized in that instant that the "fancy" would never take me. As long as Mihalis wrote to me, and as long as he was well, he didn't mention it. I asked myself many times, if it was urgent, if it was a matter of life or death for Mihalis and it depended on him, what would I do? Oh, come on, you silly thing, what would you do?

I thought about it this way, and that torturing myself without finding what was right, neither yes, nor no. What I went through about this...

Uncle Vassilis asked me every time I saw him. "Tell your master again. That's what these important people want. You have to stick to him like a tick. Don't leave it; just keep on. You don't know what's going to happen from one minute to the next..."

How could I tell him that my master was after something else, that, actually, he wanted me to stick to him like a tick? In the end, I had to lie to my uncle. I really didn't want him to think I don't care about Mihalis. I told him that he'd promised to speak on Mihalis's behalf.

However, I don't know if I had the appetite any more. I mean, if Mihalis was in danger, if we joined in the war, I don't know whether he would want to help me any longer. I saw him very gloomy when he arrived home late. Didn't seem to notice what he ate. They talked and talked seriously, the master and mistress, and even the children. They didn't tell me what was going on. As they sat around the table whispering — I'm sure they were doing it on purpose so I wouldn't catch what they were saying — without looking to see if I was around or not if I was alive or dead. It was like watching them behind a glass wall. If I spoke, they wouldn't have heard me. If I put my hand out, the wall would rise up and stop me. I had no help from them, who I could only see. Just that.

Later on, one day, the mistress came up to the storeroom. She counted everything in there, locked the door, and went down again. Another time she opened the wardrobes, took everything out, and gave me some coats to shake out and brush on the terrace while she sorted out her drawers. When I went back, she gave me one of the jackets I had cleaned. It had a bit of brown fur on the collar. I couldn't believe my eyes! She gave me lots of other things too. Some nearly new dresses, some woolens, a skirt. I couldn't help it, I asked, "Are we moving house again?"

"No" was all she said. "No," she said, noting further. Something was going on, but I had no idea what. One evening his friends came to the house, the short one among them, as they locked themselves in the office. They never used to secure the doors, but they did. My mistress told me to go to bed immediately. I turned the lights off, but I didn't go, I went on tip-toes up to the office door and tried to look through the keyhole. Somebody was sitting in front of it, though, and I couldn't see anything. I looked again, nothing, just blackness.

I stayed there outside the door, but I could only see the strip of light coming underneath it, nothing else. The piece of view as in the past began to waver and change shape, I put my eye to the keyhole, and then I could see something. Whoever had been sitting in front had moved. I could see the master's desk and some fingers counting out golden sovereigns shining in the light. Time had passed, and as I was tired, the glitter made me feel dizzy, so I made to leave. The fingers were gathering the golden coins. Other fingers were making them into packages and tied them up, then put them in order, upright, like soldiers lined up. Every package a soldier. My head was spinning, my eyes full of the many boxes, the soldiers, the fingers which were making them as if some form of magic was involved in some grotesque game. I became afraid. I left. In my bedroom, the flashing yellow hours marked out on my clock greeted me. It was ten to five in the morning.

A few days after that evening of the packages of sovereigns, the "soldiers," the master left. The evening before we had packed his clothes in a new pigskin suitcase and he took a big briefcase which he held tightly under his arm. He got into the car and sat at the wheel. Then he put it carefully down on the seat next to him, and he left.

Days passed, and it didn't look as if he was coming back. Other times he'd left for sudden short business trips for a couple of days - three at the most - and he always returned. After over a week had passed, I decided to ask Nikaki.

"Where's your papa?"

He looked at me sneakily, wearing his long trousers, like a real master.

"Journey."

"Where is he going to?"

"I can't tell you."

"Will it be long before he comes back?"

"I don't know."

I begged him, "Oh, Nikaki, you can tell me, me who nursed you and raised you. Won't you tell me?"

"No Panoria. I can't."

"How can it be such a big secret? Has he gone to war?"

"Maybe."

"Oh, for goodness sake. You're infuriating. You mean he's a spy?"

I said it nervously, as though I was telling something serious and important.

He just burst out laughing: "No, stupid. No, you idiot! Get out of here. Spying! Ha, ha! Spying!"

He left, laughing. But he didn't tell me anything.

I went to see Mr Vassilis and told him all about it to try and calm down.

"Huh! Those kinds of people don't put themselves in harm's way. Spying, for goodness sake! He is off on business that makes money. When you get involved in that sort of business, you don't know how to get out of it. Once you start...that's what it is: the start. Those people don't get lost, don't fret. He could come back with yet another car! So just keep quiet. The more they have, the more you'll get. Listen carefully to what I'm going to tell you."

Uncle had decided to leave, to go back to his village on the island of Serifos. He'd already sold most of the food he had in his grocery shop and paid off his debts. He was ready to leave. He wanted me to go with him.

"What will I do there? Are there ladies where I can get work to increase my savings for the plot of land for my house? How will I get with Mihalis? He won't have a job. I'll have to save as much as possible."

"It's a poor area. There are ladies there, of course, but they do the housework by themselves. They don't pay servants. If you come with me, you could help me in the shop. If I open one...if I can..." How could I go? It would just be a burden on him, and anyway, something inside me was telling me that I shouldn't. Maybe he didn't really want me to go with him either. I don't know. He's been strange recently. I thought about it a lot until the following Sunday when I went to see him again, but I hadn't changed my mind.

"As you wish," he said. "I am old, and I haven't got time to wait for 'houses'. War has arrived. I have no more time. Houses, and getting married, that's all for you, young folks."

He spoke with real deep bitterness, and his eyes filled with tears as he looked at me, and then he wanted to give me what he owed me, but I wouldn't take it. I don't know what came over him, but he hugged me and kissed me wildly and oddly, and became a man just like all the others. I suddenly felt dizzy and felt the world slipping away. I was fainting, but no...He gave me a push. He looked pale and shouted:

"Go! Go, woman! Leave me, pity me!"

"Uncle, what's happened to you?"

"Go, I said!"

I don't know why I didn't go. He went into the kitchen, I suppose to get some water to drink. When he came back, he was calm again and looked at me like a frightened child. Then, I don't know why, I said to him:

"Come on, Uncle, show me the mermaid again!"

"No." He shook his head. "No, it's not right. Don't you want to leave?"

"Why should I leave?"

"Aren't you afraid of me?"

"No, Uncle. I know you are good. Good, and how you wouldn't..." Something was choking me, I couldn't say any more.

He spoke though:

"Mihalis is a fortunate man." That's all he said and lit a cigarette.

On Monday afternoon, I went to Piraeus with him, and I gave him some cookies for the journey. He took his leave without speaking to me but just squeezed my hand very tightly. I was crying. I cried all that afternoon and all night and all the next day until the postman came and brought me a letter from Mihalis. He was at Delvinaki[12] near the Greek-Albanian border.

In the evening, I popped out to the corner shop where they sold stationery and bought a map, and sat through the night and studied the map and then I saw the black line — it took me ages to find it — that was the border near Delvinaki. I stared and stared

---

[12] An area in Ioannina, Epirus, Greece.

at that black line until my eyes were filled with black dots until the little black dots were jumping. Even after I had turned out the light and lay down, the black dots danced about and around my eyelashes and hurting even my irises...millions of dots which surrounded me to make me disappear...

The next Sunday, I had nowhere to go. I said that I wouldn't go out, but the mistress didn't like that, she wanted me to go out and even gave me some money so that I could go to the cinema.

A middle-aged man came and sat next to me. I didn't notice him at first because I was enjoying what I was watching. My throat was dry, and I was trembling from amazement as if I had read the most important newspaper. I saw people just like us, the same and unchanged, and houses, and a servant with a white apron and cap, the same which they made me wear. It's been three years since I wore them. Well, she laid the table, like ours, and brought in the soup tureen full of hot soup and then...then I felt a hand on my leg moving softly up. I turned and saw a middle-aged man. I jumped up, stumbled over the others who were in the row and rushed out of the cinema. I ran home and opened the door with my key. The mistress was packing things away and was standing in front of the truck. She was startled when she saw me.

"Why are you back so soon?"

I told her.

"Why didn't you just change seats, silly? You didn't have to leave the cinema!"

But I was angry, and I asked her what she was packing and why? I might have been deaf, but I wasn't stupid. What on earth was going on finally? Yes, that's exactly what I said to her.

"We are leaving," she answered.

"We are leaving? Where are we going?

"Not you. We are leaving. Sadly, we can't take you with us. You... you will find another job."

"And the master...the master left...for...

"Yes. The master left."

"And you, when will you..."

"Next week. As soon as possible."

"And the house?"

"We sold it."

She seemed upset, and I didn't ask her anything else. I could see she didn't want to talk about it anymore. But why couldn't they have told me before? I might have decided to go with Mr Vassilis... Everyone was afraid and was leaving. That was all I could think. I stayed there, and Mihalis was at the black line of Delvinaki. Me here with my little bag of sovereigns hidden deep in my trunk.

Mihalis, the money, the war.

CHAPTER 3

We Found Water on the Plot

I went up the hill again, and I stayed there all morning. The concrete columns that will support the house were in position. The workmen were hammering on the scaffolding. They made such racket hammering that even I could hear it and it made me happy. I was so glad that all this idea was becoming a reality. Stones, iron, tiles, real things, and things you can see with your own eyes and touch with your own hands. To believe that this is so, I weighed and felt the strong metal columns. They were still damp, their dampness made them seem almost alive...I was so involved with the columns that I didn't notice Mr Manthos, the builder, coming up to me. He had seen me touching the column and had been watching me. I didn't know what to think as he looked at me oddly, and he said:

"You won't find this kind of building work easily. You know that? No messing around with too much sand, too much water, too much..."

Bravo, I thought. Everyone thinks what they do beautifully. But then he pulled me back to the house where the kitchen will be, and he showed me water. Clear, running water.

"We found water, and it's going to cost us more to divert it so that it doesn't ruin the foundations."

"Why can't we leave it? It will be good for the kitchen and the garden I am planning. I shall plant some vegetables, apart from the flowers I will plant in front."

"It will be expensive. I will have to construct a well; you will need a licence."

I still don't know why I was so happy that water was found by my house. When I got home and told my master about it for his advice, he said gently, "But you have the piped water for your plants and flowers."

"But it seems such a shame to waste all that power."

He did not speak, as though he was lost in thought, and his mind was elsewhere.

I was afraid he didn't want to talk about it anymore and made to leave him in peace. He was writing a lot these days. His head hardly ever raised from his papers. When I turned my back, the brass bell sounded — the one that looks like a lady with frilly skirt — and he was looking at me. His eyes looking large through his glasses, he was overseeing me, his mind not elsewhere.

"You are sorry, eh? For the power that you say will be wasted. My advice is diverting it, getting rid of it, because..." He smiled strangely. "Because you will pay; it will be costly. Just think how much money you will have to pay out to keep the water. Think what it will be like if it runs dry...decide."

"I should remove it then?"

"That's what I would do. It's not worth paying so much more for the pleasure. Eh? What do you think?"

"Right. If that's how it is..."

He seemed pleased. "Well done! That's what I like about you. You can re-think. The more you can re-think. the better."

"Why better?"

He was going to say something then changed his mind. "You ask a lot of questions." And with that, he turned back to his papers and disappeared into them.

I went to the kitchen. It was time I prepared his chops. I'd make a little soup for myself because my new teeth were still bothering me. The dentist had said I should be patient.

By evening I'd manage to sort out the things that were going around and around in my head. Let's cut it off then. What if we hadn't found it?"

But we had...

Lots of clear water.

I had to bear with bringing the image of my house, to see the columns, damp and living, the scaffolding. I heard the beating of my heart again. That is something certain. Ascertain as that I am alive. I am alive, of course, after all, I'm good at re-thinking.

My New Lady

The world opened up another door for me. Before she left, my mistress recommended this house to me. What can I say about the sadness I felt when I saw everything from the house piled up in the entrance and the truck waiting outside. This time I won't be sitting up on high like a queen on her throne to hold the mirror. They'd sold everything, and some stranger was going to take them. He had a green trilby and was fat. He and his wife both stood on the pavement and watched the loading. My mistress was ready with her suitcase in her hand, and the children in their new suits like real gentlemen...All three of them kissed me, and they gave me the watch with the yellow hours. The truck left, and my family moved in a taxi, and I remained alone on the pavement. I swept my tears, made the sign of the cross and turned around. I saw my things next to me. Two suitcases, a trunk, the basket with glasses, and crockery which they'd made me a present of. Well, I said to myself, it is a start for our house.

I called a taxi. Did you hear that? Me! A cab! Isn't that a joke! We drove down Patission Street, in Athens, and turned into a road near the museum. A different neighborhood, different houses. Later I learned that the "higher" society lived here. They said bank clerks and so on, householders, but not as high up as those who lived in Kolonaki[13].

It seems that the neighborhood confers the class. If the people condescend to speak to you, you hear some rubbish spoken.

My new lady was waiting for me. She was younger than my last one. Tall, slim and with a sadness in her eyes. I liked her. The house was smaller, poorer, with an abandoned feel. I noticed a lot of dust in the corners. The kitchen was small and old-fashioned. The window looked out on a small garden belonging to someone else, but that didn't matter. I was happy because I could see an orange tree and a fig tree whose leaves brushed the far wall, and there were several plant pots. Much better than just looking out on bricks.

They had some problems with my usual wage. It was too much. After all, there would be less work. They didn't have either children or dogs. Why should they? It was just as well they didn't? The mistress smiled sweetly, and with her smile, the sadness in her eyes seemed to deepen. Finally, we agreed. Fifty drachmas were less, but if they were happy with me...

At noon the master came home. He was young and looked at me kindly and not at all like other men have looked at me. He immediately tried to make me feel comfortable. Maybe he would be able to help me with Mihalis. We could bring him here, and he could live the black line at Delvinaki. The master was saying something, but I couldn't hear him. The mistress told him about my problem, and he looked at me more closely, as if he sympathized and spoke more clearly.

"You look like a good girl. We don't have a lot of work here, nor children..."

They seemed to be proud that they didn't have children, but then, why did they get married? It would have been good to have a brood of children, in spite of the curse I found on the first night when I went to sleep in the small. Tiny bedroom with only a small

---

[13] A neighbourhood in central Athens (Greece), near Lycabettus Hill.

skylight up high. Bedbugs. millions of them, teeming all over the bed. Some of them fell from the ceiling. They bored through the crevices and multiplied making the bed sheet move! I went crazy! I got up to take the mattress into the kitchen to put it down on the tiles to sleep, but as soon as I moved it, they went underneath and spread out in the folds. What can I say? Disgusting.

They were also cockroaches in the kitchen. Yes, big black ones. Monsters. I killed some of them with my shoe and eventually fell asleep.

The mistress was really sorry about it and ashamed at the mess. She told me that the previous girl was filthy, which is why they got rid of her.

All work is blessed, even that of getting rid of cockroaches and bedbugs, scouring the grime because without this work, I didn't know what could happen to me at that time. I'd been to the other house for nearly 10 years. It's not easy to get out of 10 years of habits from one minute to the next, is it? But the main thing is that I was ten years older. All my memories had increased, and I had already lived 23 years in this, my life's journey.

I tortured my mind with memories, complaints, and bitterness about the world while I was battling against filth. I white-washed the corridor, the kitchen, and my bedroom. I smoked out the bedbugs from their crevices. I felt a great sense of satisfaction, like a general in the heat of battle. The cleanser and annihilator of every form of dirt, every womanizer and disgusting thing.

I wiped down the mistress's shutters with white spirit, and she watched dizzy form manic behavior. She wanted to help me, but I wouldn't let her. I felt I shouldn't have my workload lightened because I was feeling so lost. Only exhaustion could bring me the peace of sleep, which I needed. Asleep without dreams, neither good nor bad.

During all that, I received a letter from Mihalis.

My dear Panoria,

Greetings.

I am well and hope you are too. I hope that you are happy with your new house and pray that you are lucky enough to have good people to look after you and love you.

My Panoria, I think of you all the time and can't wait for the time when I will be discharged so that I can come and work too, and we can make our way in the world. If you ask about here, we had a lot of rain, lots of mud. It's one thing to read about it and another to sink up to your knees, to be planted in the earth just like a tree. If we have a chance to be near a stove or brazier then life is sweet. We talk about our girlfriends, and it's lovely. It would be okay without all the preparations. I can't write any more.

God have mercy on us.

I kiss you,

Mihalis

What preparations? The work lessened when I had scoured and cleaned every single thing. That was awful. How was I going to get tired enough to sleep? I sat down and replied to Mihalis immediately. It was Saturday, and I had a day off on Sunday. I set off along Patission Street and reached the post office, where I posted my letter. Now, where should I go? It was only four o'clock, I could see it on the large clock at the post office.

It was really summertime again. The streets were quiet, the heat was humid. I was sweating, and my clothes were sticking to me, making me feel bad.

I carried straight on to Aiolou Street in Athens. I reached as far as where the ancient columns are and the marble, below the Acropolis. A group of foreigners, two ladies and two men, had stopped in front of a stone gate. One of them from the opposite side was taking a photo of them. They looked at me, and I watched them, the youngest of them, who held the camera. He came back to the group and smiled at me. He blushed. He was wholly blonde but a bit flushed. It made me laugh, and then I got embarrassed and left. I lost myself in the small street with old houses and looked at the people living there. Here, through an open window, a woman was bent over her sewing. Over there, some children were playing. A toddler was crying hopelessly being led along by the hand of a little girl, tears and snot pouring down his little face. All these unknown people, strangers, just people from another world. However, everyone had someone to sit across from them and sleep next to in a bed. They were all so far from me, the other side of the glass wall, which was always there before me. There, from behind the glass wall, I reached the Acropolis. Here I was happy. The wall disappeared and spread off over the sea far away, and I was here on the trip we'd made when the children were small, Stratis and Nikakis. The first time Nikakis came up here, he asked, "What is that over there which shines so much? He was little, and it was the first time he'd seen the sea. We still lived in the first house. They hadn't yet become reputable people. We had picked up chamomile, filled our handkerchiefs with them, and on the way back we each bought a *koulouri*[14]. My mistress always gave us money for *koulouria*[15] and sweets when we went on an outing.

Then, without realizing, I found myself at my old stamping ground — the cemetery, in front of my marble lady. I spoke to her. "Marble lady, little mother, please keep Mihalis safe...keep him safe...keep him safe. What are these preparations?" And I told her other things too, I wanted to cry, but I didn't. Something more prominent, and more important was going on inside me, and wouldn't let me. But I saw, as if for the first time, the cypress-es, gravestones, and something like a caged bird fluttered inside me when I made the decision not to come and see my marble lady. Later on, I realized that after all those years of visiting my marble lady, this was the first time that I was terrified. When you are so afraid, you need the comfort of the living and not the dead.

I returned home on the tram. My mistress was alone, reading. The

---

[14] A type of bread with sesame in the shape of a ring.
[15] See 14 (plural).

master had left in the morning on a trip. My mistress doesn't go with him because he goes to the mountains; he's a climber. He'd dressed in short trousers, thick woolen socks, high boots and a woolen hat. He looked somewhat ridiculous in the hat. He was carrying a bag with meatballs which I had made him. He took cheese, bread, and a flagon of wine, the walking stick with the metal tip. He saw me watching him.

"Eh, how do I look? Different?

I wanted to say that he looked like a bean, but I learned to watch what I said to the people who pay my wages.

"Younger," I answered.

He was pleased, and his eyes shone. I also said, "Not that you are old, of course."

"No," he responded, "I'm not old."

He turned and looked in the mirror which they had hung in the entrance hall and fixed his hat. He moved it slightly to one side and looked at me again, saying pointedly and strangely:

"I will become old, though."

"What will you become?" As I didn't hear.

"Old. That's why..."

He said something else. Lifted his bag onto his shoulder. I opened the door for him, and he left.

"Where were you?" my mistress asked me when I got back from my walk.

"I went to post a letter to Mihalis."

"Oh, yes, your *fiancé*. Your previous mistress told me, she said he's a good boy. It's a shame."

"Shame?"

"Oh, you know, the situation. Where is he now?"

Now I don't know. He was in Serres and Delvinaki, but it's been a while since he told me not to write Serres on the envelope, but ST.G 523. So, I don't know where he is now."

"That's what happens in wartime."

"But we are not at war."

"Not at the moment, but…"

"My previous master told me that we wouldn't get involved."

"He could well have told you that, but then why did they leave for Switzerland?"

"Switzerland?"

"That's where they went because Switzerland is the only country that never gets involved in wars."

"Why doesn't it?"

"You seem clever and understand a lot, but that even I can't explain to you. It's the position they take, it's because of the money."

"What? Money, you said? What money?"

"The money which the rich, from all over the world, have deposited in their banks. There must be some safe place for it in the world. And your master…"

"My master, because he was rich and involved with finance had to go to Switzerland, that's it, isn't it?"

"That's it."

And she changed the subject.

"And after that, where did you go?"

Now, what was I to tell her? The truth? One thing I have learned is that it's the truth that they don't believe.

"After that, I went to find a girl I know in Makriyianni[16], who is a seamstress."

"Does she sew well?"

Now I am worried that she might ask me to bring her to the house.

"No, She's too careless, and she charges a lot."

"Well, go and take those clothes off and put on your white apron. I'm expecting a couple of friends, so cut a few slices of bread, and we'll have some *ouzo*."

I was really pleased that she spoke to me so nicely, because it showed she was interested in me. At the first chance, I decided, I would ask her if she could do anything for Mihalis. I was pleased that some of her friends were coming, so she wouldn't be on her own. I was happy to have something to do. I wanted people to come to this quiet house because that would delay me having to go to my bedroom where fear awaited me enthroned among the freshly-painted walls. I could almost visualise him — a big dark man with massive open arms like wings with long claws like a vulture, with big round eyes, circles, and in each eye the 12 yellow hours, just like sulphur, flashing horribly. Two yellow hands counted the minutes one by one, and one by one, the hours. I knew while I endured the thrice-accursed fear, that the more I delayed going there, the better.

Not two, not three friends of hers could come, I needed an all-night party, to have lots of people here, like a christening or a wedding, so many people that there was no more room in the house, and I wouldn't be able to keep up with serving the food platters and wine, and that dawn would find me at the sink full of washing up as had happened so many times at the other house. In fact, more recently when we were living in Kolonaki, and they would come and talk late into the night, and sometimes they

---

[16] A neighborhood of Athens, Greece.

would dance to music from the radio, and as I went in and out I would watch them, and feel as if I was also letting off steam.

I wish something like that had happened. Then I could sneer at my fears because I would have stolen that night and it would have been different, just mine.

But I'm rambling on...The two friends came, and I gave them some *ouzo* and two small pathetically small plates, just bread and cheese on one, and olives on the other.

They live a narrow life these people, sparse, everything accounted for. Three times a week we have pulses, meat just twice, on Thursday and Sunday — lots of greens, a few eggs, feta cheese, occasionally some fish, and then it would be sprats or whitebait. The master was a bank clerk. The mistress said she had some rents coming in but not much. I thought that I wasn't likely to progress far like this. I would have to get to know some girls or the grocer, or baker, to find out and see if I could find something better. They were good people. I'm not saying that it just wasn't in my interests.

The master got home late that evening from the mountains. Flushed and dishevelled and pleased with himself, he came into the kitchen to find something to eat. He was hungry, and there were some more meatballs like the ones he had taken with him, and he gobbled them up. There was no fruit, nor cheese, as we'd put it out with the *ouzo*. I had eaten dry bread with a few drops of olive oil because the mistress kept a check on that too. Later I took him a bowl of water to wash his feet. They didn't have a bath. There just wasn't room. So we filled buckets and jugs with water, and there was a low round thing like a bath, which they stood and washed in. That was where I soaped myself and then poured water, and then sponged and cleaned the place. Every Sunday, we said, the master would go off to the mountains. The mistress would sometimes invite a friend, or perhaps go, as she said to her mother's. What was I to do? Some Sundays I would go out and wander around the streets. I went all over Athens, until one day some creep followed me and wouldn't leave even when

I'd reached the door of the house. He said all kinds of things. I could see from his face, but who was listening to him. He was dark with a little moustache like a crow.

"Go to hell!" I said to him at last, and he heard that, even though he looked as though he couldn't believe his ears. I repeated it, louder, and spat at him. Then he left.

The Sunday after that it was raining. In spite of the rain, the master still went out. He hoisted his bag onto his shoulder, put on the hat that made him look like a bean and took his walking stick.

We were left on our own, the mistress and I. We'd overeaten at lunch, we had lovely food, dolmades with cabbage and lots of rice, there was plenty of mince, and we ate well. She said to me:

"Go and get dressed and go out. You can take my old umbrella so that your clothes won't get wet."

Who said I wanted to go out? And where would I go? And even if I did want to go, I was worried about my shoes, they were old and needed new soles. Just when I needed to economise as much as possible. I didn't need any other expenses. However, I realised that I had to go out. She didn't want me in the house, she even gave me money to go to the cinema. She wanted to make sure I had a good time. She was paying for my entertainment too — what could I do?

It was raining cats and dogs. First of all, I stood in the cinema queue in the dark with all the rest. I nearly burst there, it was so hot, and the people were suffocating me and pushing and jostling. I finally ended up next to a fat lady with a hat and her daughter. In front of me, another two girls and a bit further along with an old man. So, nothing wrong happened, although I felt squashed each time I felt the lady's large bust on my left shoulder as it moved up and down when she breathed. She was so close that we had practically become one person. I felt her blood flow through my body, but still, she was just one fat stranger, nothing else. It's a shame we didn't get to know each other, to speak. Something odd came over me, a great longing to talk to all those people who were so close to me. I would say that I'm a working girl saving money to build a house and get married and then I would have a place in society. I would have a hat too, and I would bring my husband and my children to the cinema.

I wanted to ask who they were? What do they do? Do they have a lot of money or just a little?

Do they work for others, or are they their own bosses?

But as I say, they were many. What would I do with so many? At least just the fat lady next to me, who jostled me all the time with her bosom that felt like two warm curled-up cats. Would it have hurt her at least to say where she lives? Only that. Where she lives. Next Sunday, I would have had somewhere to go. I would have visited her. She would have set out cakes and we would have talked. First about the weather and then about food, recipes, how I made that red wine casserole. Or how to be sure the mayonnaise doesn't curdle. The lights came up. I turned to smile at the fat lady and thank her for keeping me company, but she had already left, her daughter following behind, in a hurry to get other seats. I wanted to go close to them, to sit with them too, we'd been so close for so long, but I tripped on a step I hadn't seen.

Ah! That's how happiness is ruined, from one minute to the next, you can become ridiculous without even noticing. I fell. Yes, even me, Panoria, who was so shy and respectful of people. I, who so needed the company and respect of others, I was rolling around on the ground like an animal, everyone turned and looked at me, and then a young man, without me realising, had grabbed me and practically had to embrace me to lift me off the ground. He gave me back my bag which someone else had picked up, and he looked at me with that male gaze of longing, so I was ashamed and longed for the earth to open up and swallow me. Instead of the decorous company of the fat lady, I found myself sitting next to the young man who helped me to my feet. What could I do? I thanked him for his help, and he smiled and looked at me happily. The lights went out. I pulled myself as far as I could away from him. But nobody touched me.

It was a war film, and I got upset when I saw all the bullets and the trenches and the soldiers raising their hands and rolling wounded. The aeroplanes were going back and forth overhead and let off their bombs, and they got more extensive on the screen as if they were coming so close to us that I held my breath.

Later it was so moving when the wounded soldier was recognised by the nurse who came to tend him as her *fiancé*. Sobs rose in my throat, I didn't want to make a fuss, but I couldn't control them. When the lights went up, the young man asked me:

"Are you engaged?"

"Indeed," I said, very seriously.

"He's a soldier?"

"He is."

He said something which I didn't understand and watched him trying to guess what it was, then I realised he'd said:

"I'm going too."

Then I think he realised I couldn't hear him and started to speak more clearly:

"In one week, I shall present myself to the army."

"There's not going to be a war," I told him, "don't worry."

"How do you know?" he asked, laughing.

"I know."

"But how do you know? Tell me." and he came closer to me.

I moved away slightly, then I said:

"There won't be a war because there shouldn't be one."

He laughed, showing little white teeth like pearls, and said something else which I eventually understood as:

"If everything that shouldn't happen, didn't happen..."

The lights went off again. The hospital in the film was being bombed. The nurse was in a room where the door had jammed in the ruined hall, and she was trying to open it, to run and save her *fiancé*.

She climbed out of a window and found herself in flames and rubble. An officer wanted her to get out of there with him, bombs were falling, but she wouldn't leave with him. I was going crazy with anxiety because I believed that the wounded soldier was lost.

Later, the aeroplanes left, and the war subsided a little. They were talking about pulling the dead and wounded out of the rubble. There was a soldier, they pulled him from under his bed where he'd crawled to hide, which protected him from the bombing. They kissed and kissed, the wounded soldier and the nurse kept kissing until the lights went up. My nose was still running.

The young man was standing in front of me and said:

"Come with me."

We went to a patisserie and ordered *baklava*[17]. After he ordered, I told him:

"Please let me pay for the *baklava*."

He rolled his eyes as if he thought I was some kind of monster.

"I'm working too, I have money, and that would be a way of thanking you for your company."

"You would thank me, for...really?"

His small white teeth were shining, then he spoke, clearly, and I understood him well enough now.

"Anyway, nothing else can happen...after all, you are engaged..."

---

[17] A dessert originating in the Middle East made of filo pastry filled with chopped nuts and soaked in honey *(Oxford Dictionary of English)*.

"Yes," I told him, "I am right, aren't I?"

He thought a little before replying. In the end, he said:

"If you didn't have your *fiancé*, would you like to...not to pay for the cake?"

And I don't know how and without thinking, I just watching his small white teeth, which looked as if they belonged to a small child, I said: "I would have liked to."

He worked for a cobbler, and after the army, he planned to go back to his village near Volos, sell a plot of land he'd inherited from a widowed and wealthy aunt, and open a shop.

It rained continuously, and when we came out of the patisserie, I gave him an umbrella to hold, and he put his arm around me and held me close, as otherwise there wouldn't have been room for us both under the umbrella, and we walked for a while like this, making a diversion. Just before I got there, I left him at the corner so that nobody would see us and think I was something I was not.

We went out again the following Sunday. We went up to the memorial plaque at Philopappou[18]. The sun was shining and some children were flying kites. The longer the sun shone, the more couples appeared. I wanted to leave, but he wouldn't let me. It was going to be the last time we would meet. He kissed me. I was shocked, and my whole body was flooded with heat while a voice in my head swore at me: "Slut! Shameless slut!" Another voice tried to excuse me. "He's leaving. He will go into the army. There might be a war..."

Two days after I'd kissed this young man who would become a cobbler (I didn't even remember his name, because although he had told me, I hadn't been able to hear it correctly), a letter arrived from my Mihalis.

"Panoria, I love you! I can't stand it without you. The days are unbearable, and the nights, my body hurts from longing for you.

---

[18]   A neighborhood of Athens, Greece.

My misery has taken me over to the extent that I have taken up smoking to comfort myself…"

I took his letter up to my bed and kept it under my pillow, and I cried and cried.

The next day I sat down and wrote to him. I told him that I'd been to the cinema and I was ready to tell him about the young man, but it was as though someone took hold of my hand and said: "No, don't!" So, I wrote nothing about it.

That evening after going to Philopappou I had rushed home because it was quite late, but I didn't find anyone there. My mistress had gone out.

When I went to their room to prepare their nightclothes, I found the master's ashtray full of cigarette butts, her bed quickly made up, her drawers unlocked, and with the key left on them, her powder uncovered.

It looked as though there was something wrong to make her rush like that. Why did she smoke so many cigarettes? Did she consume them all herself? I picked them up, one by one, from the ashtray and looked at them. Some had red marks on them from her lipstick, and some did not, and all of the cigarette butts were not the same make; some were thicker, and some were thinner.

"Serves him right for being stupid! Every weekend he goes off to the mountains and leaves her on her own. Didn't he realise that sooner or later she'd go off? Whose fault is it? What a thickhead!"

That's what I thought had happened. If she had a boyfriend, it wouldn't bother me. I'd seen a lot worse. But what I needed was money. Then, there was another expense: cigarettes! After learning that Mihalis is smoking for comfort from his misery, I was bound to send him at least some cigarettes, wasn't I? Never mind that he still has 10 months and 23 days to serve, winter is coming, and he'll be cold. He needs woollens. I took all that month's salary as soon as it was given to me and went to buy wool.

I had the chance to go out on a weekday to the shops to buy

things. "I hope Mihalis is well," I thought, while I was watching all of the well-dressed women who were bustling in and out of the shops. I turned around and went in, came out and wandered around the shops. I took all afternoon to buy the wool. My mistress showed me how to knit. I began. A whole new business this was, and I liked it very much. When I was daydreaming as I knitted, I said to myself, "Yes and I will knit woollen clothes for our children to keep them warm. A hat like the master's, in lovely colours."

All sorts of things went through my mind and kept my hands company as they worked. At that time, I didn't feel so lonely. So, the summer progressed and made me long for the sea from last year's holidays. Nothing like that this year! The master left again on his own for his holiday. He went, he said, to Mount Athos[19]. Did you hear that?! Mount Athos! Was he going to be a monk? Had he learned something about the mistress? Maybe he was ashamed of that in front of his friends and acquaintances?

If the mistress had been more careful. What if I hadn't seen what I saw? Be careful! She sewed a new silk dress, the first one since I'd been at their house, and then she sewed another one. I was pleased. If the ladies of the house sewed new dresses, either they are saving from the housekeeping, or they've got a boyfriend. Here, as I already said, it was the latter that was happening. When the master was off at Mount Athos the other man came to the house for the first time. We had him to dinner. Boiled fish soup. I made *mayonnaise*. But I was sorry. It was a shame that she and her husband weren't suited and that it was necessary to bring in a third person.

When he returned from Mount Athos, sunburnt, handsome and looking very well, the master gave me an icon of St. Fanourios. He brought the mistress some worry beads made out of Cypress wood. I decided to take my courage in both hands and speak to

---

[19] Mountain and Peninsula in northeastern Greece. Mount Athos or Holy Mountain is an independent state of the Greek Republic and a centre of the Orthodox Church under the jurisdiction of Ecumenical Patriarch of Constantinople.

him about Mihalis. I gave him the reference; he would look at it, he said, although he didn't seem too keen to me. Maybe he just didn't have the right connections, that's what it looked like, and you didn't need to be a genius to understand it.

The mistress' other man didn't appear in the house, but something else happened and things began to change. We began to eat better, they bought me a pair of slippers; the first since I had gone to their house. The change was that my mistress told me that she would leave every morning at a quarter to nine and would return at two, just like the master. I oversaw her as she was telling me this and it seemed to me that the sadness had gone from her eyes. I was pleased to see it. When I'm happy I am always more brave, so I took the opportunity to ask for a raise, the time that I needed more money.

She was startled by what I said; she was almost angry. She never used to get very cross, she was good like that.

"Are you trying to say you don't like our house?"

I was ashamed and sorry, why did she take it so badly?

"No, I like it very much," I said as I looked down so that she couldn't see that I was lying, "but I need more money."

"Do you think people can always find as much money as they need? If things were like that, we'd all be fortunate! Don't be foolish. I too, long to win the lottery tomorrow, so what? And if you didn't know, I'm telling you that people are getting rid of their servants because life is getting more expensive because we are going to war and everyone is trying to save money. An extra mouth to feed is expensive, it's not just the salary."

I couldn't say anything in reply, that she said "an extra mouth to feed," hurt me badly. She was pleased by my reaction to her words and continued; "if you find you can get more money somewhere else, you can leave. You shouldn't be held back by us."

I was distraught. Once things start to go wrong, they don't stop. It wasn't only that I was eaten up with fear about Mihalis; that deep dark fear which filled my seedy little bedroom, which peered at me with its yellow hours and frightened me every night, my master and mistress had been upset because of me. What was I thinking of by speaking up before I'd found something else? But where would I find it? As if that wasn't enough, I got a letter from Serifos Island written by someone else; Mr Vassilis was ill, he had a heart problem, and he didn't have enough money to pay the doctor for medicine. Could I help?

That mermaid who was enthroned on his chest was definitely the one who had made him ill. She ate him up.

Just think about all the years, a whole lifetime, what misery she had brought him with her beautiful long hair with her beautifully drawn features, with her fishy tail...Where did he meet her? And why did he lose her? Was it because he didn't have money? Or to put it another way, is it because he carried her with him in that strange way forever? I could have made up a story, like those I made up for the children, for Mr Vassilis, his mermaid and his peculiar behaviour lately...a story where Mr Vassilis would have been continuously obsessed.

But nowadays, who has time for such things?...fear never let go of its grip! I asked and found out how to send money and went to the post office. I wrote out a cheque for 200 drachmas. I wrote him a letter telling him to get well soon, to gain strength soon, not to worry, and that I would send money again whenever he needed it.

I never got a reply. He did not reply to my letter; I never learned whether he received the money. Nothing. Days passed. Nothing. Was he alive? Dead?

I saw him in my dreams; he was naked and fat, the mermaid had left her throne on his chest, and all that remained was a red mark in the shape of her body, while she, life-size and half-woman half-fish as always, with her tail uplifted, stood next to him, just as she did in the photographs where they, the newly married, stand together and where she held him by the hand. It was a horrid dream.

Was he still struggling to live, or was Mr Vassilis already dead? I never learnt anything more about him.

On the eve of the Festival of the Virgin Mary — 15th of August — my mistress gave me some money to go to the market to shop. I took some of my own money and bought three plants, a small Bougainvillea for Mihalis, which would grow in time and spread out and cover the walls of our house and embrace him, and a carnation and a basil plant for the children. I put them on the little step outside the kitchen door.

And what can I say about the other thing that happened at home on the same day I bought the plants? I was in a good mood. I opened both the windows fully; I was on my own, as the master and mistress had left. I took my brush, dustpan, and duster to start cleaning up. I swept the dining room. I had already done their bedroom and went into the office. I tidied up there and started dusting. I lifted up some papers from the desk and shook them out and noticed underneath a fat envelope. I said to myself: "They will be photographs." I've always liked photography. I'd had one taken myself by a photographer at the museum. Behind me, there was an enormous palm tree. I had sent it to Mihalis. That was a few days after the trip to the cinema, where I'd met the young man. Mihalis wrote that I'd lost weight but that I was prettier. That's what he said.

That's what I was day-dreaming about as I sat down in the master's armchair in front of his desk. I took the envelope with the photographs and pulled out the first one. I was so shocked when I saw it. My head started spinning, those wheels began to turn inside me again, and my body was shaking: even if I'd been stark naked in front of 100 people, I couldn't have felt worse.

In all the photos spread out in front of me, I saw the master naked with his hair all tousled and a strange look in his eyes standing in a suggestive pose as if he was aroused by a woman, while behind him, also naked, was another man, who, like a wild beast ready to ejaculate over him, and had his hand on the master.

I went crazy. What was this all about? Suddenly, a part of my mind lit up as I remembered something which Mihalis had once told me. We were in a café in Makriyianni in Athens not long before he left. We'd gone inside because it was too cold outside with the north wind blowing. We ordered some spoon sweets when the door opened and two men entered. One was wearing a strange shirt and had a red cravat tied around his throat, and his eyes looked as if he wore make-up, and when he walked, he swayed like a woman. It was the first time I'd seen a man look like that. Mihalis smiled and said:

"Don't stare, it's not nice."

"But how can he look like that?"

"He's one of those."

"What do you mean 'those'?"

"Don't you know?"

"No! But he is behaving like a woman."

"Exactly! He doesn't want to be a man."

"He doesn't want? What does that mean? It's not up to him!"

He explained as well as he could about this kind of person. Afterwards, we laughed about it. It was such a strange thing that my mind couldn't grasp it; however, I tried to understand it.

My master was the same! He was one of "those!" But he didn't look like one, he didn't move like one, and, apart from his bean hat, there was nothing odd in his appearance. He would be one of the more serious ones who, as I get older, seem to increase in number all the time. I gathered all the photographs up and put them away.

I left the office after I'd swept the floor and shut the door. Then I noticed a strange smell, which was similar to what I smelt in the evenings when I went out and watered my plants.

On the 15th bright and early, they both went off on an excursion.

He went first, with his backpack on his back, and I just couldn't bear to look at him without shuddering, and then the mistress, after having a bath, dressing up, and putting on perfume, gave me some money to go to the outdoor cinema and left me two meatballs to eat and some of the small tomatoes.

And as much I had said to myself that I would reduce my excursions, I just increased them. If I went out, then I would be bound to eat a *koulouri* or a lollipop; I was hungry. When I saw them all together where they were being sold, my mouth filled with saliva and I felt dizzy, so I got out my drachma and spent it.

As soon as I went into the cinema, I saw the girl from the house across the street. For some time, I had smiled at her when I saw her and waved to her from the window. You can imagine how happy I was when I saw her there. By chance, there was an empty seat next to her.

As politely as I could, and smiling the whole time, I went and sat down next to her. She smiled at me too. She said something, but I couldn't hear it. She spoke again:

"You're from the kitchen opposite, aren't you?"

"Yes, that's me; my name is Panoria. What's your name? I couldn't hear it, so she repeated it louder: "Lambrini."

"Where are you from?"

"From Serifos."

I was so excited. I responded: "I sort of had an uncle there, but I don't know what happened to him; is there any way we could find out?"

The lights went down, and I couldn't see her anymore, so I don't know if she said anything else. The film began.

I was so happy I didn't even notice what I was watching. Some men with guns were riding around on horseback, one other undressed a lady. An old man hit someone over the head with a bottle, breaking both the container and the head! It was chaos on the screen.

When the lights came up again, I turned to Lambrini, who was with her cousin. They were talking and laughing. I went to say something, when a newspaper seller burst into the cinema and started handing out newspapers as fast as he could.

"What's happening?" I asked Lambrini.

"Didn't you hear? It was on the radio."

"We don't have a radio, and even if we did, I would not be able to hear it."

"They said that the Greek navy boat ELLI in Tinos had been torpedoed; the Italians are trying to make us get involved in the war."

The next day, I read a newspaper. They were full of the ELLI torpedoing and many photographs: the wheels began again to drive me crazy, to annihilate my mind and body.

Later, I got a letter from Mihalis.

He was alive, he was well, and he was eating well. But he asked if would please send him some woolen clothes, socks, and vests. I hid the letter so that I could read it in peace later on when, all of a sudden, there was a knock on the door and a courier appeared. I'd never seen him before.

He asked me what my position was as if he was blind and couldn't see my apron. He said: "Can you write?" and made me sign a piece of paper which he gave me, and left. It was for the master. My mistress never shed a tear, and they didn't even embrace at the door; he just looked at her, and she turned her face away from him, and I don't blame her. Then she shut the door. I was trembling. I didn't need to hear it, I knew.

The mistress would go to live somewhere else. She didn't tell me, but I understood. She'd be with her other man, but at least he was a man. She gave me one month's salary extra along with a useful reference. I should go to the agency.

So, I found myself on the streets again, with all my belongings beside me there on the pavement. Just like the other times. The only thing I took from this house was my three plants, and I had bought those with my own money, the Bougainvillea for Mihalis, the carnation and basil plants for the children.

CHAPTER 4

My House

Upon the heights, the builders were always at work. The heaps of bricks, the sand, the lime await the human hand to grab them and carry them about. See that one over there loaded up with bricks, his body bent under the weight, he is sweating, and even his legs are shaking. I feel a bit bad as I say to myself: "He is working for me, and him, and that one over there." I begin to feel a little proud: I am a lady who has people working for her. I notice the mason who is bent over carefully. Mud, brick, mud, brick: that's how the work progresses. The walls will rise up. The house is happening. It will happen. Mr Manthos talks about the spring; they're not going to close it off yet, as they need it for the site. I paid for the pipes, and later I will pay to have it cut off from here and flow downhill.

The builder called me, and we went around the site. We went through the dining room, the bedroom, and the corridor, and we arrived in the kitchen. The walls are still low, like a doll's house and houses children would build with earth and sand. Mr Manthos lit a cigarette. He began to speak: he will make the window wider as I'd asked. I am listening carefully because I want to look as though I understand what he's saying. I feel the need to give orders, to tell him what to do — after all, it is my house!

"Be careful with the door, make sure it opens fully without knocking onto the windowsill."

I tried to judge where the bricks had already made space for the opening of the windows and doors. The builder took his tape from his pocket, measured and noted it down on his book.

"Don't worry, we'll be careful and make sure of it. Whatever you want will be done: "Whatever you want..." He smiled, and his eyes fixed kindly on me, he folded up his tape measure, and I felt a rush of happiness. From then on, I felt so content and light-hearted that I decided not to take the bus home, but I went down on foot from Haravgi, down behind Zappeion, near the Stadium where my present master lives.

The chores are always the same. We ate, the master first, then me, I could chew better now. It seems that I was beginning to get used to my new teeth. I washed the dishes, and I had already put the *briki*[20] on to make coffee. Mr Alekos' son will come to see him in the afternoon. When suddenly within me, I could feel the walls of my house rising up. The muddy hands of the builder were working fast, even faster, and they put one brick on top of the other, mud, brick, mud, to make the walls rise higher and higher. They were working more quickly because I wanted it. Because I want it, it happens.

Whatever I want?

The Next Job

Another door opened and presented strange faces, strange masks. Some laugh while others cry, others again and searching for help. The world is full of hands everywhere, and that is when the wheels come, millions of wheels, big fat massive ones, with chains which churn around frighteningly and finally encompassing the world, they tighten on it enough to make it burst...

This is the sort of thing that came into my mind, I was trembling, and my head was spinning, my luggage had grown with all of my belongings; the trunk, suitcases, baskets and my plants. I sat on a chair with no back and waited for the agency to come and get me. If they didn't come today?

---

20 A small pot for the preparation of Greek coffee.

"You've got money, you could go to a hotel," the agent told me. "One night or two, it's not the end of the world. You'll see."

I avoided going to the hotel because a lady turned up, and without further ado, she took me. By this time it was evening. I hadn't eaten anything since the previous night. After all, who thinks of food at such times? The lady was an actress, a star, let's say, and she wanted me to leave her child with me. She put me in a taxi with my things and took me to the apartment. She had no problem with the wage I asked for. She sent me straight to the kitchen. The child was called Dimitraki, and as it was St. Demetrios fiesta that day, there was a party at the house so I had to roll-up my sleeves as the guests would arrive any minute.

Whatever my good mistress wanted, I would do. I was so happy that I would be with a child again, I'd found work and that there was a party at the house, I saw the people, and I would serve them, I would eat and would be paid!

Before I could get my bearings, the guests started arriving — it had been dark for some time — men, both young and middle-aged; women, some heavily made up, some not at all, wearing day clothes. It was the first time I'd ever seen guests in casual wear.

The men wore coloured jackets, and a couple weren't even wearing ties. It seems that's the sort of thing these people were used to. However, each one had a present for the child in their hands. One had a toy, another, chocolates, someone else a cake. 'Well done!' I thought. Never mind about the food, my eyes feasted on it, it had been a long time since I'd seen such a kitchen. It was a real boat, laden with the fruits of the earth. I couldn't open bottles and bring plates fast enough. These people caused a certain kind of upset. They came into the kitchen and took whatever they wanted, they didn't wait for anyone to tell them to, and it was really chaotic. In spite of my hunger, I didn't manage to take any of what I saw. There was so much toing and froing, the mistress helped and the child rushed around under my feet. He broke two glasses and a plate and his mother never said a word to him.

Those who saw him just laughed and drank to his health!

And they talked and laughed, and I couldn't hear anything but a loud buzzing. The endless buzz, and the ladies' perfumes and the men's cigarette smoking made me dizzy. I went into the dining room, and I saw them all through a blue haze.

It was like a dream, and in that dream, I saw that one of them had got up on a chair, he had pulled his hair over his forehead and started to speak strangely, waving his arms about, while his eyes bulged. Everyone was hysterical with laughter. He was pretending to be Hitler. Then he got down, and everyone clapped, and someone else got up on the chair, but this one didn't seem to be quite right. He looked like the one I had seen at Makriyianni with Mihalis that time, and there was something about him, which reminded of my previous master, the mountaineer.

I washed dishes all night. The sun came up, and they, believe me, were still dancing! I'd started making coffee for everyone.

Before the sun had finally come up, I went and got the child without anyone noticing. I asked him where he slept, I took him to his bedroom, undressed him, there in front of his cot, which was next to his mother's big bed — so luxurious and covered with lace bedspread – and I put him to bed. He fell asleep immediately.

The mistress didn't even ask me what had become of the child. The next day, by this time at noon, the guests had left. The mistress came into the kitchen, looked at me closely with her green eyes and said:

"You managed it well."

She said something else too, but I couldn't hear, so I told her. She was surprised:

"Do you hear the bell?"

"I hear it if I am in the kitchen."

She stayed silent for a while and then:

"Never mind. Stay for a while, and we'll see how you go. Now I'm going to sleep. Whatever is left over, put it in the icebox. Eat whatever you want. Wake me at four-thirty because I have a performance. Don't forget."

I had something to eat and I felt happiness in my soul. I opened all of the windows and brushed and mopped and cleaned the whole house. Three rooms, the hall, kitchen, with no window for me! I put my things out in my place as well as I could. There was no room for the trunk, so I left it in the kitchen. I put my clock out on a small shelf in the corner of the room. Its yellow hours showed me that it was three-thirty. I hadn't slept since the night before last. I put my little mirror on a small nail — along with all of the other outgoings, personally that is, was that little mirror — next to the clock, on the little shelf, I put the photograph of Mihalis, and then I cleaned round my new home. I suddenly remembered my plants. I had left them outside the door last night, and with all the commotion I'd forgotten. I ran and opened the door. No plants anywhere! Oh, Lord! Don't say I'd lost them! It seemed like a bad omen. I looked all around where the lift was, and the two other doors to the neighbouring apartments, but found nothing. I kept the door half-open with the carpet so that it wouldn't close while I was outside. It happened to me once, and I'd been badly frightened. I started down the stairs looking into all of the landings until I reached the entrance. No sign of my plants anywhere. There, the concierge called me:

"Who are you?"

Not that I heard her, but I expected that's what she would say; what else? I told her, and her face changed. She looked angry. I was listening.

"They made so much noise last night and even this morning. Everyone in the block of flats complained. What kind of state is that? Do you hear it? Off you go and tell her."

"But it was a name-day party."

"They always have parties. It would be good if..."

"If what? What do you mean?"

She didn't answer and asked me to leave.

"Oh, excuse me Misses, could you tell me your name?"

She turned around, as if she'd just noticed me and was weighing whether I deserve to grace with her telling me her name or not. She decided: "My name is Aretoussa," she said.

"Please Mrs Aretoussa, have you, by any chance, seen some plant pots?"

"Oh, were they yours?"

She had taken them into her room and she gave them back to me.

I was so pleased because I saw people in this new house, and we had a concierge, and she would be easy, I thought, to become a friend. Something told me that I was going to have a good time in this house, and I had found my plants which I quickly took with me up in the lift. Then I remembered the mistress' order that I should wake her and ran to see the time was twenty to five.

Shaking, I went and knocked on the door, the child had gotten up and he opened it. He looked at me with the same green eyes as his mother and put his finger to his lips that I should make no noise, as she was sleeping.

"I have to wake her. She told me to wake her."

She heard and moved. How pretty she was. I couldn't take my eyes off her there lying on the bed, with her blonde hair spread over the pillows, like light spilling over...

"Mistress, it's twenty to five."

"Coffee! Take Dimitri and feed him whatever he wants." His little hand was warm and soft, just like Stratis and the same as Nikakis. While the coffee was boiling, I gave him cold roast meat, prawns and mayonnaise which he ate happily. I picked up the coffee to take her. I stood outside her door and knocked. I counted ten, as

I had with my other mistresses, and opened the door. My mistress was naked as the day was born. I didn't know what to do. I nearly dropped the coffee. She noticed me and burst out laughing. Her lovely breasts were shaking around while I was just so embarrassed that I wanted to run and hide.

"Wait!" She said, still laughing.

I stood still.

"Were you shocked? Why? Am I so different from you? Leave the coffee over there."

I carefully put the coffee on the dresser near her. Her perfume was strong. She was standing near me, and she had a crystal bottle of perfume in her hand with a pear-shaped rubber bag hanging from it. She squeezed this and was covered in a golden mist of scent.

When the mist had settled, she, still looking like a living statue, but the perfume bottle down, and sat on the stool at her dressing table to drink her coffee, she watched me through the mirror, and she was enjoying my confusion. The mirrors multiplied her nakedness and she spoke calmly and clearly, as if she was wearing her clothes.

"Is the child eating? Did you give him some of everything?"

"Indeed."

"Is there anything left over?"

"There is some."

"Did you eat enough?"

"Yes, I did, thank you."

"Take a cake, as many as you like. Do you like cakes?"

"Yes, I do."

"Well then, go and eat."

I went out of her bedroom, the warmth and her perfume had surrounded me, and I stayed within this moist warm dust which tortured me and caught in my throat. I opened the windows wide in the kitchen, and I took a deep breath of the clean breeze which I hoped would help me get rid of the strange unhappiness, which had come over me in that warm perfumed cloud which had covered her nakedness. In front of me, the sky was bright red with fire.

I set a plate for Dimitraki, he ate one of the cakes, and then he went and found a rope and tried to tie two of the kitchen chairs together in order to make a train.

Dressed in a green dress with the same colour jacket, my mistress came into the kitchen, and I couldn't take my eyes off her again. It was as if she was stark naked in front of me still.

"I am off, I'm going to the theatre."

The child ran towards her and clung to her.

"No, you stay here."

He turned to me:

"What's your name?"

"Panoria."

"Panoria? What kind of name is that? I am to call you Nora, that's easier, Nora!"

"You stay with Nora, she said to the child, and do your homework."

The child struggled and cried loudly. She left.

I had a hard time calming him down. Finally, with one last piece of cake, he made up his mind and sat down on the poor little thing and did his homework.

"Where is your school," I asked him.

"Here," he said…and then he said something else which I couldn't hear.

"Speak louder, I don't hear well."

"Are you deaf?

"A little."

He came close to me, and took hold of my ear, he shouted so loud it made my head spin.

"Can you hear me now? Can you hear me? Tomorrow, you will take me to the school, can you hear, deaf old donkey?"

It was so long ago that I was called a deaf old donkey, and I was delighted. I grabbed the boy and kissed him. And we became friends. With laughter and jokes, and I fed him again in the evening, and put him to bed. I made up my lady's luxurious bed. My goodness, the nightdress was as delicate as a spider's web! I didn't know how to pick it up even, I was afraid my nails might tear it. I turned the light out. I stayed awhile in the darkened bedroom, it was almost as though I was again in Stratis and Nikakis' room in the first house they lived in.

I ate as much as I wanted and cut another slice of cake. My eyes filled with tears as I chewed, tears of happiness, I drank joy because of all these good things. Glory to God, I said, and crossed myself.

I fell into a deep dark inky black sleep. Suddenly in the death-like darkness of this deep sleep, I felt something like an earthquake. A sharp jolt woke me up, and before I had even opened my eyes, I could see red sparks jumping behind my lids.

"Nora, Nora, wake up! Get up! Nora!"

My mistress's voice shattered the sparks, and I opened my eyes and saw her in front of me dressed in yesterday's green dress, she was wild, different!

"Get up! It's war! Get up!"

I leapt up and staggered around drunkenly.

"Its war! Didn't you hear?"

"What should I have heard?"

"The sirens. Can't you hear them? Come on, get the child's milk, and let's go."

I opened the cold box and took the milk just as it was in the casserole, I put it and turned on the heat, adding a little coffee and stirred it. As I stood there shaking my legs started to turn to cotton wool, and I held onto the chair so that I wouldn't fall down, inside me, there was a voice, mine this time, and it shouted loudly so that I could hear: "War! Panoria! War!"

I gathered all my strength and straightened my apron and went as fast as I could to find my mistress in her room where she was dressing the child. Something wild and ugly fluttered in my stomach. She turned and fixed her green eyes on me:

"Can't you hear the sirens?"

I couldn't hear them. But it seemed that their sound had penetrated into my skin, and hit my stomach, upsetting everything.

We went down to the building's shelter in the basement. Everyone had gathered there. There were a policeman and others passers-by from the pavement outside. They were all talking at once, their eyes looked feverish. Some women were crying. We left and went back to our apartment, that was torturing me all this time came out.

I went up to my room, and fell onto the bed on my face and burst into tears, until eventually, my mistress came up. I tried to get up. But she put her hand on my shoulder without looking at me. She was looking elsewhere, at the photograph of Mihalis in his soldier uniform. She didn't say anything, but went down to the kitchen and brought me an aspirin and a glass of water.

We often had to run down to the shelter. Usually, I took the child's food with me and fed him, my mistress couldn't go to the theatre. Her friends gathered in the house every evening, they read the newspapers and discussed them. I read too, everything I could lay my hands on.

The titles announced: "2nd November. The border" — "written in the following pages — four bombings of the enemy." Or: "Fierce shooting at the border...Enemy aircraft bombed the interior of the country."

Ten days later, after I had sent two hurried letters to Mihalis, I got his message:

Dear Panoria,

I am alive and well!

I hope we will make our home together. We will have a life too.

Please send a thick vest to the usual address.

I kiss you, your husband,

Mihalis

I couldn't help it, and I showed the letter to my mistress. "Are you married?" she asked.

I didn't know what to say. She understood. And didn't take offence.

"Don't worry," she said, "It's just a storm. It will pass. Now off you go to the attic and put some paper over the window, the concierge tells me that he can see the light coming out from it."

We had a lot of work covering the windows with blackout material, and we covered everything, including the French windows, it was as though the house was blind.

One of her friends, an actress too, turned up dressed as a nurse one evening. She looked pretty. The next day she was to leave.

They stayed up late that night, so I did, going in and out of the dining room to empty the ashtrays, or bring a drink of water or coffee all the time.

The sight of her stayed in my mind, and a strange idea began to torture me days after she'd left. Finally, I got my courage together and told the mistress. She lost it, and looked at me strangely as if she had never seen me before:

"What are you saying? You want to go and be a nurse too? Have you had any training in that sort of work?

What should I say? Wasn't it enough that I wanted to do it so much? I would like to learn.

"You say that because you think that it will bring you close to Mihalis? Mihalis is his name, isn't it?

"Yes indeed, Mihalis."

"And you think, you poor thing, that the war is only in one place? And that you can go there, and you hope that you will find him? Thousands are spread in the army everywhere, in villages, and thousands over the mountains. The battles are in one place and the hospitals in another."

"So, I wouldn't find him?

"It's not that easy. Anyway, you have to be able to read and write. You have to go to school.

"Nursing school!"

"So, I can't manage it then?" "No, Nora dear, I don't believe so."

She thought for a bit and then said: Anyway, let's say you could manage to go, wouldn't you be afraid?"

"I will be afraid."

"Well...I."

"I'll get used to it."

"Maybe you would get used to it. But listen to me and think about what I'm going to say to you: Maybe you could manage to go, and instead of being here in my house, you could be serving some soldiers where you would be sent. But sadly, you were unlucky."

And instead of being at the actress' house I would be in some other important house, of course...

But I regretted what I had thought, and I saw her so pretty and so accepting.

"I'm not unlucky. I am not, because I have a good mistress, and..."

I started to cry. She patted me gently on the shoulder and left the kitchen. I poured and drank a whole glass of water and then sat and wrote a letter to Mihalis. That evening her friends came and said that Korytsa in Albania had been taken from the Italians.

We went out the following day.

We all went to the shops, and she bought blankets, vests, and said she was going to send them somewhere, and she gave me one of the jackets for Mihalis. She gave it to me as a present.

When we came out of the shops the siren sounded, I felt it in my stomach which began to tremble again. We all crammed into a patisserie and pulled down the blinds. My mistress ordered some cakes. When the all-clear sounded, and we came out of the patis-serie, I saw a very proper looking gentleman in a heavy coat, with a trilby and a white cravat at his throat, light coloured gloves, like something you would see at the cinema, he was so impressive, and he came and greeted my mistress. He took her hand and brought it to his lips, looking her right in the eyes. Then he turned to Dimitrakis and bent to kiss him, but the child didn't want to kiss him, and turned his face away and pulled on my hand to leave. My mistress then turned to me: "Take the child and go home, I'll come later."

The gentleman called a taxi, gave me some money, put us inside and closed the door. All through the ride I felt a strange coldness, while hoping the sirens wouldn't go off because I was alone with the child. What was I thinking? I felt trembling in my stomach. The kid huddled in my arms, and the driver turned the lights off on the car, and we drove in darkness, thankfully, we were close to the house and we arrived safely. I paid and we ran to the shelter. We'd eaten the cakes, so even though we were there for a long time we weren't hungry. The child cried. He said he was afraid something terrible might happen to his mother...and where was she? And why she went with him again? With him..." and he cried and cried until he fell asleep in my arms.

I was sitting on the floor and the well-dressed man who I'd seen for the first time today was on my mind.

I didn't even notice the others in the shelter, although I'd begun to recognise them, like the lady in the opposite apartment who would watch me all the time, while I sang lullabies to Dimitraki, whom I didn't like and who would bend her head and whisper to one of the others from our building too, although I didn't know which apartment. I couldn't stop thinking of that man who had suddenly appeared and upset us.

When the all-clear sounded, I came out of the shelter and went up, with Dimitrakis in my arms, still sleeping. He didn't awaken until I began to undress him.

"Stay with me. Don't leave me. I'm frightened. Maybe there'll be another siren."

"No, there won't be, come on, go to sleep."

"If there is? You won't hear it."

"Of course I'll hear it. I'll stay with you, don't worry. Now lie down and go to sleep."

"No, I don't want to. I will tell you...I will tell you about the wedding."

"What wedding?"

"They took me to the wedding."

"How could they take you to the wedding? What wedding?"

"I was little, but I remember it."

"What are you talking about? Come on now, go to sleep."

"No, I'm not going to sleep. When they got married. Him...with my mother..."

"Him?"

"Yes, the one you saw. He is my father. But I don't want him to be."

"I don't understand."

"Why don't you understand? I was born before they got married. Mama wore white and carried a bouquet and held me by my hand, close to her. The three of us stood in front of the priest. It smelled of incense. We had two big candles nearby, much taller than me. Then we got in a car. He and mama were kissing all the time, and she was stroking him. They left me with Sophia. It was horrible. As horrible as though I were very ill."

"Oh, come on now, calm down, time to sleep — don't think about all those things."

"I'd stopped thinking of them. Then I was happy again. She was mine again, mine I tell you — but now..."

"Don't upset yourself. Your mother will come back soon from wherever she is."

"If he beats her again?"

"SShh now, don't say silly things, people don't go around hitting each other, and he looked like a real gentleman."

"He looks like one, but he isn't. He's bad. He didn't want her to act in the theatre. That's why he beat her."

Finally, after midnight, the child went to sleep. I slept next to him, I didn't want him to be woken by the siren and be afraid. I laid down on the carpet next to the mistress bed, as soon as I closed my eyes, my head started spinning, a blabber of human voices.

Men, women, soldiers, actresses, bombs, explosions, fires, soil, mud. The mud was churning and changing into blue clouds of smoke, and there, men and women were laughing and dancing, an enormous Hitler got up on a chair and shouted, and suddenly he became angry. He was holding a machine gun and started shooting all around, right and left and the mud again and the cloud and one man beating his wife. Another, and another...All the men were beating their wives. All the children were crying...It's war. The whirlwind began, round and round, so there were wheels, only wheels made of mud, thousands of wheels. The man who beat his wife was caught up in the wheels. "Don't! Don't! She's pretty, you shouldn't..."

"Bravo, Nora, you are a treasure!"

That's what the mistress said when she found me in the morning asleep on the rug near the child. I was pleased to hear her words, and I ran into the kitchen to make coffee, and do other chores later. They were the same every day: brushing, dusting, cooking. Many times, when the tasks had been done, years and years the same thing, I thought I would have died from boredom, but it was as if someone else did them and I just watched her, to make sure she was worth the bread she ate and the money she was making.

I hadn't had a letter from Mihalis for some days. So, I sat down and wrote the fourth one:

Dear Mihalis,

it's been thirty-three days since I had a letter from you. I realise with the war, that the postal system will be disrupted. So, I wait patiently every day. My heart is with you. My mistress is perfect and gives me 500 drachmas a month.

Well, Mihalis, be brave, it's only a storm, it will pass, don't let the war destroy you. Just take care, and look after yourself as well as you can. Mihalis, make sure you write to me as soon as you receive this.

I kiss you. Your wife,

Panoria.

I took it to the post office that same afternoon, my mistress had given me some extra money to buy a pastry, and I had saved it. Thank God, I ate well in this house, whatever I wanted I could have. So, I kept my money and added that small amount to my capital which I had in a bag in my trunk, sovereigns, drachmas, I had some of everything, I had 117 sovereigns and 4.385 drachmas. The only thing was that those sirens frightened me, and I didn't know what to do. Should I take the money with me to the shelter? But how? I didn't want anyone to know that I had money and most of all the concierge, who I didn't like at all.

The more I got to know her, the less I liked her. I would never make a friend out of her. Anyway, I decided to keep the money on me. I took a strip of material and sewed the bag onto it and tied it around my waist. Of course, it was a bit bulky, but I wore my apron. Instead of once when I would take it off the moment I left the house, I wore it all the time, and this pleased my mistress. So it didn't really show much. Nobody should be able to tell. I can't say I was particularly happy with this solution, but it was the best I could think of.

Some more about the concierge. She claimed she could "read" coffee cups. She was always very friendly to me and sucked up to me, and that was why I didn't really like her because she obviously wanted something.

She kept on at me to read my coffee cup. She got paid thirty drachmas from the ladies when she read theirs. I had no intention of giving her even a cent, but I didn't want to offend her. Life had taught me to be careful and not to annoy people, you never know when you might need their help.

I didn't tell her straight up that I didn't want to, just at that moment, I didn't have any money, even though I did have...It was later that I learned that she rented rooms by the hour on the first floor.

From our balcony, when the sun came out, I would keep the child company, and I noticed who went in and out of the building, I said to myself: Oh, she will be for the first floor, her dress and face somehow showed it. "Him? Oh. No. He looks like a good husband." I enjoyed the game and the people watching. I learned to judge people.

And that was how I got the biggest shock in that strange time. Who do you think I saw? My old and first mistress! She got out of a car, all dressed up, rather fat, light-hearted and expensively-dressed, arm in arm with an army officer. My mind went blank, in a daze said: She's following her old profession! She would definitely be going to the first floor, to the rooms that the concierge was renting out. I made some excuse and went out to buy something, I went down and looked left and right, I got to the outer door, and I saw a shiny black car parked outside with a sailor at the wheel, with a flag with a gold fringe which fluttered proudly in the breeze. The concierge was looking at the car too.

Without me saying anything, she turned around:

"You see! He's the governor of the..."

"Who? What is he?"

"An important person. He came with his wife to visit the general's widow on the third floor."

With his wife? The third floor, you said?"

"Yes, silly, the little fat lady is his wife, first-class lady. She often comes to see the widow."

"I'd made a mistake? Was it someone else? I felt I had to see her again. I went into the street as far as the corner, and after a while, I could see the shop opposite pull down its blinds, and two people on the road started to run, the concierge made signs to me — it was a siren.

I ran rushed inside and got in the lift to go to the child who was on his own.

But the darned lift was occupied. I waited. I was shaking, and my heart was aching. Thank God, the lift arrived. Who should get out but the governor and his wife? It was her. She saw me. Instantly our eyes met. I could see she was shocked, she went quite yellow. She'd changed, she'd got fatter, but it was her! I was so confused that someone else took the lift up and I stood there watching my old mistress descend the few steps in the entrance hall. She and her husband arrived at the door, and they left calmly, her first and then him. The sailor opened the car door for them, saluted them and then they got inside. The concierge was asking something, but I couldn't hear her.

"Where are they going? Didn't they hear the siren?"

"The governor has work to do. So, they have the freedom to drive when there is a siren, come on, let's go down."

As I went back to get the lift I saw Dimitrakis, he's saying something, but I'm so dazed I can't hear anything.

"Hey, Nora!"

He's shouting now "why aren't you talking to me? Are you frightened?

"No, I'm not afraid...Um..."

I don't even know what I said to the child as I pulled him down to follow the others and some strangers from the street who were coming into our shelter.

Everything that I was saying was as if someone else was speaking, and I was lost deep in the past, watching a car which turns the corner, there on Makriyianni. The black car with the policeman came and took the mistress. The policeman had fixed a piece of paper to the door. Mihalis and I were standing on the corner, watching her as she left...From the car's window, all that could be seen was that yellow material that she had wrapped around her beaten face.

The car disappeared into a yellow dust cloud, dissolved and disappeared to reveal today's tarmacked road, the enormous car, and the flag with the gold fringe fluttering proudly.

Inside was travelling she who had been lost. She was so important that she didn't even need a shelter when the siren went on in the war. That's what I saw and was thinking about in the shelter when a foreign soldier came in.

He was English, blind drunk, falling first to one side, then to the other, stumbling about, and with him was a young girl, a woman? I couldn't tell you. It was the first time I'd seen her, wearing a dressing gown and nothing else. She went up to the concierge, smiling, and wanted something from her. Mrs Aretoussa bought ammonia, and she put it under the drunkard's nose, who had collapsed in a corner and was throwing up.

There were other children in the shelter. We saw them only because their mothers didn't let them play with our child, because he was the child of an actress, they said. However, I found the opportunity to bring them all together and get them to play along. We were all in the same boat. Whoever we were, whether we were the children of the actress, or the governor, or the widow.

The siren never seemed to end. There was a girl with us from the apartment next to us, and she played too — fly! Fly! I didn't always play, only when I understood what they said, but I always started their games. When the drunkard came around, and Mrs Aretoussa had mopped up the vomit, he suddenly jumped up and grabbed the young woman, or lady, or whatever she was, and embraced her and opened her dressing gown. The women rolled their eyes, and the men smiled knowingly and watched everything avidly, and the drunkard in his own world wanted to kiss her. Then, would you believe, something funny happened: The young woman gave the man such a resounding slap that he lost his balance and fell down. We all burst out laughing, along with the children. It was like being at the cinema.

But the best was when the drunkard got up, half sat down, and started to cry like a baby. He was crying. The children carried on with their game: Fly! Fly! When I heard it, I put my hand up to play, while in my mind whirled a shiny black car with my old mistress inside. He, the significant person, the governor, he surely could do something to help my Mihalis. How could I manage it? How to sort it out?

What a terribly crazy world it is. While the car whirled, the wheels started to grind me until I understood that nothing would happen from her side for Mihalis to lighten his burden in this war.

A few days afterwards, the girl from the next apartment came and showed me a photograph of her *fiancé* who had gone to war. I showed her my photo of Mihalis too. We talked.

Thank God, I have a friend. I could learn...I needed to learn.

When the mistress saw that I was talking to her, she became angry and stamped her foot. It was the first time I'd seen her like this. She didn't want me to make friends with the girls from the other apartments.

That evening, when the child and I were alone, he had heard the raised voices and said to me:

"She doesn't want you to have friends because they gossip about us."

"But we weren't talking about you."

"Even if you didn't talk about us, you will find one day. She's worried about me."

"Why is she worried about you?"

"That I won't learn what I know."

I asked him what he knows, but he didn't want to say. I understood. It would be about his father and the whole strange situation.

One afternoon the mistress went out; she took the child with her, to go and see her mother. That's a new one: Her mother had never visited us. I didn't know why. I went up the roof to speak to my friend, to learn:

"It's true. Her husband used to beat her but not about the theatre, because she had a lover."

"An actor?"

"I don't know if he was an actor. But she had someone. An important person. The newspapers write about him. But I don't remember it. My mistress knows it; that's why you've got so many comforts. You don't even weigh your sugar or your coffee, not even your oil. Even now when things have got so much more expensive...Many people are getting killed, never mind wounded; hotels have been made into hospitals. All of them.

"I wish I'd managed to be a nurse. Do you think the lady, after she knows such a reputable person could do something?

"Don't say anything. She'll throw you out. Be careful, poor thing."

Later on, I remembered what she had told me, that I was stuck with her because she didn't know anyone. I got confused again. When on earth do people ever tell the truth? When do they lie?

Despina, the girl's name, sat on the ledge of the roof. I sat next to her. Suddenly, the sun shone over Athens, lighting up the sea in the distance. My friend is speaking again. I'm listening carefully; I have to listen carefully because she is impatient and won't want to repeat it:

"Your mistress is a famous actress. They write about her in the newspapers. They even show her photograph. My boss has seen her acting in the theatre. Didn't she ever take you with her?"

"No."

"The other girl she had, she used to take sometimes so that she would help her get dressed. She has to dress differently. You see, she uses make-up and changes. If you were to see her, you wouldn't recognise her. In the theatre, she has another woman who sews her clothes, dresses her, and does her hair."

"Really? What a shame she's never taken me."

"She leaves you to look after the child. In the old days, she used to take him along too, to the theatre. But not anymore. She's afraid of her husband, and he has forbidden her to take him there."

I could have seen her. Sometimes I watch her as she walks around talking to herself. Mostly she has a piece of paper in her hands, and she stands in front of the mirror, laughs and cries...I could watch her for hours. She is very different from all the other mistresses I've had.

My friend is studying me; she has her eyes fixed on me.

"You be careful, do you hear?"

"Be careful? Why should I be careful?"

"Be careful; she doesn't hit you."

"What do you mean? How?"

"What," I said.

"I don't understand."

"If you don't understand, it is because you don't want to understand."

"What are you saying? Have you gone mad? You should be ashamed! That sort of thing only goes on between men, and don't think I'm that stupid that I don't know about that."

"You don't know anything. Women do it, too, even if they have a husband or lots of men. Just watch out because I've heard things about her..."

I didn't hear what she heard — she was lucky to understand so much anyways — and I never asked her about it. I left her there and ran to get the child from his granny; it was getting late. The sun had begun to go down and was sinking behind the houses.

Days passed. I got a letter from Mihalis:

Dear Panoria,

I'm well. Please send your socks. Our feet are freezing. We are winning, and it's all going to get sorted out. But please just send me the socks.

Your husband,

Mihalis

Only that, but at least I could relax, and I made sure to send him socks straight away.

As for my mistress, I was upset by what Despina had told me and began to watch her and trembled in case something would happen. If she were to hit on me, what would I do? Would I just stay? Would I go?

And how would I leave after I had begun to put on some weight in this house. I was rested and free, and the child loved me; he was young, and he needed me too. Where would I find something better, particularly then that we were at war? Even though I watched my mistress, I never saw any odd behaviour. She never appeared before me naked again, like she had when I was first there. I stopped having a lot to do with Despina because, although it took me a while to think of it, it occurred to me that she'd just said all those things so that she would seem much smarter than me. She wanted to show me that she knows about the world and people. Something like that.

On Christmas Eve, the actors came to the house, after midnight, with the mistress. I had made a stuffed turkey. My old mistress had taught me how to make it, and I did it well. The other children, Stratis and Nikakis, were crazy about the stuffing. The actors clapped for me and drank to my health. Something warm, very warm, started to blossom inside me, and I went and hid in the kitchen so they wouldn't see me crying.

That evening, the mistress wore a shiny, black dress, clinging and low cut. She was like someone from another world. I was proud of her and loved watching her, but when she looked at me, I started to fret, and then she gestured that someone was ringing the bell and I should go and open the door. It was her husband who came straight in. The actors froze. My mistress was the only one who got up from where she was sitting next to the actor with the wispy hair who had mimicked Hitler; her husband was speaking. My mistress replied to him; they were like two monsters facing each other, ready to attack. My lady is saying something else.

An awful, demonic-sounding laugh rumbled out of his mouth, and he advanced on the elderly actress who was holding the child and pulled him off her. He bit his hand and marked it. My lady rushed in between them to take the child, but he wouldn't let him go. Christ Almighty, they'll tear the child in two! The old actress got up and grabbed him out of their hands and held him in her arms again. The child started crying, and the actors tried with forced laughter, with caresses and jokes to cheer up Dimitraki, while my mistress tripped, got up again to get her child, and fell.

She hit her head on the corner of the table and blood flooded from her right temple. Without being told, I ran to get some cotton wool and peroxide. Then the gentleman, her husband — I suppose we should call him "gentleman" — took them from me and bent over her in a very loving way and wiped away the blood and tended to her. The actors got up to leave, one by one. I took the child to put him to bed in his room. He trembled as if he had a fever, but he didn't make a sound, although large tears poured down his cheeks. I stroked and kissed him. His cheeks were wet. I wrapped him up warmly and gave him an aspirin. I sat next to him in the dark until he fell asleep, with the wet still on my lips from his tears.

Dawn had broken, and everyone had left. In the dining room was just my mistress and her husband, and the one with wispy hair. Here was something else strange: I would have thought if my mistress had a lover, it would have been him. He always came to the house long before the others arrived, and they would sit and talk together for hours. They were pretending to be brave as well. I'd watched them as they'd become different people, speaking, speaking, speaking, many times holding a piece of paper in their hands. One day he went close to her and he embraced her. They talked all the while, but he didn't kiss her. When I'd seen her husband tonight, I was more worried for him, but no...

Dawn broke, and my mistress came into the kitchen to order three coffees. I fixed them and took them in and wondered at what I saw. All three were sitting together, talking calmly and pleasantly. I didn't hear them, of course, but I understood what they were saying to each other, I would have sworn that I had been dreaming. Just as if nothing had happened, the three of them were sitting around a table drinking the coffee I had only made for them, and I saw this. I'm asking myself: Is the actor her lover?

"You won't learn it, Panoria. You came into this life just to observe, to see living portraits which hide their secrets to torture you because that's how it should be. You have to always be confused! You will learn only what others want to tell you, you are still at their mercy. If the others want you to, then you will learn, you will see them up close, and you will get to know them. Maybe then you will learn things about yourself, things you never imagined! You will see how differently they see you, they will be able to say that you are definitely not worth what you think you are... Maybe you will also learn that Mihalis isn't worth it..."

It was an ugly voice saying this inside my head and made me into a monster. "Eh? Oh no, not that Mihalis isn't worthy. No!" And I said out loud, hitting the table with my fist, "I'm angry!" Anguish had overwhelmed me, and the only way to feel better was to be angry and shout.

For that evening, or rather the following morning, things changed.

The gentleman moved into the apartment. After a few days, my mistress stopped going to the theatre. The only one of her old friends who continued to come to the house was the actor with the wispy hair or beard. One day the old actress turned up. When I took them their coffees, both she and my mistress were in tears.

The pretty actress had gone to be a nurse on a boat which had been made into a hospital. Germans had sunk this boat and the girl drowned, along with many others.

Despina's *fiancé* was brought back from the front. They were going to have to amputate his hand. She asked me to go with her to the hospital to visit him. On Saturday, I bought some oranges so that I wouldn't go empty-handed. I wanted to know and to ask about Mihalis. I hadn't heard from him for a very long time, 56 days.

That night, I couldn't sleep because of the many things that were annoying me and driving me crazy. "Be careful you don't pester. You don't know what you might find out. Be careful! You don't want the wheels, the big heavy ones with the chains to come and trample on you, and to grind you up and turn you into mud...No way! Why should I be annoying? Come on, Panoria! Be brave! Does it mean that all of those who learned were braver than me? They're people too. We're all people and I must, I must learn."

I didn't go to the hospital, and when my mistress told me to buy oranges, I gave her mine and kept the money. I didn't go because I was scared about what I would find out. Another day had passed with no news from Mihalis. I didn't go because the child was ill for days, and we brought his bed into the living room, and I made up the sofa to sleep next to him so he wouldn't be alone, as nowadays the gentleman slept in the luxurious bed in my mistress's embrace.

The master even bought him a railway train to get him to like him. A train with an engine with a screw that you turned and then it would run, it had three wagons! A wonderful thing. I saw it and said to myself: "Please, God, let Mihalis and I will be together and have children and buy them such a train set." The little rascal didn't want it, or the master, though. When he got well, what do you think he said to me? "He took mama and gave me a train set. But he won't get better of me. You take it if you like it. I give it to you."

"I? Should I take it?" When the mistress turned up, I told her what he'd said. Lately, she wasn't looking well. She was pale, she was smoking a lot and taking some pills. It was as though she'd wilted. She doesn't even see me anymore, and when I speak to her, she seems not to hear. So, when I am telling her about the train, she lifts up her shoulders. I'm listening carefully to see what she will say. I was hanging on her every word!

"Well, why don't you take it?"

"What? What did you say?"

"I said. Take it. If you like it. Dimitrakis is never going to play with it. If you know some poor child, then take it and give it to them." I took it with its shiny new box. I was worried about what would happen when the master came looking for it. But no! Nothing was ever again said about the train, and I took it and put it away in my little bedroom, thanks be to God! See! I now have my first toy for my son.

Oh, I must write to Mihalis about this. More days passed, and Mihalis hadn't written. The newspaper, with its black letters, says 7 April 1941: The German army attacked Greece yesterday. Our forces have already experienced the most significant epic struggle. It is equal to the Persian Wars.

"What is that word, epopoeia? They do find some strange words. I've noticed that the worse things get, the more unknown and difficult words they use are."

"Is that what it means?"

"Yes Nora, nowadays that's what it means."

Another new word appeared: reduction. Withdrawal, in other words. Still nothing from Mihalis! The days pass with new words. With the word "missing." The newspaper says it will give information about those who are missing. That means, of course, for those who have had no news.

"If you want, you could write and ask about your *fiancé*," my mistress said.

Then she left. "Where would I write? To the newspaper? How would I write a letter?" As I wrote to Mihalis:

"Dear Morning News, please can you tell me about Mihalis who is the STG K 257?" Like that? No, of course not. This is a newspaper we are talking about, it must be more formal." I didn't know how to, so I didn't write. I waited. I'd lost touch with Despina...

I hadn't seen her for days. I missed her and made up my mind. I knocked on her kitchen door. Her mistress came out and said she'd gone to her village. She'd left.

"And her *fiancé*?"

"I told her and so did her sister. Finally, we persuaded her to..."

"To what? What do you mean? What are you saying?"

"I said to her, what use was he to her, now a wreck of a person? They amputated his leg — just a man with only one arm and one leg. What good would he have been? That's why I advised her to leave."

Right; a person with one arm, with one leg. My head started spinning. My body felt heavy as if it had been burdened by all of the iron and steel of the war. In the midst of all their metal, I could just see a body: Mihalis. An organization which if you pricked it with a needle would feel pain.

It was so dreadful what was happening that I didn't even cry. Just the metal, the wounded, the ones with no arms and no legs, some bodies like the trunks of trees, mutilated forms appeared in the nights during the yellow hours of my clock. From there, they poured out like worms, spreading out through the sulphurous light of its holes and presenting themselves to me in order, an army of logs, like an unending parade. I didn't cry. I just shivered, and my teeth chattered. I bit my hand to try and stop them chattering because they made my body shudder horribly.

One day, my mistress said to me: "The master has gone. You won't speak of it. Not a word. If anyone asks you, you know nothing. If necessary, you'll have to pretend to be dumb."

If it's not bad enough that I have the problem with my hearing, now I have to become speechless. "Gladly," I said. Times are hard, and I have bread to eat. I will become dumb. If that was all it was.

But that wasn't all it was. She and the child would leave. They had to hurry before the Germans entered Athens. From where, I didn't know.

On Palm Sunday, they took me with them to church. I stood next to them. I couldn't hear what the priest was saying, or what the chorus was singing, but I liked it very much. I felt a sweet warmth with all those people around me. I never got enough of seeing the faces. Men, women, children, old men, young, rich and poor - they were all there. I was there among them. Me! I lifted my eyes up high to thank God, because I was also there, so close to those people. My eyes were filled by the crystal chandeliers. How they played with the light like the water, the sun on the water. My mind ran back to the past and arrived at the sea, there with flying diamonds which glistened and made me crazy, and brought Mihalis close to me...From looking too long at the chandeliers, it seemed as though I were blind, because my eyes filled with tears. I turned to look at the icons. The faces of the saints were controlled, serious, almost frightening. What I wanted to see the crystal light again, I was scared. No, it wasn't a game being played between the light and the glass, it wasn't water, not sea and sun, it was red stripes of blood, it was dreadful explosions, and I didn't want to see them.

Later we were crushed, and they trod on my feet, and I was worried about my new shoes, anyway, we managed to get a palm cross. Pushing through with all those people and their warmth, we came out of the church gate and began slowly, step by step going down the full exit. I held on to Dimitraki by hand so we wouldn't get lost. Everyone with their palms going down the steps of the street now one by one. They were unending! So many levels and there seemed to be a continual flow of people who were going down, more and more and they pulled everyone further down, into the centre of the earth, wherein its darkness we would surely find safety.

In two days, we got all the clothes together and emptied the house. She gave me some of her old clothes, but they were still lovely, and I was ashamed to wear them. She gave me one month's salary extra, I found myself in front of the block of flats again, with all my things around me. With a piece of paper in my hand for a house where my mistress had introduced me.

The concierge asked me:

"Where are you going now?"

I showed her the reference.

"Oh, right...good...As you wish..."

As if she didn't like it. She observed me and spoke clearly so that I would hear her:

"How do you know what you will find there where you are going? Wouldn't you rather stay here?

"Here? Where? Are one of the apartments looking for a maid?"

I began to hope.

"No, but I..."

"You? What do you mean?

"Well, I know I am a sensitive person, but I like you. Stay with me. You can clean and brush up the rooms on the first floor, you'll get tips. I don't have the time. Never mind that the pain in my poor back drives me mad."

I didn't speak. I didn't know what to say. She took that meant I agreed.

"Go on, take your things down, put your plants in the courtyard. You are a good girl, you will do well."

Why did she want to say that last bit? Whenever I hear the phrase "good girl" I start feeling suspicious. I answered her:

"Thank you, Mrs Aretoussa, you are a kind woman, but you know, my mistress already spoke to the people in that house and how can I let them down? They are expecting me. If they are good to me, and pay well…"

"Nobody pays nowadays, and if they do pay all the money will lose its value, listen to me because I know what I am saying, people who know about such things have told me. Come with me, and you won't regret it.

She was looking at me as if she was studying my body. So what could I do but go down the steps to the concierge's room. Not because of what she was saying, but because I suddenly realised that Mihalis had that address for me. If I left, where would he be able to find me?

I stayed, and she set me immediately to brush and dust the foyer. As night fell, I laid the round table with a green velvet tablecloth.

Some men and two women came, Mrs Aretoussa brought the cards and a box with coloured bones. They set out the game. She showed me where she kept the coffee and sugar, and I made them coffees until late in the night. The more I went in and out, the more I noticed the players. I watched their hands. How they picked up and place the coloured bones in front of them and how their eyes lit up and showed which cards they held. I counted the money they paid out to get the bones. It could be two or three times more of what I earned in a month, thrown away in the box with the leftover bones.

The concierge didn't play. She sat next to one of the men and watched.

And what she was watching I could see clearly, it was a glass ash-tray, and there, whoever won put some money in, she watched it intently, and Mrs Aretoussa smiled.

When they left, she said to me:

"What can one do? I let them come here, and they reward me for the service."

She showed me the money in the ashtray. She took it. Counted it and put it in a purse which she put in her pocket. It was about one hundred and twenty drachmas. Well, well done her! All that for sitting for a few hours and watching other people play...

"Look here," she snarled. "If you want us to get on well and you to progress, it was some relatives of mine who came here tonight, and you didn't see any cards, understand? That's you must tell anyone who asks."

"But who is going to speak to me?"

"Anyone. You never know what may happen, and the devil has many tricks."

I pretended to be stupid.

"Why? Do they not allow them to play cards?"

"No, it's not allowed. It's forbidden, and they're playing here in secret."

"Who are they hiding from?"

"I said to keep quiet. Don't say anything to anyone who asks."

"Will they come back tomorrow?"

"Tomorrow no, maybe the day after. Don't worry about it. Look here, if you are a good girl and don't talk about this, I will give you some of the money they leave me."

She took out a fiver and gave it to me. Then I went into the kitchen and fell down exhausted on the quilt she'd given me and covered myself with my coat, the one that my previous mistress had given me, Stratis and Nikakis' mother. It was the one with the brown fur around the neck. I couldn't sleep, and I was afraid. Afraid of everything.

The war, the people. My money. I was afraid that the concierge might steal it from me. I was scared of getting involved in all her dirty tricks.

So, dawn broke and first thing in the morning I went to the first floor and washed the bathroom, washed and scrubbed the storey, I cleaned until the evening. I stopped at lunchtime just long enough to eat some salad and bread which Mrs Aretoussa gave me.

On that day, nobody came to the first floor. I locked it and came downstairs.

The concierge was out. A bad feeling had been upsetting me for a while. I read again the reference to the house which my mistress had given me. It wasn't far- should I go and have a look? And Mihalis? That's what I was thinking when I saw my present mistress stumbling down the steps, she was trembling, and she tripped, if I hadn't caught her she'd have had a nasty fall.

"They're coming! They're here! I saw them from the roof. In the dust clouds, the cars are coming..."

"Who cares?"

"Ah stupid! Don't you know anything...the Germans are here!"

And she shouted loudly so that I would be sure to hear it. I looked at her with my mouth hanging open. So, she thought I still hadn't heard.

"Did you hear me? The Germans! The Germans came! Now, who knows what's going to happen to us all..."

She said something else which I didn't hear. I wanted to know what was happening.

"Our army, our soldiers, where are they now? What are they doing?"

"How would I know? They'll be coming as well, those who survived...yes, the grocer's son came back. They said he came back from the mountains on foot."

"On foot? From..."

That was what she told me, what am I going to do, how will I ever find my Mihalis?

Suddenly I realised the truth. It was the first time that I'd faced the horror of it. The first time that my mind took it in. Mihalis was dead!

CHAPTER 5

The Walls of My House Are Going Up

Today I went out in the afternoon to go to the house when all the workmen would have left. I wanted to just sit on my own in my house. The sun disappeared behind the mountains of Piraeus, over the sea. I don't remember if I said that I can see the sea from the heights of Haravgi.

Now there are many rows of bricks, all joined with mud, joining the columns of cement. They have left all the right openings for doors and windows, here is the window of my dining room, the doorway is slightly raised from the ground and the three cement steps we will put there are missing at the moment. I had wanted to have them in marble, but it would have been too expensive, so I said never mind. The same with the lions. The two stone lions which have kept me company during my life, I won't be putting those in either, there is not going to be a balcony for them to hold up. The house will be one storey so the lions would be an unnecessary expense.

The night is falling, and I can see a star in the sky, then another. I'm still looking at my house. Only without realising it as I was standing up, I found myself sitting on a boulder. The night is beginning to obliterate the colour of the bricks on the walls. The dark continues to grow until the only thing I can discern is the window and door opening which are even blacker.

Athens has lit up. I was dazzled by the lights which spread and shone their meanings, taking my mind back to the past. We were both children then, Mihalis and I. Then when we had climbed up to the cemetery. Then when we kissed. My house became lost in darkness, just becoming a large heap of built walls which spoke to me:

You did it Panoria. You created me here because you wanted it. Because you thought of it so much. Because you worked. Because you worked, you deserve to see me. To touch me. To make me real. You did it. You must be satisfied...

The word began to run circles in my mind and began to multiply like the circles did, and the barbed wheels which grind me down and hurt me and torture me with their thick thorns, that crucified me here in front of the dark shape of my house.

When I was able to get up from the boulder, from where I was sitting, I ran down the hill to the bus stop. I ended up limping into the square. The heel had come off my shoe. I got on the bus and began to calm down as we began to travel through the streets of Athens, under the lights which spread their shimmering threads.

Mihalis

Suddenly, he appeared in the foyer, and I couldn't believe my eyes. I saw him and didn't realise it was him until he came close to me and took my hand...He wore a striped jacket and army trousers. His army jacket along with his greatcoat he had left with someone, in a stable, as he came down from the mountains, and that person gave him the striped jacket so that he wouldn't look like a soldier and so the Germans wouldn't get him. He gave him bread too.

We went out of the foyer. I gave Mrs Aretoussa a porcelain vase, a present from my last mistress. We moved again in Mrs Fotos' yard and rented an empty room which she had. That is where we could stay for now. I remember our landlady gave us a spoon sweet, made from oranges, but I couldn't swallow it. All I could do was cry from happiness. But Mihalis was different, he seemed to have gotten taller and thinner. Later in the evening, there in Makriyannis, at the tavern was when I noticed that his left eyelid trembled strangely. It was difficult for him to keep it open, it was closing as if it had a weight on it to protect his eye.

"Were you wounded, Mihalis? Why is it like that?"

He didn't answer but carried on eating and swallowing without chewing his food. He ate all the macaroni, and I gave him half of mine. Then his eyes filled with tears, and he looked at me so sadly. He looked at me with the healthy eye which was filled with tears. The other one was blind. How different Mihaliss was!

Later, we paid and left.

We went back to the yard and went into our little room, and closed the door. We too can be in our little house, even if it is small, just a room, and a divan — left by uncle Vassilis – it was where Mihalis slept, and Mr Vassilis couldn't be bothered to take it with him, he took his bed but didn't need Mihalis'. So here on this divan with the quilt borrowed from Mrs Fotos and Mihaliss army blanket, we lay and embraced and felt our blood beating in our bodies.

We stayed like that for hours, for minutes, who could say because we weren't living in this world but in a different one, whose heat burned me to the bone and melted me, on my throat where Mihalis put his lips. The flames were there and burned me to the bone, the more I caressed my love, the more I felt him...I felt him nestling close to me, hooking onto me, while the flames increased, the fire made me dizzy, my lips searched for him, the heavens had begun to tear, to open and I was sinking ever deeper into the fire...so much so, that it was difficult for me to realise that Mihalis had moved away from me, he searched and lit a match, he said roughly: "The sirens, can't you hear them?"

The eyelid on his damaged eye had fallen again and closed his eye completely. The hand which held the feeble matchlight was trembling.

"Don't be afraid. They haven't hit Athens yet. They say it's because we have the Acropolis."

"Yes, but the Germans have raised their flag on the Acropolis, and the English..."

"Come back to bed, and let's go to sleep. That's right,don't think about it."

He had lit another match and brought it up to my face.

"Aren't you afraid?"

He looked right in my eyes, and the flame was trembling again.

"I'm afraid. But if it's not our fate, don't worry about it...come on now, back to bed."

We waited until the little flame burnt all the match, later he snuggled up to me, weak and just like a baby.

In the sleeplessness of that night with Mihalis next to me it took me a long time to sleep, with the clock which showed the yellow hours and brought a thousand things into my mind, I thought:

The war doesn't only amputate legs and arms and wound bodies, it can leave a body complete but destroy the strength in it. How then can a person enjoy life? But no, it was just because of his exhaustion. Who knew what his eyes had seen? He needed care and good food.

One thousand three hundred and eighty-six drachmas I spent in those days. I paid the rent upfront to Mrs Fotos. I also bought a mattress for my Mihalis to be comfortable on. Next, I got out my good blanket and brand-new sheets. All of them a present from my mistress, the mother of Stratis and Nikakis, for my dowry. I bought cotton wool from a quilt maker and made pillows. I made a bed fit for a king, and when Mihalis saw it, he was amazed. He hugged me, and instead of kissing me as I expected, he hid his face in my breast and began to cry.

"Oh, Mihalis, why? Instead of being happy..."

"I am happy. From now on, I will only be happy."

One day when he was out. He had made friends with the boss of the tavern, where we had eaten on the first evening, you see some of the neighbours gathered there, and I told him to go too in case he might meet some people and get a job. I spoke to Mrs Fotos.

He's a man wounded inside. However much I ask he won't tell me what he's been through, what he's seen. Do the others, who came back to speak of it? Tell me, Mrs Fotos, please.

"Oh, you don't want to hear, the hairs on the back of your neck will stand up. They are crowing about what they have to say. Dear God forgives me, I don't really know if they are exaggerating to impress us. There was one here the other day at my daughter in law's you can't believe what he was saying...!"

"You see, they're all talking."

"He'll get over it, don't worry, it's his nerves."

"But are you sure he'll get over it?"

"As sure as you see me and I see you. How old is he?"

"Twenty-four."

"How old are you?

"Me? I think I must be about twenty-six. You see, I lost my family. I don't know when I was born, neither year nor month. I think I must have been about eight or nine when I arrived there. I lost a tooth on the boat, so I work it out from then."

In the afternoon of the same day, Mihalis went to the tavern — someone had told him of a job — and memories came back to me, and I found myself at the cemetery. But I didn't manage to reach my marble lady because I got caught up in a big funeral. A lot of people, wreaths, well-dressed ladies, men with black ties and dark suits, lots of cars outside the cemetery. I didn't find out what important person they were burying, and I didn't care either. I tried to get as far away as possible, I watched people, I looked with longing at the women, the many well-dressed women who were there, I struggled with myself to find the courage, to find the high strength I would need to approach one of them, not the ones at the front who were following the coffin, but the others who were following along behind them further back, who were talking among themselves — some were even smiling, until they remembered they were at a funeral and suddenly became severe - I battled to be brave enough to approach one of those and ask for work. I didn't want much, I wouldn't need to live in the house at night, I had my own place, I was married. Did they need a scullery maid? If not they, perhaps one of their friends? Yes, that was how I would say it. I had worked out all the words, just didn't dare to do it.

By the time I'd worked up the courage, the funeral was over, and the ladies and gentlemen had all left, the wreaths, the night was falling, and I left without going to see my marble lady. But other things were on my mind. Money. Why did it disappear so quickly when it was so hard to come by? I was saying stupid things, but still...

That evening we ate bread, a little cheese and shared an orange. Then we pulled out a small chest that Mrs Foto had given us, we put it in front of our door and sat down. There was a moon, and the breeze smelled of flowers. I suddenly realised that it was spring. Mihalis touched me on the arm, he wanted to speak to me. I concentrated:

"We will have the siren tonight."

"Because of the moon, the aeroplanes can see the..."

"The what? What did you say?"

"The target. Do you know what the target is?"

"No."

"It's whatever they plan to bomb: factories, harbours, airports."

"And the people who live nearby?"

"Well, what can you do? Whoever has years left to live will survive."

It was as if didn't care a dime about the people who wouldn't survive." Whoever has years left to live; have you ever heard of such a thing? I made it a cause for anger because I'd wanted for a long time to say some things. Something which had been worrying me for days: why are we living like this? One Sunday morning, we should go and find a priest and give him fifty drachmas, and get it done. He didn't say yes or no, but held my hand for a long time in his. But when we went to lie down, he did something else. He took his army blanket and laid it on the chest and went to sleep there. I move around too much in my sleep, he said, and he doesn't have any peace. Did you hear that? I walk around too much! As if...I held my tongue, and after a few days, I spoke to him again about the priest. Then he spoke:

"Leave it Panoria, let's wait, I should find work first."

"Alright, but when you do, then definitely?"

"Definitely."

He didn't mean it. I could see he didn't say it. Later the Germans came into our yard, luckily Mihalis was away at the tavern. They had one of ours with them an interpreter. With a face like a ball, completely round. He is speaking, and I am listening:

"Do you have a radio?"

"Me, a radio?" I felt like laughing

The interpreter ducked inside the door to look, he saw the bed the two chests, said something to the Germans, and they left smiling. I bravely said:

"If I had a radio, would you have taken it?"

"No, but we would have to seal it. Anyone who has one that isn't sealed, we will take it."

"Bravo, you will take it if he has it. Once we..."

"Who?" Asked the round face.

"Me and my husband." Well, why not? Was he going to ask for

a marriage certificate? However, he sounded interested. "What work does your husband do?"

"He hasn't got a job, he's looking for work."

Round face said something to the Germans, he wrote something on a piece of paper and gave it to me. "Tomorrow morning get your husband to go to this address, and they will give him work."

I was pleased with this piece of paper. Even though Mihalis wasn't here, his luck was working. But he wasn't pleased.

"Do you know what work it is?" He asked.

"Work. You will work, and they will pay you. If they pay, we will eat."

He was about to say something but thought better of it. And didn't speak.

In the night, he got up and lit a cigarette. I could see his shadow, I could see it from the little spark of the cigarette, but I pretended to be asleep, I didn't want to speak to him, as I could see there was a battle going on inside him. Not a word from me. The following nights the same thing, it had become a habit, he would get up and smoke. It was quite an expense too, all that tobacco, but what could you do? It was a comfort to him and helped him with his inner battles. But even so, one evening I couldn't hold back: "Oh Mihalis, why are you doing this?

I could tell he was agitated and startled when he heard my voice.

I got out of bed and lit the candle I had there on the chest. We didn't turn the electric light at night, after all on these moonlit summer nights we didn't need to spend more money. We managed with the candle.

"Why, Mihalis, why won't you talk to me? So, I will know, and know what to be afraid of?"

"What can you know, you who knows nothing. I wish I were deaf too, so that I wouldn't hear and wouldn't learn."

He didn't tell me what he didn't want to learn. But he came back to lie in bed, clinging as close a possible to the edge of the bed so as not to touch me. Neither he nor I slept. But we didn't move, we each wanted the other one to think he was asleep. I couldn't stop worrying. I knew that a lot of things were happening around me that I wasn't aware of. I didn't read the newspapers more, because the drachma they cost must be saved. Mihalis found them at the tavern and read them for free, but he never said anything to me. He was frightened of Mrs Fotos and the others who lived around the courtyard. Times were difficult, we had to be careful. That's what he said.

In the meantime, however careful we were, money was running out. Mihalis didn't go to the address written on the paper given to him by the Germans, and still hadn't found work. I spoke to the grocer, the baker, to Mrs Foto. I asked if they knew of any house where I could go to work in the day, but so far nothing had happened, other than that little by little we ate all the money that I had saved up all those years. My heart ached every time I took money out of my small bag.

Thus, one afternoon, I descended the steps of the foyer and could immediately smell cigarettes. Mrs Aretoussa and another lady sat at the round table with the green velvet tablecloth, she was reading her coffee cup. She looked up and saw me, and gestured to me to relax. The lady turned around nervously, and Aretoussa said something to her, which I understood: "Don't worry, she can't hear", and so she carried on with the reading.

I felt something which for some time had been worrying me. Yes, sometimes when I was with people, and I could see them and put out my hand to touch them to see if they are real and alive, and I would feel that I also existed and was alive, yes, I said there were other times when suddenly the wind thickens and becomes glass. A glass wall doesn't allow me. Then I just have to guess, I could imagine everything only by seeing the living portraits of people. I would make up my own story about each one from the little that I could see. But what appetite, what strength, what desire to guess about other people's stories when you are burning up and losing the bread you eat and the person you love? Your mind only revolves about one thing: survival.

So, I waited behind my glass wall, there in the foyer, and the glass was dull from cigarette smoke from the concierge, and the coffee-reading customer who was smoking. The two women were sitting at the round table and waited to learn their fate from the grounds of coffee were like stale drawings spread over time, especially as time didn't seem to pass. It was the problematic night hours by the time that coffee — reading was over, and Aretoussa seemed to come out of a dream and look at me and break the glass wall, and I found myself again among living people, when the lady paid seventy-five drachmas — due to the circumstances, Aretoussa had upped her charges — and left.

It was stupid of me to ask to become a charwoman or such. Difficult, an unachievable thing in this day and age, but she, always so soft-hearted, even if it were not recognised, would help me:

"Go to the first floor, you can clean and sweep up. Afterwards, you can have a wash, get dressed up. You're pretty and have quite a good figure, did you know that?"

I said nothing. "Don't be ashamed...at the end of the day you're a married woman, so what have you got to lose? There are some young girls here who..."

The customers pay one hundred drachmas, that's fifty drachmas for her and fifty for me. After lunch, on Thursday, I was to go there early.

On Thursday, the customer, the money is taken began to whirl around my head. The grinding started, I don't even know how I got back home to our little room. Nor do I know how I found myself in Mrs Fotos kitchen, holding a hard-boiled egg. I bought it in the morning from the villagers who came and brought six eggs for Mrs Georgia, the wife of the printer, who had two rooms with a separate kitchen, further along the courtyard.

Mihalis came back full of happiness that evening and ate his egg with appetite, we also had some cheese and lots of bread. He was due to get a job the following day. Twenty drachmas a day. Papers he said, he had to take some printed documents round. I fell onto him and kissed him and started crying so hard, I couldn't stop. Mihalis had become again like he used to be, my good Mihalis, he caressed me nicely, he kissed me, and as he held me in his embrace and looked at me sweetly he said:

"You see, you cry too when you are happy."

That night Mihallis found the strength to become a man, and afterwards, he slept like a log all night. I got up at dawn and opened the door, I saw the sky, standing in front of my plants, the bougainvillaea, the carnation and the basil.

Things went well with the work Mihalis found. His master, Anestis, the printer where he picked up the papers, was Mrs Georgia's husband who had the house with the kitchen in the courtyard. He paid for him regularly. We bought oil and pulses, and summer was coming.

August was sweltering. In the afternoon Mihalis and I went to the seaside. We wandered around the beach until the moon appeared perfectly round and white, to find us sitting on a rock. Mihalis had his arms around me, and I wanted to stay there, to die from happiness, while the sparks of moonlight lit up the sea.

There was a long queue of people at the bus stop. They waited in line like an army. Mihalis and I were there. Around us were lots of people. The glass world would disappear forever from my life.

That's what I believed when I help Mihalis' hand, and we moved along the queue, step by step, and then we were in a better position to see more clearly the silver road which the moon had spread along the sea, right along to its edge. That night I melted again, my soul crumbled as the sparkling crystal from the broken moon mixed with the murmuring from the sea.

Then the days became shorter, clouds gathered in the sky, and it rained, and I could smell the soil from my plants. One evening as I was sitting and watching the sun, which looked just like an orange until it disappeared behind the walls of the houses, I saw Mihalis came rushing in carrying a large packet of paper. He went straight to Mrs Georgia's house, knocked and waited, she opened the window, saw who it was and invited him in.

Afterwards, Mihalis showed me some money.

"But it's not the end of the week," I said.

"This is extra."

"What extra? Why?"

"Just because it is. Don't speak and don't shout. Don't say a word, do you hear?"

He didn't tell me anything else. All night I lay with my eyes wide open and they were filled with darkness, while my mind tried to make sense of it all. How and why, in these hard times, are they giving extra money to Mihalis?

Work was hard to come by here, the shops were closing, people were hungry. You would see well-dressed men on the street holding out their hands to anybody who would give them anything.

Those for whom it is written will live...

So why did Mihalis have money?

Another evening Mr Anestis called him to go to his house in the courtyard and left me on my own. I lit the candle and was knitting a thick pullover for him to wear under his jacket so that he wouldn't get cold in the winter. But my husband was very late back. My eyes were stinging from the little light of the candle. Inside me, something fluttered, and grew more and later it became with no sign of Mihalis. I had been debating many days, to speak to him yet again about us getting married. He had a job, we might even be having a baby. So, if we did, would we have to rush and get married then? I had a feeling...But better to be sure first and then I would tell him.

I didn't notice him when he came back. I jumped when I felt his hand on my shoulder. I could see he was speaking: "Leave that, it's late. Don't wait up for me next time."

"Why? You mean you are going to be gone in the night again?"

"I will be gone every night. We have work to do."

"And...they will pay you separately for that work?"

Mihalis looked at me strangely, so strangely that I felt something inside me turn cold. His eyes were like steel knives. His eyelid wasn't dropping as much as it did when he first returned. He wasn't afraid anymore. But I was scared, and I told him so.

"There's nothing for you to be frightened of, at least not now."

Lately, he had started talking like the printed words of the newspapers. There was something else: He was keeping away from me. As much as I asked what the work was, and how much he would be paid, he never replied.

When he sat down to take his shoes off, I ran and knelt in front of him to help him, and to find out. I had to know:

"Tell me, Mihalis, why are you like this? Does important work change a person so much? Because you are doing important work if you are working at night and they are paying you..."

"Listen, here, carefully."

Mihalis! Always behaving like a teacher. I listened:

"Your mind is always on the money. So, you need to know that there are things that cannot be bought."

It was as though he'd gotten taller, and broader, and definitely removed from me. I had taken off his shoes and his socks, and I stood up. We got undressed. We blew out our candle. Again, I spent the night with my eyes wide open and filled with darkness, while he tossed and turned. Then he hugged me tightly. He was frightened again. I, in turn, covered him with my whole body.

"Mihalis," I said in his ear, I know that not everything is paid in money. I know there are jobs that, well, it is wartime."

He put his hand over my mouth. A little later, I continued:

"You know, if necessary, I can pretend to be mute. Don't be worried about me."

The next evening, he took me with him to the printers. I had my knitting, and there they had a lovely electric light. It was like having new eyes. I sat on a stool at a distance so that I wouldn't get in their way. I didn't speak unless spoken to. They didn't even want to.

The printer had turned on the radio. Mihalis was sitting near him, holding a pencil and paper. He wrote. Every so often, the printer gave him a little piece of paper — like cigarette papers. Mihalis wrote regularly, and the printer opened up a large roll of paper with designs and marking, and wrote on it. Suddenly they stopped writing. They smiled. Mrs Georgia, with her needle in her hand, made the sign of the cross. We're winning. We are doing well, they told me. Only that.

When we went to our room to sleep. Mihalis spoke:

"Don't say anything about what you saw, do you hear?"

"I hear."

"I guarantee you. If you speak, they will kill me. They will kill you too."

"Who will..."

"Shush! Don't ever repeat it."

Mihalis brought money in regularly. We ate what the printer and his wife ate. We didn't go hungry all that winter, and we weren't cold either. On the coldest nights, we warmed ourselves at the printers, who lit a brazier.

And during the day I wasn't just sitting in the little room alone.

I went to the printers to help Mrs Georgia with her chores, and more than ever I wanted to get tired, so that the day would pass quickly. I had hoped we had a child, and then I would have joyfully told Mihalis, but we weren't. So, I didn't say anything more about going to see the priest to get married. I waited for him to say it.

One evening he came in upset and tearful. He hugged me close to him and struggled not to cry, and couldn't speak.

"I am leaving."

"What? What are you saying?"

"I am leaving."

He spoke only with his lips. That was how he spoke ever since he started to work at the printers because he couldn't talk loudly, those weren't things for other people to hear.

"Where are you going? Aren't we at war anymore?"

"We are. I'm going. It's a wonderful chance. I am going for work."

"How for work?"

"Shut up, don't shout! Are you mad? Do you want to get us killed?"

"No, no! See, I am not shouting. I don't want us to get killed. But where are you going?"

"Far away. They trust me. Me, Mihalis. They trust me. Indeed. Can you imagine it! Me, Mihalis, they trust me. I must…"

I don't know what else he muttered in his happiness until he burst into tears. But even then, he didn't stop talking while walking around the room. He took my suitcase and emptied out my things. He took his new shirt, which I had given him as a New Year present, and folded it to put it in. Then changed his mind. No, he wouldn't take a suitcase. He would only take what he could wear: two shirts, two underpants, the thick woollen pullover I had knitted for him.

He had to leave at three. The hands of the clock showed their yellow hours and stood in the right positions that one would point at the three and the other at the twelve. My heart exploded and shattered inside me.

Mihalis was at the door and pushed me back inside. "No, not even in the courtyard. He pushed me hard inside and locked the door. He wasn't afraid anymore. He didn't need me. He was alive.

He left me a piece of paper. I was to go there, and they would look after me. They would take me into their service. Can you believe it! Who would have thought, in this time of hunger and corruption that they would have found me a house? How come they didn't find one for me earlier? Why was Mihalis leaving? I decided to go first thing in the morning as soon as I could.

I hid the paper in my bosom, and that was when something collapsed inside me:

"Mihalis, take me with you. How can you leave me?"

I got up and opened the door. The courtyard was pitch black. There was nothing to be seen. I was afraid and went back inside and locked the door. I went to bed with the candle still lit to watch its flame. That was all. That one flame became two, two became three, four, and they started to multiply in my mind, to whirl me around, they wanted to burn me so that I could be happy. Just that. Be happy.

I was woken by a firm knock on the door. I thought for a moment that Mihalis might have come back. The sun had come up. There were two Germans. They had an interpreter with them. They nearly broke the door. The interpreter spoke. I was so dazed I didn't understand anything. I just trembled. One of the Germans pointed to Mihalis's old shirt. I didn't understand what he was saying, and the interpreter repeated it. I put my finger in my mouth. "I can't speak", and I pointed to my ears "I can't hear." They signed to me, "Whose is the shirt?" I don't know, I'd found it, and I use it as a duster. I grabbed the shirt from the German and pretended to be dusting, "like this." He laughed, just like the devil. He took my hand. It was hot and sweaty. I pulled away from him with all my strength. He pulled me to him again. He would bruise me. Now. Now. Something is screaming inside me while he holds me. I pushed him. He showed me his pistol. He will kill me. The other two were laughing.

I nearly shouted and spoke. I don't know how I didn't, but mutely I grunted and pushed, only that. Grunted and shoved, until the other German came between and with one hand, grabbed a hold of me and with the other, grabbed him and pulled us apart. He said something to him, and the two Germans and the Greek turned towards the door. Mother of God, help me, they're leaving! No, they're pulling me outside with them. They showed me the printer's house further along in the courtyard. What do you think I saw there? All their possessions were thrown out of the house into the yard. Even the brazier. I couldn't see the radio. They pulled me. Outside the yard, I could see a lorry. "I don't know, I don't know" I kept on gesturing while they pulled me to the truck and pushed me to get into it. A hand stretched out and pulled me into Mrs Georgia's.

There were others, but not the printer. All the men had tense faces and their eyes were fixed on me. Don't speak, Mrs Georgia signed to me. The lorry set off. I am sitting next to her, nobody is talking. They are all like people from different worlds, ghosts. One thought kept flashing through my mind:

"Mihalis. If he hadn't gone away, he would also be here, along with all these ghosts."

Now the only one to be a ghost, dead, is me. Only me. I, who at least am not a ghost yet. Who am alive. Who feels the taste of bitterness in my mouth. My hands were frozen.

My whole body was suffering from the rocking movement of the lorry from Zappeio to Syntagma in the centre of Athens. I knew the place. But I saw it in a blur, like through a misty, dirty window. Just that. We turned along Vasilissis Sofias Avenue, which was called Kifissias before, on our way to Kolonaki. But no. We're not going so far. In front of the railings of a gate, the rocking of the lorry stopped. The ghosts began to get out. Some elderly gentlemen — a ghost too — fell down. The German who was standing by counting those who got out, gave him a kick on his backside to make him get up. Oh no, he shouldn't do that. I got down too. The ghosts were already going through a metal door. One by one. The German was in front, and I was the last.

The interpreter was looking at me. He turned around and looked at the metal door which was swallowing up the others, and turned to me: "Go!" He gestured, and at the same time, he carefully indicated that I should stay behind, go back, and hide behind the lorry.

The German was pushing the last ones with the butt of his rifle, and when Mrs Georgia stopped and was going to say something he hit her on the shoulder with the gun, and she made up her mind to go through the metal door too. "Go! Gestured to me the interpreter again, Go!"

Slowly, backwards, along the edge of the road, I went further and further back. The lorry completely hid the metal door from me. I went even further back. I got to the corner. I turned, and I couldn't see the lorry, just an empty free road in front of me. I used to walk quickly. I didn't run. I got to Vassilisis Sophia Avenue and didn't look back.

The streets were empty. It was still early morning, and I walked and walked. Nothing and nobody was following me. I began to run, slowly at first because I didn't want to appear suspect, and then faster. Nobody was suspecting me. Faster and faster, I passed through Syntagma Square and arrived at Zappeio. I am still running. I'm at the columns. I am out of breath and stop. It was raining. Only then did I notice it was raining.

I am soaked. My legs won't hold me up, but I'm still walking. I am too frightened to go back to the courtyard. What if they've gone there looking for me? I started off towards Phaliro, and eventually, I see the sea. I'll go there; that's it! Why didn't I think of it before? That's where I should go. That's the only place I can go to...

I walked on. I could see the sea coming closer and closer. Then...

Then I don't know what happened, but I turned back running and slipping in the mud, through the rain, and arrived at the courtyard. I went into our room and went straight to my trunk, scrambled around inside, found my bag with my money, and took a breath. Then, I remembered the piece of paper with the address. Had I lost it? Oh no, there it was, still in my bosom, wet and damp but still readable.

Just then, Mrs Fotos appeared in front of my open door. She was holding a bottle and a funnel. Even if she'd seen a dead person walking, she couldn't have been more shocked. She lost it, couldn't even speak.

"Err...you came? How? How? How did your get away? A little oil..."

She showed me the bottle, and I saw the demijohn we had; it was open and spilt oil was all over the floor.

"Take them; they're yours."

I gave her all the pulses we had.

"Where is Mihalis?" she asked.

"I don't know."

"Didn't they get him?"

"No, he left in the night."

"They didn't get the printer either, he must have left too."

Suddenly she got angry:

"Great! The men do what they want to do, like men, and then leave the women to pay the price!"

She looked at me.

"And you, what are you going to do now?" I asked her.

"Leave immediately." She was suddenly worried, as though only that time she remembered the danger. "Go now! Don't hang about! I'm in a hurry to lock up. I am going to my sisters for a few days."

I took my smallest case; everything else I left, including the plants in the yard. I gave Mrs Fotos some money to water them and to keep them and keep the room for me. Maybe Mihalis will come back suddenly; perhaps the war will end. We left together and split up in Plaka. She went in one direction, and I in another.

It was still raining. With my suitcase in my hand, I went to find my new masters. I would find protection there. Michalis and I got away. I would work; I will eat; I will live. I will live so that I can wait better. I was in a great hurry. I ran through the rain, splashing through the water and the mud to get there as soon as possible. To get there…

CHAPTER 6

My House Almost Finished

The house is progressing; now we are in the inside walls. Bricks, mud, bricks, mud. The builder works consistently. I watch. It's real, what I'm seeing. We're now getting water from the town supply. They put a pipe and a tap here on the edge of where the garden will be. Everything is going ahead very fast. In a few days, they will put in the doors and windows, and they've already delivered them! Some of them are thick, and some are a little thinner, all waiting their turn. All the materials are waiting for their turn, and one by one, they find their place.

I can only look. I talk to Mr Manthos. It will be Swedish wood for the doors and windows, mosaics on the floors; they are easier to clean if I want to wax the floor in the dining room. He cares a lot about my house, and he's really working hard on it as if it were his own. I choose that one for the entrance, darker for the dining and the other room. In the kitchen, I think it would be better to put that light green with the little yellow dots. Lovely, happy looking! Mr Manthos agrees.

Later I tried to see how the house will be when it's ready, with its mosaic floors and its windows and doors open and waiting for me. But I don't know why my mind couldn't do it. I had got stuck on the inside walls, the bricks and the unending rows of them and the mud that would hold them together. I was upset. Why did that detail not let my mind acknowledge it?

Why couldn't I enjoy everything as I should, as I deserved? I struggled all day to rid myself of this feeling of sadness. All day, I tried to imagine myself walking through the open door of my own house, treading happily on the mosaic that I chose...

I suddenly felt tired, as if I had walked for hours, days, months, years. Yes, just that: years. As if I had walked for years without taking a breath. My legs were hurting, and I was tired. I only wanted one thing: to lie down and sleep for days, months and years. All those years I lived, I wished they would pass, just disappear. Only then would I wake up. I shouldn't have started to build this house. I should have been able to keep it in my mind and watch it getting higher inside myself.

The Last Master

I didn't meet a couple at this address; it was just a master. My master, whose hair had already turned grey, with his blue eyes which fixed you with one look. He took me in, and I told him everything that had happened with the Germans. He didn't ask about Mihalis, nor the printers.

"It's good you got away..." he said. It seemed that he knew, I didn't hear the end of his phrase. Then he spoke clearly and looked me in the eyes: "You will stay with me and look after the house. I know that I can trust you."

He showed me the house. It was the first time I'd seen such a mansion. Old and full of things. Enormous paintings on the walls, with some beautiful faces. Some of them wore clothes in which the bust was on display. In the dining room, almost all one wall was filled by a painting of a lady in a ball gown.

She looked both proud and sweet at the same time; you'd almost think she could speak. The furniture was heavy and carved, real monsters, with lion's feet, with eagle's heads on the backs of the chairs. Never mind the books! They reached up to the ceiling in the office, and the table was covered in papers, newspapers...He understood I was dazed by it all, and spoke:

"You won't touch these. Unless I tell you to."

The kitchen suited the house; it was light and cheerful, and my room in the house was one of the regular places. There were many of them, and two were locked.

"The house is large; there's a lot of work," he said.

"So much the better," I replied.

He was pleased and patted me on the back kindly; then he left me.

Later, when I'd sorted out my things, I went to find him in his office; he was writing. He was writing fast on a piece of white paper, then pushed it away, and took another and filled that one too.

I stood at the door and waited. How could I speak?

He seemed to be in a rush to fill the pages. I waited some more. In the end, I pushed a chair which was near me. Then he realised I was there and raised his eyes:

"Are you here? Good, go into the kitchen, and I will come there and tell you what to do."

He didn't have a lot to say, he just wanted to show me. He told me what he wanted me to cook for him. What else? Lentils, beans. He gave me oil, and showed me how much to put in. I boiled some potatoes. But that which made my heart rejoice was when I saw there were dried figs and raisins. I could eat as many as I wanted, he said; he had two sacks of them.

My master went out a lot. But he always came back at mealtimes, regular as clockwork. He sat at the head of the walnut dining table, and I brought him the porcelain soup tureen for the pulses. He put the food on some plates with gold stripes and blue and green paintings, on plates that, when I held them in my hands, terrified me that I might break one of them. He had beautiful and expensive things. Opposite, the lady in the painting watched him eating in silence. I was always nearby, ready to give him whatever he needed.

When he had finished, he lit a cigarette. The glass wall which separated me from people began to grow between him and me.

I saw him through the cloud of cigarette smoke. I saw my master getting further away, to become tarnished and dull, to become like a painting, old and stale like the lady opposite him.

One day he asked me if I knew how to read and write. He was startled when I said yes, that I read the newspapers.

"It is good to read."

He didn't say anything else, and I had my work to do. I brushed and washed, polished and dusted…I had a lot of work. The house was enormous; I'd be afraid to be there on my own. Most of all I was scared of the two locked rooms. But surely at night, I was at peace? Then it was worse. My whole soul and body cried out for Mihalis. I brought him into my mind, I begged him:

"Mihalis, please tell me where you are. Tell me that, wherever you are, there are no Germans? Did you get away, my dear? How did we get away…? Tell me, did you know? Was that why you left?"

"I knew it, but my work didn't allow me to say. You weren't to know Panoria. That's why I told you to leave quickly in the morning."

I spoke to him out loud. I like doing that; somehow it relieved my mind and gave me hope:

"Never mind, Mihalis; don't be sad. Everything passes, and you will come back. I'm satisfied with where I am. My master gives me 800 drachmae a month — did you hear that! 800 drachmas. A lot of money. I will save it…You'll save money with all that important work you do. We will build our house much faster than we thought we would Mihalis…"

"Yes, what is it now?"

"I am going to put the two lions, whatever you say."

And that's the sort of things we said — me, that is — until my mind was whirling and my body was exhausted, and then I would cry myself to sleep. Sometimes I would be scared, and I would shake horribly until the heavy wheels, with their chains of war, those that wrap around the world until it bursts, until they come to grind me.

One day, with the glass wall which had arisen between the master and me, I felt a strange yearning, and the strength of its sudden appearance helped me to break the wall. The moment that my master put out his cigarette, after his evening meal, I spoke to him:

"Sir, I want to ask you something."

"Yes, my child, go on."

"I wanted...I wanted to know...You would know..."

"What would I know?"

"About the...the..."

"About your *fiancé*?"

"Yes, about him. Please, where is he?"

"He's far away. He is fine. He is with the free Greeks."

"Where are the free Greeks?"

"You don't know? He didn't tell you anything?"

"No. He didn't tell me."

"Good, that was the right thing."

He looked at me with his blue eyes — they were like the sea without its depth, something like that — and then he spoke:

"If I tell you, do you know how to keep a secret?"

"I know."

"Do you swear?"

"I swear it on Mihalis' life."

"He is in..."

"Where did you say?"

"In Egypt."

"What is he doing there?

"He's fighting."

"Fighting? Fighting again? He might get wounded again?"

"Why? Was he wounded in the war here? I didn't know that."

"No. No. He wasn't wounded. But maybe he will be."

He looked at me again with those eyes without depth, and said slowly and clearly:

"They are not fighting only with guns against the enemy. They fight in other ways."

Days and nights were troubled by that phrase "in other ways" that he said. So, I asked him:

"Is he in danger where he is?"

"Less than here."

He continued to smoke his cigarette, and the glass wall between us shot up again, and as long as it stayed, I saw him again just like a painting and made to pretend to clear the table. I waited...Nothing. He didn't want to say anything else to me. I wanted to leave the dining room, to go to my bedroom to discuss all that, to see if I could make anything of it. Then, I glanced at him for the last time. I saw that he wanted to speak to me. Inside me, something fluttered, suddenly...fluttered strangely.

Before he managed to say anything, I said to him:

"Is it the siren?"

"Yes, can you hear it?"

"I felt it."

"Did you hear it or not? Tell me."

"No."

"So how?"

I told him: "Just something inside me..." That seemed to impress him, and he laughed quietly and oddly; he looked at me; he didn't budge from his seat.

"The shelter is downstairs in the basement. We have stored it up. Take the keys if you want to go there."

"And you?"

"I never go there; it bores me."

Fine then. Nor will I. It bored me too. But "if it's written..." I was pleased that I didn't go. From then on. since I went into that house, I never went to the shelter, and I felt strangely proud about that.

However, I was very lonely. Of course, I was buried within the mansion with its paintings which all watched me, with the beautiful lady in the picture who seemed to want to make sure I did my chores correctly. Of course, I was afraid to step outside the house because of the Germans. The master said that it would be better if I didn't go outside for a while. So, I never saw anyone but my master, and one other good person, a villager who came twice a week and brought greens from the mountain, eggs, oil, potatoes, cabbages and other vegetables. But he didn't say much either. What little he did say was hard to understand because he mumbled the words and they got mixed up in his big moustache which hung down over his mouth. He was more like a living portrait than a person.

If the school wasn't next to us, or better the schoolyard boredom would have been greater...there, every midday, there was a long queue. Some friendly people came to every lunchtime, ladies and gentlemen, each with a can in his hand, and waited quietly for their turn.

Under the roof in the corner of the yard was the cook. Next to the cook, a man was wearing a cap. He counted the spoons. One spoonful for each can. He made sure nobody got more. When the gentlemen and ladies had got their spoonful, they left.

I asked one day what was going on.

"Clerks," my master replied. "The bank gives them food."

"Free?"

"Free."

"Why don't they cook at home?"

"Because they don't have anything to cook."

He remained silent. He didn't want any more talk.

But I ran to the window to see. I wanted to see them every day; they were the only people I saw any more, in this world. The ladies and gentlemen were coming every day for their spoonful of food. They were coming with their cans and waiting patiently in the rain and cold.

One day, when it was hailing, I watched some children on the corner of the street — in the beginning, when they were sitting down, I thought they were dogs. There were some barefoot, their feet like spiders, with their faces blackened and thin, all eyes, watching. When the ladies and gentlemen came quietly with their cans, filled with the spoonful of food, the children fell upon them and grabbed whatever they could, upsetting some of the cans and spilling the food on the ground. Other children gathered — I don't know where they came from -- and they fell down on the muddy pavement and tried to pick up as much as they could of the spilt food and cram it in their mouths; some others were like pigs and lay down and licked the food and mud from the ground.

All that day, I wanted to cry. To battle against that evil, in the evening when the master went out, I put the soup to heat on the fire and left the little door open and sat and watched the flames.

I sat like that for hours to get warm, only that getting warm was no small comfort.

Then something else happened during these days: It was night. I couldn't sleep. I brought Mihalis to mind to discuss, and I was thirsty. I left my room to go to the kitchen to get some water. Then I saw the door to the terrace half-open. I could swear that I had closed and locked it, as I do every night. I remembered, though, some sheets that I'd hung out, and said to myself, "Why not go to bring them in?"

It was pitch-black on the roof; the only white was the two sheets on the line, but past them, I saw a tiny light. A cigarette. The master. He's smoking. He didn't see me and I froze, going neither backward nor forward.

Eventually, he threw his cigarette away; it made a circle like a star and disappeared from view. I went to leave so that he wouldn't see me. Then I changed my mind and walked forward. He was standing right on the edge of the roof. He lit a second cigarette, smoked some of it, and then, as he had with the first one, threw it away. He lit the third cigarette, and the same thing happened. I left the sheets there, went back downstairs, leaving the door slightly open as I had found it, and went back to my room, but there was no way I could sleep. Was he mad? And I was all alone with a madman in his house? Later I had an idea and slowly opened the window slightly, still in the dark, of course, and tried to see the road. I struggled to see in the dark, but there it was again, a small light like the previous ones, that made a small circle and then disappeared.

I was so happy that my master wasn't a madman, because something extraordinary had happened. I closed the window and got into bed; I spoke to Mihalis again, and we discussed it all. I made him realise that I'm not stupid. That I was not crazy. I understand now what they are doing: he, my master...and the shadow on the pavement.

The next day, I was at the window again to watch the queue in the schoolyard. The German soldiers had appeared and guarded the corner.

The ladies and gentlemen quietly took their food. The children came, too. They sat on the ground on the pavement opposite and watched, with their enormous eyes, cans full of food which passed them; they didn't move. I noticed that none of the adults from the queue turned to look at the children.

I asked my master:

"As they are giving out food, why don't they give some to those poor, hungry children?

"Because they're not employed by the bank."

"So, they have to die? Don't they see what state they are in?"

The reply made me cold all over:

"It's the only way. They will die. So many are dying every day."

And he wanted to say something else:

"Be careful. Do you hear me?

"Yes, I hear you."

"I don't want you to give anything to anyone from the little we have. I forbid you." I was looking at him and wanted to say something, but he beat to it:

"If you give something to one person, you can't do anything. If you give to all of them, you won't have anything, and you will die. It's either them or you. Understand it. Better to close the windows not to see, because you may see far worse things."

The master used to bring a piece of meat back every Saturday for the meal on Sunday. I had no idea where he had found it, and I never asked. One weekend he brought me a different kind of meat, and I mentioned this to him.

"Yes, I think they fooled me. They gave me dog meat; never mind; cook it. It's probably edible."

On Sunday, when he had eaten — I did what I could to make it, the dog meat, tasty – he lit a cigarette again and spoke, smiling:

"Go on, eat some. Well done. You cooked it well — everything is an idea, isn't it?"

I didn't hear what else he said. But I also ate dog meat. There were some leftovers, and we had it again on Monday with some salad.

And thus, with even more loneliness, the winter passed and the days began to lengthen. I asked my master if I could go to see Mrs Foto. "Yes, you go," he said, but not to be late.

I found her thinner, in a mess, a different person. We sat on her stoop. I was lucky, she said; many people had died that winter. She lost a niece of hers from weakness. I asked about Mrs Georgia.

"She never came back. They may have killed her, and that would be better than her being humiliated."

"Why humiliated?"

"A relative of hers came here a few days after they'd caught her, to get her things. She'd been tortured, he said, in gaol. They beat her badly to betray her husband and the others involved. They hung her up and burned her soles; they extracted her teeth...If she hadn't talked they would have killed her. That's what the relative said. He took her things and left. She never came back."

"They killed her?"

"No idea."

"If she talked?"

"If she talked? Mrs Georgia would never have talked...So much has passed, if she had talked..." She shook her head...and I was shocked because I found myself thinking that it would be better if they had killed Mrs Georgia, because otherwise...

Anyway, my master was in danger, I was in danger, and they were looking for so many others, apart from my Mihalis, who was far away, like her husband, of course. I took a breath. I don't even recall if I gave Mrs Foto money to keep the room for me, or I told her to look after my plants because I couldn't take them now, but someday I would come and fetch them, and I found myself on the road and on the way back to my boss and his home...I could hide there in my shell. I didn't need to see or hear anything else about the world.

I unlocked the door, rushed inside and went to my room. I closed the shutters and pulled the black curtain in place and turned the light on.

If it hadn't been for all that, if it hadn't been for Mrs Georgia, wouldn't I have been happy enough here? I have a brass bed with a good mattress, with lovely, almost new, blankets. I had a walnut wardrobe with a full-length mirror. There, suddenly, I saw my face. I had lost weight, one, two, three, wrinkles had appeared on the edges of my lips. "If I had stayed there, if I hadn't left and would have pulled my teeth out too, I wouldn't have been able to see my wrinkles, they would have smashed my face and it would have hurt a lot. How much pain can a man bear? And if they had humiliated me? And..."

I am no longer alone in the mirror. My master is standing behind me, there in the open door. I was shocked! He'd never been to my room, and I didn't like it that he'd found me in front of the mirror.

"Sorry, did you speak?"

I had decided to make a habit of saying "Did you speak?" That way, I could be sure because people often spoke and I didn't hear them.

"Yes," he said, smiling.

He probably didn't speak but said 'yes' just to please me. He was a strange man, clever, a real demon!

"Tonight, you will make macaroni."

"With what cheese?"

"We have some."

"We have? Where did we find it?"

I shouldn't have said that, it just escaped me. It wasn't my business to ask. I was paid to work and eat; my opinion was unnecessary.

He behaved as if he had given me his order and of course didn't answer my question. Quite right too.

We had a guest. I got some clean sheets, my master unlocked one of the closed rooms and I made up the bed. There were lots of photographs there. A young man dressed as a sailor on a warship. The same young man in civilian clothes. With a girl on his arm. Again, the young man over there with white trousers, a shirt with no jacket and the same girl with him, wearing summer dress and holding a dog.

There was a table in the room, with two armchairs, a wardrobe by the wall and a radio. My master was going in and out all the time and didn't let me enjoy myself and have a good look around at all those new things in peace. He seemed worried.

The guest arrived. He was an old man, all skin and bones, with an ugly face. I didn't like him, because when he smiled, you could see his yellow teeth, like an animal. He appeared with a suitcase in his hand. I made to take it when I showed him to his room, but he wouldn't let me.

When they had eaten, they went into the office, and I made them some coffee from chickpeas. They were talking and smoking. The glass wall shot up then, with their discussions and their business, and over here on the other side was me. I never felt the need to make up a story about this ugly person who had suddenly appeared before me more urgently. He was a merchant, apart from the other work that he may do with my master. I mean, the work with the cigarette, that evening on the roof, he could have been the shadow on the street. However, I don't want to dwell on such things. Something trembled deep inside me, and I seemed to see

Mrs Georgia with no teeth. I got scared. "No spying…"Oh, dear! I said that awful word.

No, I say, I don't want to…it's not my fault…I don't want to pretend to be mute again…I am afraid I'm afraid.' I tried to pull myself together. 'Come on now, forget all that. Pretend there isn't anything like that. Think about what story you are going to make up about this ugly face. So, he's a merchant…what does he sell? Ah, I found it…thank God…the Black Market. After all, in the evening we suddenly had cheese for the macaroni, and we had white bread too… so there you are! There is some joy in the topsy-turvy world.' The pleasure which I didn't expect to feel so much or so profoundly when I ate the white bread and macaroni with cheese. It made me feel like crying when I ate so well…crying from joy. Thus, a merchant in the black market. He goes through so many dangers to find those things and to fill his wallet. Such work needed a lot of courage. It's no joke. 'As for the other work he does here. Ah, it seems I can't stop thinking about it. Why did he lock his bedroom door this morning when he left it before the master came down? And why didn't he let me clean it, nor let me carry his suitcase? I am afraid I'm terrified. I fear that is not going to go away, however much food I eat.'

The master is standing in the kitchen in front of me, looking at me with those blue eyes. He's speaking: "You never saw the man who came here. You don't know him. Do you understand?"

I understood. But there you go, I saw him again at midday. He came in as if it was his house, and went straight to his room where he left some parcels he'd been carrying — food, maybe? — locked the door and came into the dining room and sat down at the table opposite the master. I brought the food out. He started to chew with his yellow teeth. What did he chew? What was he eating? Meat! Beef, not dog.

Something has definitely changed in the world, and I could see it only through the bread and meat from the black marketer and spy and…"Christ, what next? Oh, the master knew, of course, he knows all about it and never thought that I should know. How can I find out?" One day, when he called me to bring a cloth so that he could dust some books that he had gotten down from a high shelf, I wanted to talk to him and ask him. But how should I begin? Oh yes, like this:

"Have you written all these books?"

"Not all," he laughed. Did he think that it was a joke? He wrote for so many hours, days, months, years, continuously. He wrote fast, his hand moving quickly over the paper, so why was it a joke that he could have written those books?

He showed me a shelf nearby with some thick books in brown leather, all the same: "All no, just those."

I plucked up all my courage. 'How was I going to say what I wanted to know? What I needed to know?'

"Would you lend me one of those books to read?"

He laughed, very pleased. I wouldn't have said that he could have been happy with my question, but he said: "But they are not stories."

"Stories?"

"Yes, like those you will definitely have read in the newspapers."

"Stories are what one reads in the papers?"

Something else that he found funny. He certainly was in a good mood today. He continued:

"You said something true, without realising it."

"About the stories and the newspapers?"

Actually, I had realised it, I was not as stupid as he thought.

"Yes," he said.

What can I tell you? All the time he was reading my mind, he was brilliant, a monster.

"Those books there are...too heavy for you. They are studies."

"Did you say 'studies'? What are you studying?"

"Human beings, their acts, what motivates them."

"What? Who? What did you say?"

"Well, I should say that I study their behaviours and try to find the cause...I struggle to enter the souls, their minds..."

"But why? What would you gain if you did learn all that? Would it teach the world and make people better? To not have wars...they wouldn't kill, they wouldn't..."

"Maybe...later, even that could happen. Science...it would take a long time for me to explain it all to you. Maybe some other time we could talk about it..."

He went and sat in his office, took the books which I had dusted, opened one and was lost in the depths of what was written there. He forgot about me. The image of him became blurred behind the glass wall which had risen, mercilessly now.

Anyway, it was nice to even have a little conversation, even if it wasn't about what I wanted. "Another time...another time we could talk about it," and I was happy with the little he'd said. It did help my mind to work better as it had a goal: "How and why must my master study humans?"

Then, an answer came, the same as his, sweet like a song, comforting and full of hope. Maybe...Maybe later people will become better. Possibly there will be no more wars, or murders or torturers. That last bit I dare not say in front of him. I was afraid. He also said something about science...I went further. "Yes," I said: "As long as my master and people like him study humans — there must be others because he couldn't do all this work on his own — then all the ugliness will be gone." Then, when I was ready to be happy about how humans are being studied, the drill started again. For humans, the need to be considered so much means that humans are the lesson. "What kind of teaching? And how can you learn, you poor thing, how to progress? It's a shame I can't read so that I can learn too." To learn...I couldn't get anything from the newspapers. The Germans were victorious, all victorious and the Kommandant gave out new orders all the time, and they always bombed their targets on the allied front "successfully." Goals and objectives. The word Mihalis taught me that evening when we sat on the stoop in our room in the moonlight...

And from what I saw and from what I was able to understand, the Germans had won. One day — I wanted to talk again — I said to my master:

"The newspapers wrote that the Germans have won, but they don't say anything about the other war, the one you said Mihalis was fighting in."

"I thought that you are clever. What are you asking me?"

He looked at me seriously, and I was afraid. He continued:

"The newspapers write stories. We said that, didn't we? Truth is something else. How could they write the truth anyway as the newspapers are run by..."

"By who?"

"The occupiers, the Germans."

"Oh, I see."

"As for the war waged by the free Greeks, how can they write about it? It's secret and is being carried out to destroy them."

"Yes, right, thank you, I understand. Those you call 'the free' are fighting for the Americans and the British."

"Exactly."

"When they've finished?"

"Theoretically, when will be the victory, theoretically?"

"Why only theoretically? Aren't you sure?"

Maybe he isn't. He doesn't speak. He is thinking. Then:

"It's a long story."

It was as though he regretted that, because he may have realised how I resented that he didn't want to tell me the long story. He spoke again, but he didn't seem to believe what he was saying. It was as if he was saying it just to say something.

"We will be with the victors, I can assure you of that. We'll get rich, they will pay us recompense for all that we've lost."

"Recompense. Recompense. What a lovely word. It really made me feel full of hope!"

My master continued with these lovely words:

"All those who were in the war, those who are where your Mihalis is will..."

I felt choked up with joy: They will get rich. They will be glorified. All those who have fought will become talented people. There you are, Mihalis was right then when he didn't want us to get married. He was planning on all this happiness for me. That's what he was fighting for. It was all going to happen. As long as we live. As long as we are alive. I felt like falling down and kissing my master's feet, but I was too embarrassed.

Burning up with happiness, I whispered: "Thank you." I ran up to my bedroom because I wanted to be alone with all this jubilation, for once, without fear. Even the yellow hours of my clock which were always waiting for me there could make me afraid.

On Sunday, I went to see Mrs Foto and opened up our old room, found the brush, and swept and cleaned with Mihalis' old shirt, which the Germans had seen. My landlady looked at me as if she was waiting for something. I realised that, but it was too late. Otherwise, she would have said I should give her something. I could have saved a few raisins, or some dried figs, I could have hidden them from my master.

When I went to give her some money, a little that I had on me, she said with difficulty:

"You know about the rent. You will have to give me a bit more."

"How much?"

"Don't you see what's happening? Money doesn't have any value now. Does your master pay you with paper money?"

"No, there are times when he pays me with sovereigns."

"Everyone pays like that nowadays. Can't you give me half a sovereign? You have money. You eat. You are warm where you live."

"What was I to do? I made up my mind: I would give her half a sovereign. She told me about her man. He lived with her for years without marrying her and then he left. He was rich. He left these rooms in the courtyard to rent out. But that was all she had. These rooms.

Then I left Mrs Foto. As if I didn't have enough misery about her situation — because her man left her and lived with her without marriage — and my heart was heavy, as if I didn't have enough with all the new worry gnawing at me, I saw outside, a person lying on a doorstep. His bare feet were black and there was some encrusted saliva on his chin. Passers-by were looking at him and shaking their heads. A lady with a child covered the child's eyes so he wouldn't see the open blue eyes of the man.

And those who had stopped, began melting away one by one. Later on, another man came by, stood close to him for a while, and then left. Eventually, there was just me left with the dead man. His bright blue gaze didn't let me go and my stomach began to hurt. I bent down and closed his eyes. His eyelids weren't yet completely cold.

It was as though that was what my legs were waiting for. For so long they hadn't wanted to walk at all, and suddenly, without me feeling something — as if I was someone else — I started running. I arrived at our door without even realising how, or which streets I had taken. There I ran into the guest, the ugly man, who opened up with his own key and went inside. He looked at me strangely to see me so upset. He said something, but I couldn't understand what. I ran into my room and locked the door.

In the evening, my master came into the kitchen. He is speaking to me, and I am listening carefully:

"Why were you running when you came home? Was anyone chasing you? Speak up, I need to know."

"Death."

He looked at me oddly.

"Death. A dead person."

The dead don't move. Don't talk rubbish."

"A dead person, I'm telling you."

"Where was it?"

"Down on the pavement."

"Yes, and?"

"I was frightened."

"Why were you frightened? You haven't seen a dead body on the street before?"

"No."

"Bravo! Well, you are lucky then. It's over now, so forget about it. Put it out of your mind."

"I just can't, his eyelids weren't even cold."

"You closed his eyes?"

I was embarrassed and didn't reply. My master is looking at me. He doesn't say anything for a while. But then:

"Now listen carefully to what I am going to say to you. If you see something else like that — although there will be fewer as we are nearly..."

"Nearly what?"

"At the end."

"Of what?"

"The trials."

"Whoever is still alive now is a survivor."

"Why? Is the war ending?"

"Nearly."

"And Hitler?"

"He is a madman. He will fall fast."

"All those soldiers, where will they go?"

"Back to their countries to die from hunger. It's their turn."

"Their turn to die? And the other war, the secret one?"

"That is also ending."

"So, we are near, you said?"

"That's what I said. But take care because I want you to hear something else."

Oh, why didn't he leave me to enjoy this moment? Why didn't he leave me in peace to think about it properly, to discuss it with my Mihalis, to take it all in, for my soul and to feel the sweetness? What else did he need to tell me? I wait.

"Next time don't take the initiative when you are in the street. If you see something strange, turn away. Get lost, go far. Do you understand?"

"Yes."

"Nor dead people nor living, nor children nor dogs."

"There are no dogs."

"You noticed that? They've all been eaten. The cats too."

"The Italians bought them. Mrs Foto told me. They made them into a stew, like rabbits."

"We ate dog, I hope we won't have to eat cats."

He looked at me carefully, his eyes darkened suspiciously:

"I don't believe you spoke to that lady about the stranger here?"

"No."

"You didn't see him. You hear me? You don't know anything about him. Now go please and bring your things from there to here. You don't know what might happen, maybe someone will steal them and then you'll have to pay out for no good reason."

"I am not paying for no reason."

"I said: bring your things here!"

"Alright. I will bring them, but not yet."

"Why not yet? What do you mean, "not yet," I said now!"

"But...for Mrs Foto...she needs the rent."

"Ah, now you've overdone it. Be careful. As long as you are in my house I expect you to do what I tell you. Silly! Sentimentality, in these times!"

I was shocked. Maybe he wants to get rid of me, to be free from all this "trouble." Trouble?

I didn't know what I was saying, but in my daze, I saw that he was smiling.

And it was as if he had given me the biggest and best present.

He is speaking. I am listening.

"Listen carefully to what I am going to say to you."

"Yes, I am listening."

"Do you want to live and progress in your life?"

"Yes, I do."

"So, try and become a bad person. Do you hear me?"

"Yes."

"Otherwise, you won't survive. If you can't become bad, it's too difficult, you'll have to try. If you try, you can do anything and manage to make the best out of the worst situation. Do you hear me? You'll do your best? Now go and get the food ready."

Another drill pushed into my head. I would have to try hard to be wrong. Otherwise I wouldn't live, and of course, I wanted to live. That's all I need! All this going round and round in my head, I found that my first try to follow my master's advice had begun to be successful. What I mean is that suddenly I thought how sad Mrs Foto would be when I take all my things from there, but I didn't want to do it and leave our little room. My Mihalis and I lived there, and I wanted Mihalis to be able to find it again. Because sure he would return soon, as my master had said. I would make a new dress and stand in our yard. Opposite me would be Mihalis.

"Yes, Mihalis, I kept everything just as you left it. We can live together again in our little room."

"But I have money, Panoria. Let's go somewhere else. We will be able to live better there."

"We would live better in our own home. We could build it quickly, don't you worry."

"But until then, no. Come on, let's live here, I don't want us to live here anymore, where?"

"You mean about Mrs Georgia?"

"Yes, about her."

"But it's better that she is dead, and better that she won't be humiliated."

"And her husband?"

"He will marry again."

"Oh. Right? Good, Mihalis, as you wish. Better to leave here and go to a better house until we have built our own. Better to leave. To leave."

I shouted it all and even did a deeper voice part for Mihalis. My mind was spinning, and my body was aching from the desperate need for my husband.

One evening when I had a talk with Mihalis, I was thirsty and went out of my room to get some water. I saw a light in the corridor. My master must have forgotten to turn it off. I reached for the switch to turn it off and then I saw the guest's door was half-open. There was a light on as well. Then, the guest appeared in the doorway in his pyjamas, with a revolver in his hands. I started to scream.

"Don't kill me! Don't! I didn't do anything! Don't kill me! He came at me. I can't see anything but the revolver getting bigger and him growing bigger. I wanted to scream, but I couldn't. I'd lost my voice. He's even closer to me, I can feel his breath on me, and it smells of cigarettes. He put one hand over my mouth, and I can feel on the back of my neck the cold metal of the gun which he was holding in his other hand. I grunted and kicked him on his legs and felt something falling down. He lets me go to bend and pick up the revolver which he's dropped. I go to leave, but hands hold me firmly by the shoulders and push me towards the kitchen.

My master turned on the light, fastened the door and stood in front of me. He's speaking. I can't understand anything he's saying. It was such confusion in my mind; millions, many wheels were grinding me completely to crush me to dust. As much as my master's lips moved, I couldn't get out of this awful whirling to be able to pay attention to him. He understood. He even got me a glass of water. I drank it; it refreshed me. I am struggling to see what he's saying. An ugly light is shining in his eyes.

"Shame on you! Do you want to burn me! Are you with the others?"

"Me? With which others? Which others?"

He looked at me. He is unrecognisable:

"What did you say then to the Germans that they let you go?"

"Me? To the Germans?"

"Don't pretend to be stupid. The other day, he who was hunting you...death...speak! Why did you come out of your room?"

"To get some water."

"Why didn't you get water before you went to bed?"

"I didn't think of it."

"You didn't think of that. But you can eavesdrop though..."

"But I can't hear."

"You can hide and watch. It's the same thing."

"But I didn't see anything. I just went to turn off the light in the corridor."

"If you are telling the truth, I will know. But if you are lying then know that they will get all of us, but you first of all. They will torture you. You will die..."

"Again, they will get us? They will...again?"

"Again? What do you mean?"

He was trembling and had turned yellow. I wanted to speak, to explain to him what I meant by "again" how again frightens me with death with...'Oh God, Mrs Georgia!' My tongue was tied. He grabbed my hands. He twisted them like pliers:

"Speak!"

I couldn't. My tongue was tied and was burning me up, my whole body was in flames. They were rising from the soles of my feet...

"Speak!"

Nothing, I was burning, the hammers were beating, beating, burning me everywhere, everywhere...

"Speak!"

He hit me on the face. It was like a bomb had gone off in my head. He was hitting me...until everything went dark around me. All the fires went out, and I fell into a dark hole. There, I was surrounded by cold snakes writhing around me, I was frozen all over, and the ice reached my stomach and made me feel nauseous. I controlled myself as much as I could. Managing, and all the while, I am struggling to loosen my tongue. While I struggled like that, I realised I had gotten up off the chair I had fallen, and I ran to the sink and vomited.

Then I felt lighter. My tongue was loosened, and I turned to my master, but he had fled the kitchen.

I washed the sink and cleaned myself up. I sat on the chair again to wait for him. I was afraid to leave the kitchen. I stayed and awaited my fate. "Would he get rid of me?" I waited. Nobody appeared. I sat there. I daren't even to go to my room. I would have to go along the corridor, and that was dangerous.

I stayed there until the light of the day spread slowly and surely, sweetening the kitchen.

I got up, my legs were trembling and wouldn't hold me, I felt pain and itching and a weight on my left cheek. I went to the window to open it. I saw my cheek in the window glass. It was swollen and black and blue. It had been bleeding, but the blood had dried. I turned on the tap and put my head underneath, I stayed there for a while. Then I went and sat on the chair again. There was no way I was moving from there, even if the world was to end!

My mind was trying to tie up loose ends, all that I'd heard from what they'd told about what was happening in the world. I re-membered what Anneta had told me one day about the big spies, how they would play a double game. "Was the guest perhaps one of those? Otherwise, why would he carry a revolver? Yes, he brought food, and what was it the master had asked me? If I was with the others?...Oh, I wish there was no glass wall to separate me from the rest of the world. I could have learned."

Eventually, my master appeared in the kitchen. I have no idea what happened to the other one. I didn't see him again that day. My master looked at me with his blue eyes, deep in my eyes. He noticed my cheek. I could see he was upset, and without wanting to, I found myself watching the gold snake, the ring which he wore on his right hand. He spoke. I listened.

"You got up already?"

"I didn't get up, I sat here."

"All night?"

"All."

He thought and then:

"Why didn't you want to speak?"

"I couldn't."

I told him everything; how my tongue was tied, about my head.

Then something very odd happened.

"Do you like me?" he asked. "Even though I hit you, do you like me?"

And I was ashamed that such a gentleman would ask such a thing.

It was the first time anyone had apologised because they had hit me. I took his hand and kissed it, but he pulled it away. He didn't want me to do that.

"Do you like me?" I asked him too.

And then he took his usual stance:

"Forget everything that happened. Only tell me that all you told me about the Germans was true. How you got away then. Is it true that you pretended to be dumb?"

"It's true. I swear it, I swear it on my life, on Mihalis!"

"Let's hope so. Then I have one thing to ask of you."

"Alright."

"If something happens, I want you to do the same. Understand?"

"I do."

"Don't go to that woman's place again. What's her name?"

"Mrs Foto."

"I will send someone there to get your things."

"Alright."

I was shocked and unhappy. But what could I do? I took a sovereign from my wage, and I took him his fake coffee to his office, when he saw my cheek again and was upset, I mustered all my courage and said:

"Please..."

"Speak."

"Please...when you send for my things, please tell whoever goes there to get her to give him my plants."

"You have plants as well?"

"Only three. Bougainvillea, carnation and basil. They are..."

"What are they?"

"Nothing. They keep me company."

"Alright, I will say about the plants."

"And..."

"What else?"

He was impatient. I struggled to swallow my saliva. I gave him the sovereign nervously.

"What now?"

"It is for rent. I owe her...she is in need."

"Shut up. Silly! Take your sovereign back. Off you go. Move. Go!"

I didn't go. I couldn't. I had to speak to him.

"Keep your sovereign" he repeated. "You may need it."

Then he smiled strangely. His eyes had become distant.

"Never mind...I will give her the sovereign."

And he looked at my cheek again.

"Off you go now."

He became serious again, and the glass wall rose up between us. I remained alone behind the wall, with a strange happiness inside me; a sort of bitter joy, if there is such a thing.

The next day, a barefoot boy turned up with my things.

My boss then bought me a flashlight, and we went to the store-room, which he unlocked - the shelter, we could call it - he had reinforced. They were so many things in there: armchairs, chairs, a large table, shelves with books, paintings, some parcels, a baby's swing, old toys, a big wooden rocking-horse with only one eye, a rusted lion on a board with four wheels. I looked, open-mouthed, at this treasure flickering in the round light of the flashlight. A whole house-full, you could say.

Then I felt his hand on my shoulder. I turned. His eyes had become even more in-depth, black, totally black, and they shone strangely:

"Come on, hurry up. Leave them there. I'll give you the keys one day, and you can come down and clean up. If the war ends. If we are still alive."

"Why do you say if we are still alive?"

He didn't answer, he was in a hurry, and it was clear that he didn't want to look at all of those things. But I couldn't tear myself away from there. A strange yearning was bothering me: The lion with the wheels...

"Come on! What are you looking at?"

He saw what I was looking for, he thought it was funny, and he started to laugh: "You want that? Take it! It's a present from me!"

I took the lion in my arms. I also had some other presents for my child, for Mihalis' child. I opened my basket and put it inside, along with the box with the train, the gift from Dimitraki.

The master locked up, we went upstairs again, and he left. I went back to my chores. It was as if nothing had happened. Just that I put my plants outside the kitchen on a little step. They were in bloom, the basil smelled lovely, and inwardly, I thanked Mrs Foto. That was the last I saw of her, and the last of our little room too.

The next day, he called me into the guest room. I was to give it a brush and clean he said.

"Be careful of those things. Don't touch them. Leave them as they are."

It was the radio. There were lots of wires, all tangled up like a mad woman's hair and spread all over the floor, where there was another radio, this one was new but still all tangled up with wires.

"The radios..." I began. He interrupted:

"They don't work."

"Are they sealed?"

"Exactly."

He said it strangely. He indeed hadn't said anything.

"The other gentleman?"

"He left."

"When is he come back again?"

"Never. That's the end of him."

"He died?"

"Maybe."

"They killed him?"

"You ask a lot of questions."

I took the dirty sheets where the ugly man had slept and felt queasy. 'What if he was no longer in this world? And how did he die? Did they torture him?' I held the bundle of sheets in my arms. It was a big bundle and nearly reached my face, and suddenly gave out such a smell of cigarette smoke and dried sweat. 'What if they tortured him? Oh dear, how strongly these sheets smell... cigarettes, sweat, alive, male odour.'

But, as I go to leave with the sheets in my arms, my master taps me on the shoulder. I turned.

"Then you can make the bed up again with clean sheets."

"Is someone else coming?"

"Maybe."

'What's going on here?' The story I'd wanted to make up which came because of the human smell on the sheets, was stopped before it started.

Nothing happened any more with the man with the revolver who was a merchant in the black market, a big spy, and almost certainly dead. Then we had someone else. Nothing ends until the war ends...

Before I went to sleep that night, my master ordered me: "Take water with you tonight and don't put your nose out of your room. I don't want to have to lock you in. I wouldn't like that."

Lock me in? To imprison me, in other words? I trembled. Cold snakes came again. Why did he have to say that he locked me in? Something inside me woke up, got angry and stubbornly pushed me to go out of my room to go and see what was happening. If it was necessary, I could help him. I could do something too. Even if it's only pretending to be dumb. Important things were happening here, and I was alone and locked in and useless, like a dog tied up in the garden with a chain...Where would I find peace? How could I manage to go to sleep? I got up, and, instead of opening the door with the power of my anger, I opened the window. In front of me, I saw the night sky full of stars. It was full of stars, the eyes of the world, who watched me and shone to comfort me even from so far away.

I said: "Mihalis, husband, you are so far away too, further than the stars, in other worlds. You see and hear and are full of life. Come Mihalis, come and tell me...I want to learn."

I stayed at the window for a long time, and spoke with Mihalis; we said a lot. Even about the schoolyard opposite which now at night shone from the reflection of the moonlight upon its white tiles.

The ladies and gentlemen didn't come any more to queue up for the soup kitchen; on several occasions, Mihalis and I had asked the boss about that.

"And what did he say?"

"He said that those who lived managed to survive. The others..."

"What of the others?"

"The others, he said, hadn't survived and so the soup kitchen was no use to them."

"True," said Mihalis seriously.

"Do you know children come to school, to the yard. I like seeing them. I have chosen, don't laugh Mihalis, a boy and a girl...a couple."

I felt a bit happier thinking of the school children. I thought of them more than I saw them because the morning when they arrived was when my master got up, and so I had to see to him. Midday, when they came out, he had arrived waiting to eat his lunch, and I couldn't just sit at the window and look outside. You see, when there was a soup kitchen, they used to come late, and by that time we had already eaten. Now the present view was much more pleasant and let the mind travel sweetly to warm households, to specific and lovely things. I see how odd it is that it can do it at such times when I can't manage to enjoy the peace unless it's stolen. Only in the interval could it travel, and then they would come into the yard and run and play and shout. That was my other great joy: the children would shout so loud that I could hear them.

That night did me good, thinking of them. Then I didn't want to go out of my room. I couldn't sleep. I was watching the empty road behind the window. It was like everyone had died. The stars above spread their comfort on the emptiness. I tried to talk about the names we would give to our children. We could ask my master to be godfather to our first...I observed the empty road. It looked as though something was moving. A shadow. Of course, that's him. "He's coming quickly, he's coming...He's gotten to our door, he's standing there. It opens, and he's inside."

I quietly closed the window and ran and got into bed. "What is this now?" I thought to myself. "If he's Greek, isn't he afraid to be out at this time? It's forbidden. Is he German?"

"He has the key to our house? How? What happened? Is he one of those very big spies that play a double game?" Then I fell into a deep sleep and dreamt of Anetta. One Anetta who was dressed as a man, with a briefcase. She had found her old man, and he'd found her work...and I had gone to her house, and she tried to make me wear men's clothes so that I could go to work too.

I cried. I was frightened. I didn't want them to catch me and torture me. I didn't want to die...I told her: "I wouldn't be able to save myself, even if I said I was dumb"...I wanted to shout and I couldn't...I tried to speak, and I couldn't...I had become silly for real.

In the morning, the master had to shake me to wake me up.

"What's happened to you? Why didn't you get up? It's too late."

"My head..." And I was happy because I could speak after that awful dream.

"Take some aspirins and come and make two cups of coffee."

The late-night guest was a woman. They were after her, it seemed, and that's why she arrived at that time. She looked bad-tempered, and smoked continuously. I made them another couple of coffees. Later on, she went with my master and they locked themselves in the room with the radios and wires. That day, he didn't go out. Nor did he go out in the evening.

At lunchtime, opposite each other at the big table, they didn't speak. A dark flame flickered in her eyes. Something inside me fluttered again, and I felt the wind heavy, ugly. Oh, Jesus Christ! Later on, in the afternoon, something worse happened. There was a knock at the door. I could hear it even though I was in the kitchen. I went to open it, and the master leapt along the corridor and raised his hand: "No! No! Don't open it. Go into your room. And, as we said, you are dumb!"

He didn't need to tell me twice. I closed my door and locked it and sat on my bed and waited. I was not surprised that I'd had that bad dream. I waited. I was just an idiot. A frozen idiot with only a heart which was beating fast enough to burst in the stupid body of mine. How long I stayed like that — more dead than alive — I don't know, but at some point I saw the door handle turn slowly and I crossed myself hurriedly, with my eyes fixed on the handle. But it didn't move again. The door didn't open. Nothing. I had to wait again. I couldn't sit on the bed any more. I felt like a grill. Yes, a grill over hot coals and with that grill they roasted me in hell with the sinners to torture me. I knew I would talk. But what would I say? My throat was burning. I didn't have any water.

couldn't go to drink some. I was thirsty, very thirsty, I was burning up...How long did I have to stay like this? Until when? When would they open the door? Would they give me some water? Or would they just leave me to die of thirst? I had a glass there with me. But it was empty. I picked it up and looked in it. Empty. Dry. Useless. I went to the window. I asked myself, "Should I open it?" If the wind blew, perhaps I wouldn't feel so thirsty.

But no, I was afraid. If they came and took her or the master... No, not him, No. They mustn't. Say they were to take him, leave, and start out on the road without having seen me. If I opened the window and then...they would see me.

I sat down on the bed again. On the grill...I thought I would die there. What else awaited me? And if I killed myself? Nobody would know. They wouldn't take me, they would...But how? I could have opened the window and jumped down. It was very high. But if I didn't die at once? If...

Now, without me noticing, the handle turned, the door opened, and the master stood there in front of me, smiling, and his eyes were shining:

"Come on, it's over the..."

"What?"

"The alert. All's well."

"We're saved, there was nothing to fear. It was nothing. Were you scared?"

I looked at him, and I felt such a sudden rush of joy that I was still alive, and I found my strength.

"Were you scared?" he asked again; he thought I hadn't heard him.

"No...no...I was just thirsty."

I went into the kitchen and poured and drank three full glasses of water.

"You will put food only for me."

"The lady?"

"The lady left."

I felt lighter and happier. I served the food to my master. The real lady of the house was opposite him in a picture frame.

She smiled quite proudly and calmly because the other one had left with her black glasses, the owl who had upset everything. It was all quiet again. It was as if the war was over, as if Mihalis was about to appear any minute. My master looked at me with his deep blue eyes.

"Are you relaxed now?"

"Will anyone else becoming?"

"Not anymore."

"It's nearly finished?"

"And...those who were sent away, will they come back?"

"They will come back."

"When?"

"Soon."

That night, I slept all night without dreaming, like a person who has worked well and hard, got tired during the day and was sure of his food. Without worries. In the morning, I got up at dawn, I shook out the furnishings, swept, mopped, and scrubbed floors. The master smiled when he got up and saw all that. He didn't speak but went into his office and wrote until lunchtime. In the evening, I waited for him, and he came back late. I could tell immediately that something extraordinary had happened.

"They are leaving," he said. "They are going and not coming back. The big day has finally arrived. Tomorrow..."

"Tomorrow what?"

"We will be free. The English are not far away..."

"Why English? Why do we want them?"

"That's the way it is."

"We always have to have someone here? So how can we be free?"

He looked at me but didn't speak. He was amiable that evening. He took me into his office and spread a large map in front of me. He showed me where we were. A tiny bit of the earth with lots of seas. I saw Alexandria and all of Egypt where my Mihalis was. I had told him that when he came back we would get married.

He strangely looked at me. I was startled.

"What? He's not alive? Did something happen to him? Why don't you speak?"

"No, nothing has happened to him. He is alive. But listen to me, my girl. Your Mihalis has become a significant person. Very important. He left the job we'd given him, and he became a trader."

"A trader?"

"He is in a different world. He makes a lot of money."

I didn't ask anything else, yet my master lit a cigarette. He continued:

"Mihalis turned out to be different from how we thought. In the beginning, he worked well. Later on, he preferred to do different things. Easy gain won him over. He is a smuggler."

"A smuggler?"

That word sent me back in time to Mr Vassilis. It was from him that I'd first heard it. Mr Vassilis refused to smuggle and lost the woman he loved so much that he had her tattoo on his chest and wanted to die with her: those things whirled round in my shocked brain. I asked shakily:

"Is he smuggling things like tobacco, which are bad for people?"

"What do you know about that? No, smuggling is not just about tobacco. There are all kinds of smuggling."

"Could he go to prison? Has he become a bad person?"

"No. He became clever and able to live in today's world. And..."

He looked at me. He continued. I was attentive.

"If he comes back and marries you, you will also be rich..."

"Me? Are you teasing me, master?"

"Not at all. That's one of the things about war. It gives people opportunities."

The word "smuggling" went around in my head and worried me. The wheels came to grind me up. 'Mihalis is rich!' I thought, 'Without the smuggling, he wouldn't be rich, and I am close to him.' And the home that we talked about began to get taller and wider and become a real mansion. It had a big garden and wrought-iron gates which would be supported on white columns. On top of the columns, I would place my two lions to defend

Mihalis, the children, and me.

The Germans had left, and we again drank proper coffee and ate white bread. The master smoked some cigarettes which smelled of vegetation and had a box with a cat's head on it. I asked him again:

"Can I write to Mihalis now?"

"Later. When our acquaintances return and tell us his address."

"Do you know a lot about them?"

"I have my son there."

"The one who is in the photographs in the guest room?"

"Yes, him."

"I hope you welcome him home soon."

"Thank you."

His blue eyes rested on the opposite wall, their depth filled with the picture of the lady.

"Is that lady your wife?"

"Yes."

"She is wonderful."

"She was."

He didn't say anything else. I gathered the coffee cups that he'd drunk and took them into the kitchen, feeling happiness bubbling up inside me. He spoke to me of his son, of his wife's son, as if I was a person close to him.

Now, every time he came home, I watched him and waited for him to tell me if anyone he knew had returned, if his son had come back, if he had learned about Mihalis. He realised that and seemed annoyed by it.

"I don't have any news yet. But it won't be long now..."

I waited for 'it won't be long now...' and it was lovely, the joy of waiting. So much that I got my courage up and decided to go out one evening. I wanted to see Athens with its lights on, to see free people. On Sunday, I said I would go out.

"Where will you go?" he asked, surprised.

"To Mrs Foto. To see what's happening."

"Go on then, but make sure you are not back late."

He gave me some money to buy a cake, it was too much and I said so.

"Buy one for the lady too; what's her name? And be sure you are not late back. Before the sun has gone down, you must be here."

I was still feeling happy when I arrived at the courtyard because I went through streets full of people, I saw children playing in Zappeion, men and women, girls and boys everywhere, I tell you, all over. The square was black with people who wandered around... and it was beautiful, so beautiful it made me want to cry. I felt that, yes, I too am a person and I am also here in this lovely square along with all these people. I walked up and down three times. I enjoyed it so much, as it was of my making! I was also free and wandered freely around with other people...

The door to the courtyard was closed. I pushed it and opened. There was nobody around. I knocked on Mrs Foto's door, and a strange woman immediately appeared, wearing black. She looked at me hard with little yellow cat-like eyes.

"What is she to you?" she asked.

"We lived here with her."

"She's dead."

I didn't hear properly, and I asked again.

"She is dead," she repeated.

She said something else which I didn't understand. I was dazed...I stumbled, and the woman took me inside. She gave me a chair; Mrs Foto's chair, and everything in there was just as she'd left it.

She'd died from appendicitis. She was exhausted. She couldn't take it. The woman was a relative of hers, and she'd lost two children, one in the war and the other in Athens. The Germans had killed them at...

"What did you say?"

"...a roadblock. Where have you been living? Don't you know what a roadblock is? They shot him as he was standing there, just by chance."

That much I learned, and I was thankful that the woman wanted to tell me. When I was leaving, she said:

"It's better for you, since you can't hear. What do you gain by learning all this? Just thank God that you were warm and fed." Then, as if she had just thought of it, she said:

"Didn't you hear, the bombings?"

"No."

"Not even the dreadful thing that happened in Piraeus?"

"No."

She made me sit down again and told me all about the bombings, the harbour, the shops and the houses. The church which was destroyed. The women and girls who ran to the shelter.

"All gone, for good," I said, "They will pay for it altogether."

"Who will pay?"

"The Germans, who else?"

"Silly, it wasn't the Germans who bombed Piraeus. It was the

Americans. Do you hear it? The Americans, who wanted to hit the Germans..."

"And hit us?"

"Yes."

I don't remember how I got back into the street. I felt almost drunk from all that I had learned all at once. I was confused by all the new words which swirled around my brain: roadblock...reprisals...Americans...exhaustion...and again: roadblock...reprisals... Americans...

All that made me feel unbearably hot, and made me dizzy along with the dust in the roads which had turned yellow, blurred from the setting sun. In all that confusion and blur, I noticed that some people were running as if they were being chased. I started to run too, at least I would get home a bit earlier. From one corner, a crowd of young men appeared, and they were holding cardboard signs with giant letters written on them. I was seriously frightened now. Thank goodness I was near home. I ran, unlocked the door and rushed inside.

The master was waiting for me in the hall.

"I am glad you got back. Now, go and pack a few clothes, we are going away for a few days."

"Where are we going?"

"Never mind, just hurry up and do what I say."

I hurried. The car arrived, an old banger which made me feel queasy from the strong smell of petrol. By nightfall, we had driven far from Athens, to the main house at the village that used to bring the food we ate during the German occupation. It was the master's estate. The villager, his wife and their children lived there and cultivated it and looked after it. I was happy to be among people again, and I helped the wife with her chores. I looked at the master. He had spread his papers all over the table next to the window facing the sea. He was writing.

I found myself again by the sea; shining blue. I looked at the open sea, I travelled its distance with my eyes and said to myself: "That's where Mihalis will come from. Mihalis, a rich man…"

I particularly liked watching the sea at sunset, when it filled with shards of broken gold which swirled with the waves where I could see them, and I could see in the golden distance our mansion which was rising, with its marble columns at the entrance to the garden, with the two lions on top to protect us.

I didn't learn immediately why we had left Athens, until the villager's wife told me: There was trouble, people were being killed, Greeks were fighting Greeks now that they were free. The master wanted to be away from all of those troubles, which is why we'd left.

I asked him when we would return home, and he said:

"When things calm down." He didn't say anything else, but I wanted to know.

"But what is happening? Now, we are free…"

"That's what happens with us Greeks after wars, so that England can control us so that we are in her debt."

"Why would we be in her debt?"

"Now, what do you want? Should I teach you about high politics?"

He didn't want to say any more and later, much later, I learned more or less what had happened that December 1944. The master told me one version, and Mrs Foto's relative told me another, when I went two or three times to visit her, and yet another from the wife of the villager. I thought I would go crazy. Each one said whatever they wanted.

We returned home three weeks later. Things had calmed down in Athens. It was only in the mountains that the Greeks were fighting amongst themselves. I went to the cinema that winter, one afternoon when the sun shone as if it were pouring a new green coat of paint on the Cypress trees at the cemetery and brought a type of shine to the tiles on the roof that warmed my body and soul.

Then I went to visit the marble lady. It was as if my heart sang a comforting song. The marble lady stayed the same however many years passed; neither the sea nor the marble lady was spoiled with all of those awful things that had happened. Even when the years passed, the same evening of passing the marble lady on my way home, I stopped at the kiosk and bought paper and an envelope and sat down that evening and wrote to my Mihalis.

> *My dear husband,*
>
> *Years have passed, the war is over, and my money has increased. It's time to build our house. I went to the cemetery today. On the way out, I asked the marble masons about the two lions which we will have at our home and they said they will do them just as we want. They only need someone to draw them on a piece of paper.*
>
> *Come back now Mihalis. Time is passing and we are getting older. Let's not waste it. Do you remember the clock? The one that watched over us on the nights of the occupation, with its yellow hours? Well, it broke, and I took it to get it mended, but the watchmaker said that it had worked for many years, there was no chance to get it repaired. He said I should get another, a new clock that has just come out. He showed me some. One had a cuckoo which came out of a little window. I liked it a lot. When you come back, we'll get it.*
>
> *My master told me that you have become rich. I can't believe it! But it doesn't matter if you have really. It's the same thing for me.*
>
> *I will be waiting for you forever.*
>
> *I am always your wife, and I send you a kiss.*
>
> *Panoria*

The master sent the letter off to Egypt to his son, and he would make sure it got to Mihalis. He wrote in a few days, which seemed months to me, time passed so slowly. He'd written to say that he gave him the letter and that Mihalis was well. I was waiting.

The days passed, and I waited. The months passed, and I waited. Although time went on, I didn't ask the master. I didn't want to burden him unnecessarily. If he knew, he would tell me.

Many times, it seemed as if he had something to tell me, but he didn't say anything. Nothing. Not a word.

The glass wall had not only risen between us, but had widened and spread, it became a glass wind which bound me on all sides, which imprisoned me and froze me and never seemed to break or pause to let me rest awhile. Nothing. It didn't even allow me to speak to my Mihalis, nor make me cry. Nothing.

Days and months passed, it was a year since I had written the letter, and the master's son came to our house with his wife and their child, Tassouli. Not a word about Mihalis.

But that evening after their first visit, my master gave me a present. He brought something small out of a box. He had ordered it from his son to help me hear better. That's what he said: To help you understand better" not that I didn't hear...but better. He showed me how to fix it to my left ear, which was the worst.

I put it on top of my heart as it said in the instructions which were written in a foreign language, but the master explained them to me. Later, when he spoke, it made a sudden loud noise in my head, I told him, and he spoke more quietly, I could still hear him. For the first time, I could hear his footsteps. I walked too, and I could listen to mine. Even the doors: they made a strange creaking which I heard for hours, without being able to work out where it came from. I realise in time. From our home, there in the homeland. Suddenly I remembered our cat, Whitey. Our pure white cat with the furry tail and yellow eyes...bright yellow and shiny like the hours on my clock which had broken. About twenty-five years later, for the first time, I wondered what had happened to Whitey in the catastrophe?

I thought that then, along with the people, animals must have run terrified though through the fires: cats, dogs, chickens, pigeons...

Just think, I said to myself, some little things with torture our minds sometimes...and I opened my bedroom window. I wanted to hear the noise from the street, to be part of the cars, the people walking on the pavements, the mixed noise of life which sounded differently, "ding!" A bell chimed, then a whistle and an engine revving up.

There were times when it seemed that my ears would fill up with trumpets and the teasing and noises which made me feel alive. People came close to me, and I could even hear their breathing. As for the music, another type of enjoyment came from that. I put the radio on — the one from the guest room, the master, had had it repaired, and he did the other one, along with all its wires like a madwoman's hair, I have no idea where he put it. The more the radio played, the more the music spread her invisible hands, her velvet, coloured, shining hands stroked me and comforted me.

One evening something strange in the music affected me. The time came when I couldn't control my legs, they managed me, and started to mark the beat. My legs danced without knowing how to dance. As if that wasn't enough, my hands started to tickle, and I had to clap them together to calm them down! One, two, one two three, long live music!...My body flew around, waltzed and bent and twirled. I wanted to laugh, to shout, to sing, to make noise. A strength started building up inside me, and it got bigger and stronger inside me and made me crazy...

Then I got scared by how different I'd become. I turned the radio off. I went into the kitchen, sat on my chair and listened to my heart, which was beating in my body loudly enough to break.

Night has fallen. I didn't turn the light on. And sat looking at the window in the house opposite which was lit up. I didn't put the radio on again for a long time. I was afraid of myself, petrified.

At nights, I took the hearing aid out. There were lots of cries in the night, and the park was full of people. They came and overflowed my bedroom, people of every kind, and it was as if they were all looking for me, stretching out frozen white hands, a buzzing filled my ears from the words they spoke all at once, as though each one of them had a mouth filled with thousands of bees which buzzed. You are no longer alone. We are all with you. See our hands, they are asking for company...company...company.

No, I didn't want so many, nor their company. They wouldn't leave me in peace, which is why I took the hearing aid out. Thus, the world was silenced, and those white hands fell down unnoticed, and the bees disappeared.

That's how the days passed with the new things that had happened to me. The son and his wife and their child come to eat every Sunday at midday. I tried my hardest to make them the best possible meals. The house always had company. I heard better, so I could understand what they were talking about even from the hall when I turned the hearing aid up high. I learned to manage it. But that which I hoped to hear, I didn't understand. However, I handled the hearing aid, however long I lingered in the hall, however much I watched my master because without him saying so I understood that he didn't want to say anything to me. With my eyes. Like a dog I watched him, I waited for him to tell me some news. Nothing. The war was over...Nothing. The ones who had been sent abroad had one back and the master's son and others. Nothing. I waited. And nothing.

Every Sunday I regularly went to the cinema. There I enjoyed being surrounded by all people behind, in front and behind me, I felt somehow protected, a kind of warmth, and I also heard different conversations here and there. Later on, the company increased with the shadow of those who talked on the screen. Of course, they spoke in a foreign language, but I could hear the voices and their sighs. Thus, one day, I heard the words and whispers of a middle-aged man who came and sat next to me. He brought out a bag of sweets, and he offered one to me. I told him I didn't want one, but he insisted and eventually I took one. After I'd eaten, he came out with his story: I was to go with him to the country where he had a house, and we could spend the night together...he would have given me three pairs of stockings.

"Go to hell!" I told him. Got up and found another seat, but I found myself too far in front, and I couldn't see comfortably.

In the evening, I don't know what came over me, I told the master.

"Can you imagine! Three pairs of silk stockings..."

"You didn't go, of course. The stockings were too little payment, what if he said something else, that he would marry you?

"Why are you asking me such a thing?" I said, shocked.

He looked at me with his in-depth look and continued:

"Would you have gone?"

"No, how could I have gone...But what do you mean?"

"I say, you would have gone, that you would have sold yourself!"

"Me?"

"You."

"I don't understand."

"You would have sold yourself happily to a smuggler," he said calmly.

I realised what he meant and was dumbstruck. I wait. I feel that the moment has come. I will hear now, I have to learn. Come on, Panoria, be brave...now you are going to learn...

My master was in his study, and he was smoking. It seemed as if he was waiting for me to ask him something. But I can't. Whatever he has to tell me, let him tell me and get over with.

I wait. Nothing. My blood is beating. My master noticed me there where I was standing in front of him.

"Sit down."

He showed me the armchair next to him. I was too shy. I had never sat in front of him. Certainly not here in the study. My mind was working well and said:

"No, it's not necessary."

"It is necessary. Sit, we will speak."

I sat.

"The same would have been if you would have married Mihalis."

"If I would have married him? What do you mean?"

"You are not going to get married!"

"Why? Is he dead? And you didn't tell me?

"He is not dead. I told you before. He is well and alive, he is here in Greece."

I am lost. It took me a lot to be able to speak:

"He is here in Athens? And did not tell me?"

"Calm down please, and listen to me."

I listen. I didn't lose a word because of my hearing aid. The master saw Mihalis. He went himself and met him. He spoke to him about me. Mihalis said that our affair was a childish thing. It was in the past and forgotten. Now he is married. He married the daughter of his business partner. He is involved in lots of enterprises and plans to enter politics.

"How did you say this last one, he plans to...enter politics?"

"Yes, he plans to be a candidate in the next elections."

"Mihalis is a member of parliament"?

"Yes, Mihalis."

"But you told me he is a smuggler."

"He was. Then he became an entrepreneur. Also, a benefactor."

"Benefactor?"

"Exactly, he has plenty of money and makes a lot of different donations to charities."

My small mind works hopelessly trying to understand.

"Then if his first smuggling was so successful he is happy..."

The master looks at me, calmly. Finishes his cigarette in the ashtray.

"Others can, and others can't make it a success."

See how Mr Vassilis couldn't and Mihalis could. So Mihalis had strength. Strength. I wouldn't have thought it, then when he came back from the war. Then with his nerves...

"Your eye, Mihalis...what happened?" He was bent over his macaroni and ate and ate...

 The master is speaking:

"Now you have to try and get him out of your mind. It's better that you didn't see him again. So many years have passed, and Mihalis is married..."

"Yes, it's better," I said not to disappoint him.

"That's right! I am glad to see you being so logical!"

"Yes, I am...but I want to ask you something else..."

"Go on..."

"If Mihalis hadn't been a smuggler and hadn't married, would be as rich as he is now?"

"No."

"If he'd waited to marry me, would he have been able to make... what was it, a donation? Tell me then, because I need to know.

What do you think? Did Mihalis do well or not?"

"He didn't do well...for you and me. For so many others, though, who needed him...The most important thing that Mihalis did is this: What they needed from him, he managed to give them.

I wanted to say something else, but he didn't let me.

"Forget about him. You have money, and you are capable. An honest man will turn up for you. You will live your life.

"Yes."

 I got up from the armchair where I had never sat before. I will live, of course. I wanted to leave straight away from the study. I will live...And shut me in my bedroom. Of course, I will live...I took out the hearing aid that had helped me to hear and learn. I will live. I closed my eyes. Darkness. I will live.

CHAPTER 7

My House Is Finished

Doors, windows, glass, a terrace on the roof all done. We said I won't be putting the two lions. The house is a bungalow. The locksmiths came, and now I have all the keys in my hands, each one with a little piece of paper attached which said which door it is for.

Spring. The sun is dull, and can only just be discerned, a ball of light in the sky. The master and I went there by taxi, he was carrying a bottle of sweet Mavrodafni wine to celebrate, and I had made a cake. I offered a slice to the master first, and the master-builder next and then the labourers who were levelling and flattening the soil in the garden. That is where I will plant my three plants. The bougainvillaea had grown very well. Its branches had reached out of the window and looked like breaking down the wall. It was time to take it out of the kitchen, the master said. We didn't have anything to open the wine bottle with, but Mr Manthos managed it with one of his tools. It would have been adorable if I hadn't been so humid. A heavy humidity.

The builder clinked his glass with mine. "Well, Mrs Panoria, you should make the decision…"

The master smiled and said something to him. I can't hear that. It is quite a long time now, more than five years, that I don't wear the hearing aid all the time. In the past, you see, I really wanted to much to listen and learn. Now it just all makes me dizzy. I have heard and determined enough, if not too much. Although today I should have put it on, I forgot.

There is sweat on Mr Manthos' forehead, drops. He looks at me kindly but with a sly little look in his eyes, a flash of impatience. The master said to him:

"Leave her alone, we'll talk about it some other time…"

I gathered the glasses and went and washed them in my new sink. It's hot, and the heat is spreading its warm leaden hands around my throat and is choking me.

Then I locked my house up. I put the keys in my bag. The master was going somewhere and left me in the taxi near home.

Mr Manthos had left earlier. He stood there as though he was waiting for something, but I was too hot and didn't speak to him. He left. The heat continued to stroke me with its leaden hands. I wanted to get away from them, but I was afraid to go home alone. So, I walked. Among people walking like me men, women, young people, old people. Some were in. A hurry, others were walking more slowly. Some two by two, and sometimes three, they were talking together. But there were people on their own too. Many were walking along, not just me. The night time now, the lights are flashing from a cinema. I could see the pictures, one enormous woman, half-naked, with her breasts showing a man held her in his arms, and he was kissing her. Other people on their own were standing and watching that kiss. I bought a ticket and went in. The heat inside was higher, it stuck to me. I can't see clearly what is happening on the screen, the shadows mixed together, blurred, got bigger, and smaller, they made the shape of flaming wheels to finish me off. Don't, don't please, pity me…

I got up. My legs were shaming. I can still feel the wheels in my mind. Outside all the lights have been turned on, and I am walking in the lights. I can breathe better. A mild breeze has started up. It cools me down. Thank God! The storm has passed. I feel at last how alone I am, and it's better that way. I am standing still and looking around me. How did I get to be so far away from home? I started back, the master's house is in the other direction. I walk again passing through all the well-known neighbourhoods, I turned in the corner, and the lights are getting fewer, I am walking more slowly on the pavement, my legs are hurting, and they've swollen up.

It's late. I walk. In my daze, I nearly fell over a ladder that was leaning against a wall. There was someone up it, next to the ladder was hanging a bucket full of glue. The man is pasting posters on the wall, he spreads one out. A man. The wall was filled with signs about this man. The man gets down and pulls the ladder further over to fill the next wall with the posters.

I am going to the opposite direction of him. Over the whole length of the wall he has pasted the posters, the faces multiply and the portraits — posters seem to follow me, they accompany me, they are lit up by the street lights, the big black letters with the name of the ministerial candidate came unstuck nearer me, they seemed to surround me: Mihalis, Mihalis...the posters of this person came alive, they spoke to me, they sent words to enter my ears, to run in my blood, to beat in my temples: Deaf donkey... deaf, deaf...It's me, don't you believe it? It's me...me...me...deaf donkey, deaf...

The further I walked the more the faces multiplied, they came unstuck from the walls and fell and filled the pavements, the road and they whirled around me, I don't know where to go, to make a path to get away, get away...I try to run, and I can't...I tried again, I managed a bit better. One two steps, three, come on, run...to get-away...But what is the point in running, when they prefer to hunt me down? I ran, and they followed me, there were millions of faces, all the same, always the same, saying the same words: Deaf donkey, deaf...They surround me again, and the eyes and mouth and nose are all getting mixed up. They whirl round and round, becoming white dots. A mass of white marks, many wheels, are coming onto me now. I am running, running to save myself. I trip and fall. Deaf...deaf...the voices are getting louder, I struggle to get up, and I manage it. I am running again to getaway. No, they won't let me, they are still multiplying. The wheels are turning, the face...they have covered everything, all the houses and shops and people...there's nothing, just the faces and the wheels...The voice: deaf...and millions all together...they are catching me up...they're pushing me against a door so that I will die there...maybe some passers-by will close my eyes for me...my eyelids won't have got totally cold...yes, they are still warm...

I didn't die. My master picked me up from the doorstep of the house where he found me. He brought a doctor. I am in bed. My master looks at me seriously. He is saying something, but I can't hear him. He gives me my hearing aid, which was on the table, to wear.

No! No! I signed to him, I don't want to. I feel strange, as if I had become a spider. I am in the middle of a cloud.

I am leaning towards the cloud which is warm, thick, and made up of the breath of all world. I'm turning...the dust is unending... the people are endless.

One day I came out of it. I got up, and I just felt lighter. Nothing else. I put on my hearing aid and presented myself to my master. He was pleased to see me.

"Oh, are you better? How did you end up like that? Where have you been?"

"In the street."

"What were you doing there?"

"Looking at things."

There was a newspaper on the table, he picked up and opened it.

There was a face again. The whole page. He noticed it and look at me. His eyes had got even more in-depth, but he didn't speak. Despite his intelligence, he didn't know what to say to me. I was sad.

I went out of his study, brushed and mopped, dusted, cooked just like every day, like all the days of my life.

Mr Manthos came, they locked themselves in and talked. Then they called me in.

Come on Sunday, we will expect you.

When the builder had left, the master was cross.

"I just don't understand you. In spite of being happy, where you see all your hard work coming to fruition, and what a great thing you've managed, a whole house...And it's a very nice one, bravo. Mr Manthos did perhaps the best work in his life. So, on Sunday..."

He said other things, and I became a spider again. I went back to the warm cloud to play among the breath of the world...all that night.

The next day I got up and went to Haravgi, I sat on a stone outside my house to look at it.

Just that. To look at it. A passer-by stopped and looked at me, I was embarrassed. I got up, got out my keys and opened the house to show him that the house was mine, not anyone else's. He relaxed and left.

Then like a thief, I went again out of the garden gate — the garden that will become there, not just my plants. I stood on the road, in the same place the stranger stood, then I closed up and left. I left quickly, stumbling and tripping as if I was hunted...as if an army was after me, a crowd of me dressed in khaki, all with the same face. All shouting at me with the word "Deaf donkey" And I ran and ran. I took a taxi — I couldn't run anymore — and arrived home early. There I found a woman, she had been talking to the master and was just leaving. When she closed the door, my master said to me:

"This is the woman who will come when you leave."

"When I leave?"

"When you get married."

"You are throwing me out?"

"What do you mean, am I throwing you out?"

"But I am not..."

I opened my purse and put my house keys on the dining room table near him."

I don't want them."

"What don't you want? Your house?"

"I don't want it."

"And Mr Manthos who..."

Suddenly a light went on in my head:

"Mr Manthos built it for himself."

"I don't believe you are..."

I didn't let him speak:

"I am, I'm very well. Mr Manthos built the house well so that he could enjoy it. If I didn't have a house then he..."

"Stop, stop...it's not..."

It is! He wants it for himself. Well, he can have it! Take the keys and give them to him. I didn't need it. I don't need it, and I don't want it. No! No house anymore! Never! Give it to him! I can also give a...what did you call it...a donation. Donation...donation. I am rich too. You see! I'm rich...I offer support. Take it. Take it. He is welcome to it, they are all welcome to it. I give it to you, I give it to everyone. It's payment for all I've learned. I like paying... paying...

My master held me by the shoulders with both hands. He shook me:

"Pull yourself together! Are you not ashamed of yourself? What ridiculous things you are saying? Stop it now!"

"Let me go! Let me go! I'm sorry, I didn't mean it...I..."

He let me go. Then he put his hand out and gently stroked my head, slowly and comfortingly. He did something that nobody had done for me until now. It touched me and I had to cry. I cried a lot and looked stupid.

"Come, come, now...the bad has gone," he said, as if I was a child, "it's over the ogre has gone."

"You cried, you feel better now, take your keys back."

I didn't take them. He realised that I had made my decision.

"Well alright," he said, "I will arrange with my lawyer to rent it."

"Why should we rent it out? I don't want it. I don't want it, I tell you."

"Well, what do you want, for goodness sake?"

He was angry, I was scared, but what was burning me up now, I had to tell him and make my position clear.

"And...when will the new woman start?"

"Oh, please God, help me, so he doesn't throw me out...he shouldn't...it must not happen...please!"

"If you are not leaving, then she won't come...What can I do? It's better this way. I don't want a new face around the place, particularly that my son is leaving..." His son was going to America. He'd found an outstanding job and would take his wife and child with him, for some years. The master would be on his own again, alone with his books and his studies of people.

He seemed as though he was in a hurry to go and carry on with his studies. He didn't say any more. He left me there in the middle of the dining room, with the pictures of all of the talented people in their uniforms, with the lady on the wall smiling proudly. He carried on through, opening the double doors and reaching the back wall. He turned and sat at his desk and bent over his papers. I watched him from afar. But between us, the glass wall had not risen. I was sure it wasn't going to rise up again. I realised at the moment when I gave him the keys to my house, when we had to turn off the water and cut the power, his words were beating me. "You have to learn to refuse. The more, the better..."

There were two things I refused: The two stone lions, which were going to support the balcony...really. I didn't have them, so that I wouldn't see them, but that others wouldn't see them either. So, they were saved. They remained untouched, enthroned inside me, holding up my heart.

***

THE END

ABOUT THE AUTHOR

Julia Iatridis (Neo Faliro, 1910-1996)

Daughter of Spanish Director of Symphony Orchestras and Professor — Director of Piraeus Conservatoire for 60 years, Jose Bustinduy and Eleni Georgandopoulou. Studied music at Athens State Music School.

Award for her short story on World short story competition by New York Herald in 1954.

The novel Stone Lions was filmed as a serial in the Greek state television in 1969-1971 with great success.

From 1950, she published approximately twenty short stories and was honoured by an award for short stories of a group of 12 writers, the State Award for the Best Greek Novel and for the Best Biography.

She translated into Greek a significant number of works of Spanish writers and playwrights, with many of her works appearing in the Greek theatres. Works, like the second part of Cervantes' Don Quijote, Jimenez, Unamuno, Valle Inclan, Federico Garcia Lorca, Perez Galdos and Alejandro Casona.

Key books

1955: Three Persons. Her first book.

1958: Rider against the Wind. "Kostas Ouranis Award" for the Best Greek Nook.

1963: The Stone Lions, the second award for the Best Greek Novel.

1964: Order from Above, short stories.

1971: Pyrigonos: Literary biography of Lope de Vega in Greek.